Tales from the Otherworlds

A MIDDLE GRADE FANTASY ANTHOLOGY

ANTOINE BANDELE   BRITTANY HESTER   KISH KNIGHT

LOUP GAJIGIANIS   MARIE MCHENRY   KEN KWAME

RYAN J SCHREODER   FRANCESCA MCMAHON

KRS MCENTIRE   ZIA KNIGHT   JESSICA CAGE

EDITED BY

ANTOINE BANDELE

EDITED BY

FRANCESCA MCMAHON

BANDELE
— BOOKS —

Publisher: Bandele Books
Interior Design: Vellum
Editors: Antoine Bandele, Francesca McMahon
Illustrator: Arthur Bowling
Cover Design: Mibl Art

ISBN: 978-1-951905-24-8 (Ebook edition)

ISBN: 978-1-951905-27-9 (Paperback edition)

ISBN: 978-1-951905-26-2 (Hardback edition)

First Edition | December 9, 2023

Contents

Will of the Mischief Maker   1
By *Antoine Bandele*

About the Author   21

The Queen's Kitchen   23
By *KRS McEntire*

About the Author   43

A Trip to Sunma   45
By *Jessica Cage*

About the Author   69

The Guardian's Twin   71
By *Kish Knight*

About the Author   97

No Way Out   99
By *Ken Kwame*

About the Author   117

The Green Man Falls   119
By *Francesca McMahon*

About the Author   145

The Beams of Faelleria   147
By *Ryan J. Schroeder*

About the Author   173

King Impulu & The Sky Pearl   175
By *Zia Knight*

About the Author   197

The Portal to Aril   199
By *Brittany Hester*

About the Author   223

Fae-Took   225
By *Marie McHenry*

About the Author   243

Magiks and the Tale of Two Kings   245
By *Loup Gajigianis*

About the Author 277
Enjoyed the Anthology? 279

Will of the Mischief Maker

BY ANTOINE BANDELE

Eshu didn't care what the other Orishas said; the mortals had it right. They had bicycles, trains, cars, and most importantly, planes. Heck, even a sluggish air-balloon would've done the trick, no matter how slow it was. That would've been much better than climbing an endless golden chain to the heavens.

Sprinkles of water dewed Eshu's face and saturated his long, drooping hat. He thought it was the condensation of the clouds that wet him, but as he scaled farther and farther upward, the rushing of waterfalls filled his ears.

It might've been ages since he'd been up there, yet he knew he was close. He knew this not only because his loincloth and hat were getting soaked through, but because the strain in his arms was giving way to fatigue.

A few more grabs, pulls, and lifts later, and Eshu finally broke the plane of the tallest and thickest clouds. And it was about time —the strength in his hold was threatening to leave him, forcing him to tumble back to the Mortal Realm.

Before I get done here, Eshu thought, *I'm going to make some changes to this damn sky chain.*

A collection of floating mountains spread out ahead of him,

dotting the deep-blue canvas between the sky and heavens. The water that had ruined Eshu's clothes came flowing from the waterfalls that fell into the clouds to cast rain on the mortals below.

The Orisha grunted and wiped his face clean for the dozenth time. Then, with a long, resounding breath, he lifted himself over the small plot of earth, which served as an anchor for the sky chain.

Eshu took measure of his surroundings. It had been a while since he'd visited the Sky Realm. He remembered then why it had been so long. Everything up here was so ethereal, so peaceful, so perfect.

And absolutely a bore.

That's another thing the mortals got right. They knew how to spice up a place, make it their own. His fellow Orishas, however, especially the ones who lived way up in the clouds, had as much flavor as the human's oatmeal.

Squinting, Eshu surveyed each mountain atop their floating islands. He scanned for a specific peak... a snow-capped range that housed a certain Orisha of interest. And just there, between the sun's ray and the moon's glow, a perfectly angled cap of snow glimmered like a shining pyramid of silver-white.

"*Wà si mi,*" Eshu said, and a staff snapped into his hand from nothingness. He twisted the wooden shaft around his body, and his clothes dried in an instant.

"All right, old friend," he murmured. "Let's see if you're still up there."

With another flourish of his staff, a cluster of clouds gathered around his floating plot of earth. He smiled. Now that he had made the climb, he was free to travel as he pleased, free of the chain that suppressed the full use of his *Ashe*—his magical energy.

He tipped his toe on the first patch of cloud to test his purchase. When his weight found proper balance, he skipped along the clouds he manifested before him, one by one.

Eshu chuckled the entire way to Obatala's domain.

Knock, knock, knock.

Eshu slammed the bulky door knocker against the giant snow-swept doors for the dozenth time.

"Obatala!" he called out through cupped hands. "It's me, Eshu! Your old friend!"

There was no answer.

Eshu pouted in exaggerated annoyance. He didn't come all this way just to be ignored. And had he been any other Orisha, Obatala's cold-shoulder would've stuck, forcing him to return from where he came.

But Eshu wasn't like the others; he was the Gatekeeper, the Master of Thresholds. No path was ever obstructed to him.

It also helped that he was the one who installed the lock on Obatala's door to begin with.

Drawing out his staff once more, Eshu gave the grand doors a light tap. The enormous slabs of birch gave way to Eshu's magic without protest, lumbering inward. Snow dust shook off the opulent doors like a new day of winter, and light spilled into the empty foyer.

Eshu had a hard time keeping his eyes from squinting. Every surface in the tall room blinded him with its grand white staircase, white rugs, white banners, white vases, and white doves—the latter of which glided between the large windows and their wide sills.

"Hello!" Eshu called out once more.

His only response was his own echo.

So then... time to search.

In the Mortal Realm, the palace would've measured the size of a small city. But the daunting task of exploring its many halls, libraries, and chambers was nothing for the Master of Mischief. Every door opened to greet him like an old friend—though none of them offered up who he was looking for. He wasn't rude about it, of course, knocking before entering each room, sometimes with an "Eshu here," or a "the Gatekeeper seeks your audience," or his personal favorite, "is this where they keep the wine?"

Though none of the rooms housed Obatala, Eshu did find several curious items. In one chamber, he discovered a zoo of pale snails sloughing down marble walls; in one of the larger courtyards, he spotted a trio of albino elephants snacking on grass. But most interesting of all was a workshop filled wall-to-wall with ceramics.

The room had all the markings of an inventor's busy hands: loose boards, clay pots completed and in progression, and, of most value to Eshu, the figures of human bodies.

The sight brought a smirk across Eshu's lips. *Good, this should go perfectly.*

He continued onward.

Of course, as such things go, it was the last room Eshu searched that turned out to be the right one. It was at the highest tower in the highest study: Obatala's dream room.

In hindsight, he probably should have checked that one first.

Eshu couldn't tell where the room ended. When he stepped through the doorway, he had to float instead of walk, as there was technically no floor—or at least no floor he could discern far, far below.

Jutting prisms the size of a human movie theater screen studded each wall. And, like a movie screen, they depicted different images, first-person point-of-views of what Eshu assumed were human perspectives. Some of the windows showed a person flying through the sky, others: someone being chased, or people whose teeth were falling out.

"Is that the Gatekeeper I see?" a gentle, yet baritone voice said from above.

Eshu raised his eyes to the endless ceiling to find the giant of a towering Orisha descending upon him. With each passing moment, Obatala reduced in size until he was only slightly taller than Eshu himself.

He doesn't have to do that, Eshu thought.

He didn't mind being small, preferred it even, despite his fellows favoring more colossal builds. Then he remembered how considerate Obatala was. Even if Eshu voiced a complaint, Obatala wouldn't hear it. The ancient Orisha always wanted to put others at ease.

Obatala looked different from what Eshu remembered. How long had it been? A few centuries? A millennium? Whereas before Obatala looked no different from Eshu—save for his typically larger size—now he was devoid of all pigmentation.

Eshu had seen this blight on mortals before. They called it vitiligo, or was it albinism? Wasn't that Obatala's new role now? "*The Shepherd of the Imperfect*," the other Orishas called him.

"I almost didn't recognize you, old friend," Eshu said as Obatala continued to waft in the middle of the grand crystalline room. "Did you do something to your hair?" Eshu had only meant to quip at first, but one of the prisms shined off the distinctly bald head of Obatala's pale skin, a head that was once curtained by long, flowing hair. Now his scalp looked like a pearly bowling ball. "Oh, apparently you did..."

Obatala gave him a kind smirk and an airy chuckle. "It's good to see you too, Gatekeeper. A moment, please?"

He slothed a hand toward Eshu; Eshu glided out of his way.

Behind him, a section of the prism-wall reformed to show a new image: the point-of-view of someone at their desk toiling over complex mathematical equations.

"Whose head are we in right now?" Eshu asked.

Obatala pressed his hands along the fractured image. "This is Doctor Oladipo. He's been trying to work out a cure for glioblastoma."

"A glio—what?"

"A form of cancer."

"Right." Eshu nodded idly. "I always get my cancers mixed up."

Obatala inhaled deeply, then spoke a chant into the wall. With each of his words, the man's pen picked up speed along his notebook.

"He has the information in him," Obatala muttered between chants. "He just needs to manifest it. It's been so hard communing with the mortals. I usually don't work with them when they age past adolescence—they tend to trust in their dreams less and less as they grow. I've not had a breakthrough with one so old since Charles R. Drew decades ago."

"So, why not try communicating with them when they're younger?"

"Oh, I do, as you saw when you entered my domain. But so often the mortal adults ignore those early dreams. And sometimes I'm forced to resort to these... less than perfect circumstances." The scene within the prism changed. The doctor's hands pounded on his desk, and he bunched up his latest piece of paper to discard it.

"Doctor Oladipo always forgets the dreams I send as assistance." Obatala dropped his pale head. "But I can't give up. It's the least I can do for all my wrongs."

"You're not still hung up on *that*, are you?"

Years ago, Obatala had gotten himself drunk when he was charged with the construction of human bodies. He had never forgiven himself for the birth defects and disabilities he caused by his cavalier wine-downs.

"Always." Obatala brushed by Eshu and floated to another portion of the chamber. "You know, Olodumare wouldn't want you traveling between here and the Mortal Realm. I don't even know how you manage it."

"What kind of trickster would I be if I played by the rules? Besides, the Big Guy's been gone for a hot minute now."

"If a 'hot minute' is a few centuries, then yes."

"If you'd visit the mortals from time to time, you'd know the lingo, old friend."

"What are you up to, Gatekeeper?" Obatala cut to the chase with a gentle, curious tone.

"I'll admit it. I'm bored and I'm looking for some company."

"Hah!" Obatala's laugh shook the entire room. "I've never known you to be so easily bored. Have you exhausted all forms of mischief in such brief a time in the Mortal Realm?"

He spun to another prism display. This one showed a cafeteria with the viewer surrounded by a group of children who jeered about the way the child tapped their foot on the corners of the linoleum tiles as they spoke.

"I am trying to help this one gain some social confidence. But more and more, her dreams are tarnished by these other children. Just a few months ago, before starting school, you should have seen the things she was dreaming about. Oh, look! She is transitioning." Obatala's wide and brilliant irises lit up all the brighter. Even in his exclamation his voice was soft and muted. "She is going over Einstein's equations. Not just reciting, but actually forming her own thoughts around it."

"See, friend," Eshu patted Obatala on the shoulder, "where you see faults, I see talent that could never be achieved if this child were born like all the others. How many mortal children do you know who can reform facts as their own thoughts as fast as this one?"

Obatala hummed under his lips. Eshu couldn't tell if the sound was meant to communicate agreement or irritation.

"Tell me," Eshu pried as innocently as possible, "when was the last time you fashioned a human body?"

Obatala shook his head, and a shadow passed over his eyes. "Never again."

"You fear what your hands might make? Well, old friend, I could help you there..." Eshu waved his staff at the nearest prism and reformed an image of Obatala with long hair crafting human bodies. "When's the last time you've tried making a vessel for a non-mortal? One of the Orishas, for example."

Obatala sucked at his teeth and moved around Eshu to another prism. "I knew you came here for a reason. No, Gatekeeper. I will not mold a body for you."

"Come now," Eshu groaned, following along like a pestering child, "it's the only way I can interact with the mortals properly. You, of all of us, should know of the desire to assist them."

"I can't. I refuse."

Okay, so direct questioning wasn't going to do it. Eshu let a silence fall between them as he shifted to a different tack.

"I know what plagues you each day, each season, each era," Eshu began solemnly. "You never got to properly finish your work all that time ago. Not before Oduduwa took over—"

Obatala spun rapidly on Eshu, and the entire chamber darkened like a stormy night. "Never speak that name in my domain."

Eshu threw up his hands. "Of course, of course, excuse me. But think of what you could do! You should have a direct hand in the creation of new human bodies. They could be in the image you truly wanted, what you intended."

Obatala's gaze shifted between another prism and Eshu, seemingly conflicted.

"Listen." Eshu floated in close to Obatala, then murmured, "I'm not asking you to go back to an assembly line. Just one. And for me, not for a human soul."

"Well..." he started to relent, but his pursed lips told of a brewing stubbornness.

Eshu drew in even closer, merely an inch from Obatala's face. "If anything goes wrong, nothing bad will happen. I'll hop out of the body, and you can always try again another time."

"I have wanted to try it out once more..." Obatala said almost to himself. "That much I'll admit."

Eshu careened around Obatala, just at the edge of the Orisha's ear. "Come now. I know what the other Orishas say. I know why you seclude yourself at the highest peaks within the highest clouds. If you made another human body, one of note, none of them could speak against you."

"The Great Monarch hasn't been with us for many ages. I would need his approval to begin with."

Perfect. He was no longer denying his want, no longer

denying his capacity to do the task. Now, he was just looking for permission.

And Eshu could give it to him.

"Well, old friend, you are speaking to the Gatekeeper. I'm the next best thing. I saw your workshop coming in—your ceramic work. You've been trying again, haven't you?"

Eshu snapped his fingers, and the room's prisms transformed into the image of Obatala's workshop. "What's that just there?" He nodded to a clay piece in the shape of a bird. "Were you trying with animals first?"

Obatala nodded. "That is the dodo. The humans did away with them decades ago, and I was trying to—No. No, I cannot. I just don't have it in me anymore." He gave Eshu a condoling touch on the shoulder. "Thank you. I appreciate your kind words. But you'll have to go now, old friend."

"You know something, maybe you're right. After all, your best works always came off the back of... liquid inspiration."

"Do not goad me, Gatekeeper. I have been sober for more ages than I can count." Obatala narrowed his bright, pulsating eyes. "If I were to slip back now... who knows what I would do, what I might manifest."

Eshu turned with a shrug. "Ah, I didn't realize you had sworn off the drink like *that*. I might as well do away with this gift I got for you."

Obatala's eyes glinted. "Gift?"

Eshu continued bouncing away from the chamber in a floating skip. "I don't see how my gift could interest someone who claims to be free from liquor."

Obatala sniffed the air. "Is... is that palm wine I smell?"

Eshu beamed as he said, "*Wà sí mi*," and a bottle of milk-white palm wine popped into his hand from thin air. "It even comes in your favorite color. Straight from Osun State."

Obatala stretched out his hand, then drew it back in. Stretched it out once more, then drew it in again. "That's where the Oyo Empire used to be, yes?"

"One and the same. And I'll tell you what, the mortals have gotten even better at fermenting it."

"Oh, I've not had some of that in many, many, ages... not since the Great Monarch's Decree of Separation." He drifted toward Eshu as he licked his lips. Eshu smiled. This was going to be too easy.

But then the pale Orisha stopped, lips slightly parted. "Wait. You took this from the Mortal Realm? You have shown yourself to one of them?"

"Nah..." Eshu replied. "I couldn't even if I attempted to. I'm just a whisper to mortal ears. Trust me, I've tried to communicate with them for centuries, just as you have."

"Oh... good, good." He turned away from Eshu—and the bottle—composing himself once more. "Shango has told me the same about the mortals' elevated skills in fermentation. *He* tried getting me to drink some as well." Despite his retreat, he kept giving the bottle sidelong glances over his shoulder. "What's the catch?"

Eshu drew back with an exaggerated hand to his chest. "No catch at all. I just want to see you do what you do best—what you were *made* to do, old friend."

Obatala stroked his chin, seeming to pull at the long beard that used to be there. He glanced at the changed image of his room, which still depicted his ceramic workshop.

Eshu was so close. His celestial comrade just needed some encouragement. A reminder of better times.

"I'm sure you recall when we used to drink near the Osun River. We used to play *ayoayo* as we watched the sun set in the Mortal Realm. Do you remember?"

Obatala chuckled inwardly. "Oh yes, I remember. Those were simpler times. Before the Great Monarch set me to molding human bodies. And before Odu—" The Orisha was about to break his own rule by speaking the name. "Before I made a mess of everything."

"Let's have a bottle together. For old time's sake, at least."

The grimace on Obatala's face and his body drifting toward Eshu were at odds, each seemingly pulling against the other. "No, I cannot. I have too many responsibilities now. I can't be drinking."

"Fine, then. No drinking. But what about a game of ayoayo?"

Obatala took in another deep breath, then pierced Eshu with a stare of irritation. His first *true* glare of irritation. Eshu simply floated there with mirth, unfazed by the intense gaze.

"A game..." Obatala trailed, his expression softening. "A game I could do. You have been practicing since last time, I hope."

Eshu smiled. "You know it."

***

And so the Orishas played their game. The rules were simple: two rows of six holes filled with four cowries each. The objective was to "sow" more "seeds" than the opponent. First to twenty-one won.

The game was a simple one, but one of Eshu's favorites. On the surface, it was an elementary game for children, but in reality, it was a trickster's haven.

And Eshu loved setting his opponents up to make poor moves.

At that moment, however, he made sure to let Obatala win a few rounds. This was key. Of course, Eshu didn't let him win so many rounds—or so easily—that his ruse would be uncovered. Just enough to make Obatala think he had the edge. And for added distraction, Eshu peppered in some light chit-chat.

"You really gotta come down to the Mortal Realm with me sometime," he said after a particularly daring play. "They've got this thing called social media. Complete waste of time, but oh so fun."

"Oh yes." Obatala made his next move and smiled. "There's this one, erm, application the mortals keep dreaming about... it's called Insta-Spam? No. Insta-Lamb? No, that's not right. Insta-Yam? Something along those lines."

"Close enough." Eshu clutched his stomach. "Oh, some yams sound great right about now..."

Orisha couldn't eat food in the same way mortals could. Sure, they could pass meals across their mouths, but it was like tasting the ghost of something, not the full thing. One couldn't fully enjoy the flavor of mortal food unless one had a mortal body. That was something Eshu was looking forward to. He just needed to keep his wits about him, and a mortal body would be his.

As they got deeper and deeper into the game, floating in the middle of the chamber cross-legged, Eshu caught Obatala's gaze slipping to the palm wine, which hovered at their side. The trickster had deliberately taken swigs from it after each of his losses, smacking his lips so that the sweet tang could waft between them —and hopefully ensnare Obatala.

"How about we make this next game a bit more interesting?" Eshu finally asked. "If I win the following round, we will take a drink together. A little taste."

"And *when* I win," Obatala said, "What do I get then?"

Eshu stroked his chin. "*If* you win the next round... I'll lighten your load a little. I'll promise to come visit at least once every decade to help with your dreams. A thousand mortals for each of your victories. Directly, that is."

Obatala ran his hand over his bald head as though flipping back long strands of hair. "I would benefit from the help," he intoned. "Okay, Gatekeeper. You have a deal. But you've lost most of your games. Your victory seems... unlikely."

Not as unlikely as you think, Eshu thought, but what he said out loud was, "That's because I wasn't properly motivated before, old friend. On this next round, you had best come correct."

Obatala tilted his head. "Come correct?"

"Some more mortal-talk. Don't trip—I mean, don't worry yourself."

And so they continued their game, and Eshu handily won

round after round. He had seen how Obatala played, recognized each of his moves and his preferred paths to victory. Eshu cut him off at every pass, winning every round by definitive leads. And with each of his victories, Obatala took a sip of the palm wine.

His first few were meager attempts at drinking, but with each loss, he took deeper and deeper swallows. Even on their seventh game, which he had surprisingly won, Obatala still took a drink—out of habit or because he was feeling himself, Eshu couldn't tell.

"All right, that's one-thousand of your mortals I'll over-watch," Eshu reminded him.

Obatala gave him an expression of mild confusion, then said, "Oh, right! Yes, yes."

By the twelfth round, and the twelfth chug of palm wine, Obatala had begun slurring his words.

That's when Eshu enacted his next gambit. "Okay, good games, good games. Now that you've loosened up, let's see if you've still got the touch." Eshu snapped his fingers, and a ceramic torso manifested between them. "I took the liberty of bringing this torso mold here from your workshop. Let's see what you can do with it. Complete it, if you can."

To Eshu's surprise, he was met without protest. Obatala, with the limp hands of one under the influence, started work on his mold. His hands stroked along the lumpy surface, turning it from something amorphous to the distinct figure of a human chest, human ribs, and human abs.

"Impeccable work, old friend." Eshu ran his hand over the outer layer of skin. It felt like the real thing, even down to the little hairs. "The belly is a little flabby, however."

Obatala shrugged. "I think it gives it a nice look... a unique shape."

Eshu wasn't about to get fussy about a little pudge, so he let it go. He couldn't talk anyway. He had a bit of a muffin top himself... Maybe that was Obatala's motivation. Plus, beggars couldn't be choosers, and this was more than he was hoping to achieve with Obatala in a single day. Skies, Eshu was expecting this whole ordeal to take at least a few years, maybe even a few decades.

His old friend must've been *really* lonely.

With Eshu's next win, Obatala gave the torso arms, and the win after that came the legs. All that remained after the third win was the most important piece, and the most difficult part.

Eshu snapped his fingers once more, and this time, the ayoayo board winked out of existence, replaced by a lumpy mold of an unfinished head.

"All right," Eshu said, "the last piece. You're almost there. If you can complete your work, I'll test drive it for you, take it down to the mortal realm and make sure it's well put together. What do you say? Make me a face that you think will suit me."

Obatala, now properly filled with the wine, wheezed and took up the challenge. Though the torso and limbs had only taken a few minutes, the head, and particularly the face, took several hours. Eshu, in patient silence, watched his old friend at work, and he couldn't have been prouder.

Lines cut through Obatala's forehead with the valleys of concentration, his lips pursed, his hands steady. Anytime he stopped to examine his work, he took another drink of the palm wine—Eshu assumed he did it to relax. Yet the measured way he moved his hands, the utter concentration in his slitted eyes, filled Eshu with joy.

And he hadn't even revealed the best part of the whole charade yet.

To pass the time, Eshu adjusted the dream room's prisms to show different landscapes with a flick of his finger like changing a human's television channel: an underwater cove with sharks that had glowing streaks along their heads, a swampy marsh with dark trees backdropped by vivid indigo, a volcanic vent smoldering molten rocks. Then he called forth several masks he had been working on. The other Orishas would've called his projects forgeries. Eshu preferred to call them homages.

He was in the middle of working out how to replicate the

mask of Orunmila, the Orisha of Divination—and one of Obatala's neighbors—when the head was finally completed.

"You know something?" Obatala lifted the head aloft, turning it to see it in different angles of light. "It's not my best work... but I think it'll hold up."

Eshu floated across the room to examine the face. Not his best work, he said? It was *perfect*. Exactly what he needed: friendly, approachable, and most of all, unassuming.

"Do you mind?" Eshu nudged his chin to the completed body.

Obatala held out a steady hand. "By all means, Gatekeeper."

Eshu, taking in a deep breath, closed his eyes and concentrated.

He visualized himself as the body, forced his will through its bone, sinew, muscles, and skin alike. The longer he fixated on the human sensations of proper touch, proper scent, and proper sound, the weight of it all settled.

Being a human was both marvelous and exceedingly limiting.

He felt things he couldn't fully touch as an immortal. He expected human skin to feel clammy or moist with how much they sweated, but it was instead smooth and delicate. And the simple act of staying afloat amid the room took twice the effort than it had before, not only because the body was on the heavier side but because humans were filled with far less Ashe than the Orishas, which made them so light. Plus, Eshu had to keep reminding himself that he needed to actively breathe.

Then he opened his eyes.

My goodness, how blind the humans are, he thought.

It took several minutes for him to make out where he even was. The room's prisms, which had now returned to their default crystalline visage, blurred before him. The perfect clarity and field of view he was used to was cut in half. It was like being thrown into a dark tunnel with only the smallest morsel of light at the end.

His damned human eyes took their time, but eventually they

cleared enough to make sense of the pale figure ahead. Where he expected to find the warm smile of Obatala, instead he was met with the countenance of sorrow.

"You know," Obatala said darkly, "This was the last body I started before I went into my drunken episode. The very last. I never thought I could do it again, could finish it..."

"But you have, old friend." Eshu placed his new hand on Obatala's shoulder. The effort felt slow and sluggish, and the Orisha's skin radiated with a heat Eshu wasn't expecting.

Despite Eshu's gesture of goodwill, Obatala still frowned. "My followers... what will they think of me? They know I don't drink. They know I abhor it. When the other Orishas find out, I'll never hear the end of it. I should never have taken a sip."

Eshu would have felt guilt at these words, but instead, he smiled. "Never fear. Your sobriety is still very much intact."

Obatala lifted his head; his eyebrow quirked. "What do you mean?"

"While true this was indeed palm wine," Eshu grabbed the bottle and poured it out, "it is *not* fermented, and thus, non-alcoholic."

Obatala's eyes descended with the liquid, which fell to the bottom of the room where, eventually, it splashed on the floor far, far below.

"You mean to say," he said, realization dawning on him, "*I* did all that myself."

"You did it all on your own, old friend."

Obatala stared at his hands, transfixed. For centuries, he must've thought he could never put them to work as they had been at the beginning of humankind. Now, he knew he could.

Eshu nodded his approval. He might've been a trickster, but that didn't make him heartless. With a small salute, he turned away from Obatala and drifted out of the room. He'd better get back to the Mortal Realm now. He could already feel his Orisha powers waning, and, with his new mortal body, he felt the need for a very long nap—a foreign concept to an Orisha.

"Where are you going?" Obatala called after him.

At the threshold of the dream room, Eshu waddled through a half turn and gave his old friend an awkward salute—it was going to take a while to get used to the human body. "I wasn't being dishonest when I said I'd test drive this body for you. There's someone I want to visit who needs a lesson of their own."

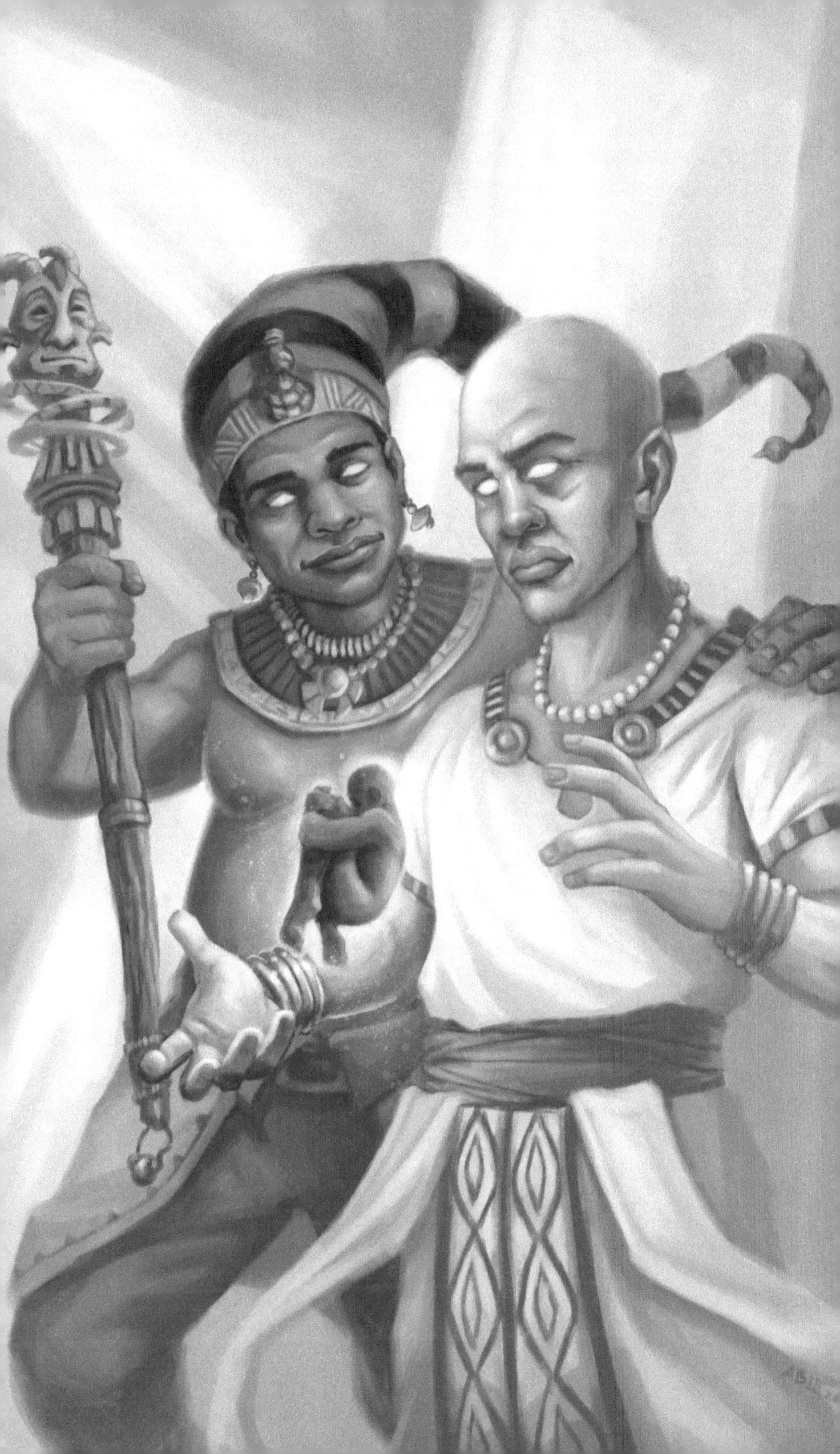

ABOUT THE AUTHOR

Antoine lives in Los Angeles, CA with his girlfriend and cat. He is a YouTuber, producing work for his channel "Antoine Bandele".

He is also an audiobook engineer and publisher.

Whenever he has the time, he's writing books inspired by African folklore, mythology, and history.

antoinebandele.com

The Queen's Kitchen

BY KRS MCENTIRE

Joy's earliest and best memories took place in her grandmother's soul food restaurant.

During summer, when school was out, Joy, mama, and her brother, Justus, would pile into mama's car and drive to Queen's Kitchen long before the sun came up. They would stay at the restaurant until it was dark outside again, but Joy didn't mind. She played under the tables and chairs with her brother and cousin as the grown-ups prepared to start the day.

As Joy grew older, she helped her grandmother polish tables, wash dishes, and set out menus. She was proud of how well she helped the adults. There never was a slow day at Queens Kitchen. The large, busy eatery was the most popular spot in town. People came from all over the city to get a plate, sometimes waiting in hour-long lines outside the door. Grandma's food was just *that good*. People said it tasted like magic. Joy didn't know about all that, but the sounds of forks hitting glass, friendly conversation, and laughter felt like music to Joy. The warm, hearty food cooking in the basement smelled like home.

Joy wasn't allowed in the basement. The door was always locked. Aside from the cooks, grandma, mama, and auntie were the only people to ever go down there. Whenever one of the children got close to the basement door, Grandma would rush over to guard the entrance like a dragon guarding its lair. She was especially diligent about watching Joy's older cousin, Keisha, who claimed to have snuck in the basement before.

"Grown-ups are working their magic in the kitchen," Grandma would say. "They don't need distractions."

Grandma was a tall, plump woman with long, salt-and-pepper hair and a youthful sparkle in her eye. She was the center of the restaurant, the crowning jewel of their family, and she guarded that basement door like it was full of secrets. Joy's older cousin, Keisha, was convinced it was.

"There is something strange going on in the basement," Keisha said quietly to Joy, as if she were a co-conspirator in her mad ideas. She had a long list of theories about the restaurant's basement. Most of them involved aliens or ghosts. Joy thought that, at fourteen, Keisha would be a lot less likely to believe in magic. Or maybe Joy was just more mature than her.

Joy, Keisha, and Justus were sitting at a small spare table between a large sink and the door to the basement. Keisha fiddled with her bracelet, a fancy, sparkly thing that looked much too expensive to belong to a child. Grandpa was at the sink in a newsboy cap, washing a few dishes, humming a song, and occasionally glancing at the children to make sure they stayed put.

The table was out of the customer's view, so the adults let them hide away and play. Plastic food and tiny pots and pans were sprawled out on the table and ignored as Keisha shared her latest conspiracy theory.

"Think about it," Keisha said, looking over at Grandpa suspiciously before looking back at them. "This restaurant is huge, but only mom, auntie, and grandma ever go down there. How can three people cook enough food for all of these customers by themselves? They don't ever stay down there long enough to cook anything."

"They hire cooks." Justus, the youngest of the trio at ten years old, sighed as he pushed his glasses up his nose. Despite his youth, he had a practical and analytical mind. "We already know what you think."

Joy lifted her hands and wiggled her fingers dramatically. "Ghosts are making the food."

Justus giggled. "Aliens live in the basement." The siblings laughed together.

Keisha scowed at them. "I *know* what I saw." Keisha claimed to have snuck into the basement when Joy was very little and Justus wasn't born yet.

"You said you saw nothing," Joy said.

"Exactly! There was no kitchen, no cooks, nothing. Just a dark, empty basement," Keisha said as she fiddled with her bracelet. "I saw grandma go down there, but when I followed her, there was nothing. I didn't even see Grandma. It was like she'd been... abducted."

"By the aliens," Justus said with a grin, shooting Joy a cheeky smile.

"By *something*," Keisha insisted.

"Think about this logically, Keisha," Justus said. "Do you really think if something weird was in the basement they would go down there?"

"And if it's empty, why do the grown-ups go down there at all?" Joy put her elbows on the table and rested her chin in her palms. "Besides, I can smell food cooking and hear the cooks moving around behind the door. If they weren't cooking in there, I wouldn't hear a thing."

Keisha lifted a finger. "What cooks, Joy? We get here early every day, before anyone else. Have you ever seen anyone go down there to cook? No, you have not. There is no kitchen down there!"

Joy listened to faint voices coming from the basement and the *clings* of pots and pans from behind the basement door. She smelled the scent of cornbread baking and meat frying.

"You were a little kid, younger than Justus is now. You might have been confused." Joy could hear the *click click click* of her grandmother's shoes approaching. She lowered her voice before she continued talking. "Besides, not seeing anything isn't proof of ghosts."

Grandma eyed all three of them as she walked past. "I have ten dollars and an apple pie for whoever can help grandpa wash the most dishes."

Joy and Justus lept from their seats and followed grandma to the sink.

"I'll be right there," Keisha said. Her hands were balled into fists, and her forehead was wrinkled in frustration.

"Hey, beautiful." Grandpa's face lit up as grandma walked into the room.

"Hi, love." Grandma grinned and gave him a kiss on the cheek before rushing back to the dining room.

Joy washed eleven plates before Keisha came back from the bathroom, a triumphant and mischievous smile on her face. Joy could hear the faint sound of something going *jingle jangle'* in Keisha's pocket. She waited until grandma and grandpa stepped away before confronting her cousin.

"What did you do?" Joy whispered.

Keshia grinned as she pulled a pair of keys out of her pocket and passed them to Joy.

Joy's eyes grew wide with shock. She shoved the key into her pocket and looked around to make sure no one saw. "You stole grandma's keys!" she growled quietly.

"If you don't believe me about the basement, then you should go look for yourselves," Keisha said. "Unless you're chicken."

"You *know* I can't get past grandma." Joy rolled her eyes.

Keisha put her hands on her hips and flapped them like a bird. *"Bawk bawk bawk!"*

"Stop it!" Joy said. "I'm not scared. I'm just smart. We see the grown-ups bringing food up from the basement all day long. There is a kitchen in the basement and nothing else!"

"Then go take a look at it yourself."

Joy rolled her eyes. "You *know* they'll stop me."

"Not if you're fast." Keisha winked, rushed off into the dining room, and leapt on top of a freshly washed table. The guests gasped in shock. Mama, auntie, and grandma rushed over to get her down and scold her.

"Keisha!" Auntie bellowed. "You know better than that!"

"What has gotten into you! Act your age!" Mama said.

Auntie tried to scoop Keisha up, but Keisha lept away. She fell from the table and proceeded to cry as grown-ups crowded around her. Joy couldn't ever tell if she was really hurt. Her cousin had always been a good actor.

Joy's hand fell to her pocket. She gripped the cool, metal keys and took a tentative step to the large, wood door that led to the basement.

It's now or never. Joy thought. Her heart beat in her chest like drums as she pulled out her key and opened the basement door.

The stairway to the basement was darker than she expected. The stairs were narrow and steep, but there was a faint blue light below. If people were cooking in the kitchen, she wondered why they had most of the lights off.

Joy tried to shut the door quietly, but it slammed behind her. She grimaced, convinced her grandma and mother would come to punish her. The doorknob had a double-sided lock, which filled Joy with relief. She locked the grown-ups out.

Even if they had an extra key, Joy had bought herself some time. Enough time to prove Keisha wrong about her silly ghost theory. Joy slid her hand across the wall, hoping to find a light switch. Unable to find one, she crept down toward the pale blue light.

The narrow staircase squeaked under Joy's weight with a loud *creeeakkkkk.*

After her first step, she could no longer smell the food. The smell of cornbread, greens, potatoes, chicken, beef, and stews could be smelt from outside the door, but not here where the kitchen supposedly was.

She took another step. All she could hear was another *creeaakk* of the stairs beneath her feet. Nothing else. No clanging of pots, no banging of pans, not even the voices of cooks issuing orders to each other. The faint voices she heard through the door every day were gone. Could mama, aunty, and grandma really make all of that food themselves? Why did they tell Joy that there were people working down here if that was the case?

Joy made her way to the bottom of the staircase. It was a large, empty, dusty basement. There was no oven, stove, or food, just a bunch of plates and silverware on a long table. The only light here came from a dull blue lightbulb that lay on the small end table in the corner. Fear twisted in Joy's gut as she struggled to see in the dark. She was starting to think Keisha's alien theory might have some truth to it.

She approached the lightbulb with curiosity. It wasn't attached to a lamp or plugged into a wall. When she got closer, she realized it wasn't a lightbulb at all, but some type of glowing rock or crystal. Joy had never seen anything like it before. She didn't see a wire attached, so she assumed it must run on batteries. She peered closer and considered picking it up.

The door on top of the staircase swung open and crashed into the wall with a boom.

"Joy!" her mother's voice called, "Joy, get up here right now!" Footsteps raced down the squeaky stairs.

In a panic, Joy picked up the glowing stone to put it in her pocket. It felt warm, then hot as her touch caused it to emit even more light. She gasped as it shone so brightly it all but blinded her. She shut her eyes, tensed her muscles, and waited for her mom to scoop her up, but no one touched her. When she dared to open her eyes she was no longer in the basement. Jo's mouth fell open in shock.

The spacious room looked like the inside of a palace, with glossy marble floors, tall white ceilings, and immaculate furnishings. A chandelier hung from the ceiling, and its colorful stained glass windows reminded Joy of old churches.

There were dozens of tables, covered with fancy blue and gold tablecloths. Large groups of people sat at each table eating. There were old people with ice gray hair, young families with babies in tow, people in fancy attire, and others in simple clothes.

Some of the people in the room were dressed in suits and dresses nicer than any Joy had seen before. Some of the food reminded Joy of grandma's menu, but other items were foreign. She eyed a large goose that sat in a roasting pan, head still attached to its seasoned and cooked body.

"Welcome, child." A woman's voice said from behind her.

Joy spun around and saw two people sitting on large white thrones, overseeing the festivities. The woman wore a sparkly, golden dress and had gold accents in her black, curly hair. Her chestnut brown skin and gray eyes reminded her of grandma. The man wore a tailored blue and golden suit, his short hair cut partially hidden by a large crown.

Joy took a step back, eyes wide. *What was this place? Who were these people?* She looked down at the stone in her hand. It felt cool and ceased to glow.

"I didn't expect to meet you until you were much older," The man said with a warm, eager smile. "There is no need to be afraid, Joy. We are family. Welcome to the Adaeze Kingdom."

Every eye in the room was on Joy. They whispered, but she couldn't make out their words. She felt out of place in her jeans, sneakers, and t-shirt. Even people who weren't wearing fancy clothes still seemed to dress a lot nicer than her here. She put her stone in her pocket and gulped. Her mouth was dry and no words came to her.

"I see you found your grandmother's moonstone," the woman said as she stood up from her throne. Tall and lean, she was even more beautiful standing. Her dress had a small golden train that flowed behind her as she walked toward Joy. The woman offered Joy her hand, her elegant manicured fingers had gold tips that were just slightly lighter than the golden hue of her skin. Her hair was big and proud, but her eyes felt familiar. They were so much like grandmas.

"I don't know how I got here," Joy admitted. "I must be dreaming."

The woman shook her head and offered a kind and gentle smile. "You are not dreaming, child. This is a homecoming. You are finally waking up."

"Are you a princess?" Joy asked. "You look like a princess."

The woman laughed, "My name is Asha. You definitely look more like a princess than me. Just a spitting image of my daughter when she was your age."

Joy could feel her cheeks grow warm. In her dirty play clothes, she knew she didn't look royal. "Your daughter?"

"Would you take a walk with me?" Asha asked.

Joy nodded and followed, eager to be away from the crowd. She was careful not to step on the train of the woman's dress as she made her way past people who whispered and leered at her. Joy thought she saw a man with antlers on his head. *It must be an elaborate costume,* she decided. But there was something off about most of the people. From eyes that were a little too red or blue, to bodies that moved just a little swifter than she'd ever seen, something about these people put her on edge.

Asha led Joy out of the dining room to a long hallway and opened a door that led outside. Joy gasped at the scene before her. They were in a tropical paradise. It reminded Joy of her family vacation in the Caribbean.

There was a beach in the distance, a warm breeze, and plenty of palm trees offering generous shade. A pathway from the door to the garden led to the waves. Joy stepped outside and allowed the sun to warm her skin like a blanket. Flowers of the richest red, blue, and orange filled the garden, and Joy watched as butterflies and hummingbirds zipped around.

Joy squinted at the birds. There was something odd about them. They were so fast she could hardly see them, but they looked uncharacteristically petite.

"Hello!" A tiny voice called out to her. It took Joy a moment to realize the voice came from one of the birds.

Joy screamed and stumbled back, almost tripping over her own ankles to get away from the possessed bird.

The bird zapped away, equally afraid of her. "Wow! You're a loud one," It said. "What if I screamed like that when I saw your face?"

"You can talk?" Joy asked the bird. But as it slowed its pace she realized it wasn't a bird at all. It looked like a small woman with wings, her long dark hair pulled back in elaborate braids that floated in the wind like feathers.

The tiny flying woman pushed out her bottom lip in a pout. "Yes, only *I* know that what I choose to say is more important than how loud I can say it. No need to yell at me."

She flew away and disappeared amongst the branches of a large tree.

Joy looked back at Asha and raised an eyebrow, hoping for an explanation.

"Don't be alarmed," Asha said. "It's a fairy. An Aziza, to be exact. They are your kin, too, child. Not all of the blood that runs through your veins is human."

They took a seat on a wooden bench near the edge of the garden. Joy watched the waves wash onto the shore. From here, she could see that the building they had left did, indeed, look like a modern castle with ivory walls and pillars that raised to the sky.

"I've never seen a castle on a beach," Joy said. "I mean, not unless it's made of sand. When you say that fairy is my kin, are you saying I'm from this place?"

"Your grandmother, my daughter, was next in line to be queen. You have Aziza blood, and on my husband's side of the family, you have dragon's blood. Our blood flows through your veins, child."

Joy eyes her suspiciously. "If grandma is your daughter, why do you look younger than her?"

"Time works differently in the Adaeze Kingdom. Your grandmother has spent more time in your mortal realm, so she ages as such. Would you like some tea?"

"Sure." Joy looked around the garden, unsure of where they would get tea from.

Asha held out her hands, palms up, and two golden teacups materialized upon them. She offered one to Joy.

"You have magic?" Joy asked while taking the cup.

Asha grinned and tasted her own cup of tea.

Joy sipped the tea, which was warm and sweet. "Why would grandma leave a place like this? You live like royalty."

"Finish your tea, and I'll show you more."

The tea did wonders for Joy's nerves. She was no longer thinking about being stuck in a strange new world, or even about getting in trouble with mama. She just wanted to enjoy the breeze and learn more about this magical world.

"If you want to understand why your grandma left, you should see what our kingdom is like. I have a friend who can give you a tour of the kingdom."

"A friend?"

"I'll call him over. Let me know when you are ready."

Joy chugged down her tea and sat her teacup on the bench. "Ready!"

Asha stood up, raised a hand to the heavens, and murmured to herself. Her voice was so low that Joy couldn't hear her words, but as she spoke the wind picked up and the palm trees started to shift and sway from the force of it. A beating sound like nothing Joy had ever heard before filled the air around them.

"Is that...thunder?" Joy tried to place it. But thunder wasn't quite right. Joy's hair, in two proud braids, started to blow about. The ocean waves became heavier. The sand started to shift, and even the grass and flowers in the garden stirred about. When the cause of the sound finally made it into Joy's field of vision, she gasped in shock.

A large beast emerged in the sky with scaly green and white skin. Every flap of its wings roared like thunder, the wind from its force sending chills through Joy's spine.

Joy had seen dragons in movies, but the real thing was bigger than she could have ever imagined. Joy was certain its blood-red eyes were larger than she was.

The dragon swooped down, and Joy's heart fluttered with fear. She turned, ready to race to the castle for safety.

"Be still, child." Asha said as the dragon swooped down, and Joy's nose wrinkled at its smell. It was a strong scent that didn't exactly stink but didn't smell like roses either. It reminded Joy of rain and smoke. The beast smiled as it landed, curling up the edges of his scaly lips to reveal sharp white teeth.

Asha picked Joy up, grunting under Joy's weight.

"What are you doing?" Joy demanded. Her muscled tensed and she shrieked in shock as Asha moved toward the dragon.

"Calm down," Asha whispered. "I want him to see that you are with me. You are a friend and not a threat."

I'm going to be dragon food, Joy thought.

Joy shut her eyes, waiting for the end, as she felt the women leap into the air. Wind crashed against her face. When Joy finally gained the courage to peek she realized they were on the dragon's back as it raced high above the palace.

Joy gripped one of the dragon's scales, sandy white and slightly larger than her hand, and held on for dear life. She wondered how they didn't fall off at such high speeds. Did magic help keep them on the dragon's back?

"Once upon a time, many years ago, your grandma was in line for the throne," Asha said, apparently unbothered by the fact that they were hundreds of feet above the ground. While the castle was easily the most impressive building around, there was a large town not too far away with dozens of quaint yet beautiful buildings and houses.

"Your grandmother, my daughter, was an odd princess. She spent her free time in town befriending peasant children, in nature with the animals, or in the palace kitchen with the cooks. She loved to cook most of all. They let her experiment with food because, well, you can't say no to the future queen." The woman laughed. "It wasn't until she was twelve did she realize she could save time by simply making food with her magic."

The dragon flew over a tropical forest. Beyond the forest, there was another small village.

"She was altruistic. On her birthdays, rather than receiving gifts for herself, she invited people from Kingdoms far and wide for grand dinners. Though her birthday dinner galas made our parents nervous at first, even the village peasants and nobles from foreign lands were welcome to your grandmother's table. She was an adventurer too, exploring every inch of the world, meeting people from every small village and large kingdom. But there was one place we never expected her to find because we didn't know it existed."

The dragon swooped toward the ground and landed near a circle of small stones. It reminded Joy of a smaller version of Stonehenge, but these were not normal rocks. They seemed to hum and glow with energy. The small stones were about the size of the stone in her pocket and they had a soft blue glow. One large stone sat in the middle of the circle of smaller stones, glowing brightly.

Joy jumped off the dragon, eager to have her feet on the ground again. Asha followed, and the dragon curled up like a giant cat and rested as it waited on them. She took a few steps away from the beast. Just its toe was larger than she was.

"Come, child." Asha walked to the stones.

Joy's hand fell to the crystal in her pocket. It was warm. She felt dizzy and her head hurt, but her heart raced with adrenaline. She took a step toward the glowing center stone. It looked like a large version of the crystal in her pocket. Each of the tiny stones around it shimmered just like the one in her hand.

"Your grandmother discovered this place," Asha said. "This is how she first entered your mortal realm."

'You mean to tell me each stone leads to a different city?"

"Nothing so mundane, child. Each moonstone leads to a different world. First, she brought the Fairies here. Their home was in danger, you see, and we afforded them a safe place to live. Next, she brought the dragons. She met elves, dwarves, vampires, werewolves, and merfolk in various worlds, but when she found your mortal realm she loved it most of all."

Joy wrinkled her nose. "Why would she love our world most of all? It's nothing like this! We don't have any magic where I'm from."

"Every world has magic, child. But over time, magic can start to feel routine. You forget how miraculous your own world can be," Asha said. "Sometimes you have to find the magic again, or bring some of your own. As for why she chose your world, please remember this, child. Love can make any home a castle and any person a King. In your world, she met a boy, fell in love, and didn't want to leave him."

Asha held out her palm, and smoke appeared above her fingers. The smoke danced and swirled until it formed an image of a woman. It took Joy a moment to realize it was a younger version of her grandmother. In front of her stood a man in overalls and a newsboy cap.

"Grandpa?" Joy asked.

The queen nodded.

"Has he been to this world before? Does he know grandma is from here?"

"He found her when she first arrived in your world, but he's never been here." The queen snapped her fingers, and the smoke faded away. "It would be dangerous for him to travel by moonstone because he doesn't have our bloodline."

"So mama can come here?"

"Yes, your mother and aunt have been here. I wonder if they have forgotten..."

"How could they forget?"

A sad smile filled Asha's face. She wouldn't meet Joy's gaze. "Your grandmother, she has no problem remembering no matter how long she spends in your world. But the others... I wish it wasn't so, but they quickly forget this world. I'm not sure why. Maybe its because they didn't grow up here like your grandmother did. I do feel like part of my family is missing."

Joy looked at the mountains in the distance and the vast, green tropical forest. "I could never forget a place like this" Joy turned to face Asha. "Are you saying I'm not fully human?"

"You are partially human, but your lineage allows you safe passage by Moonstone. The blood of fae and dragons run through your veins, that is why you can come here."

"Moonstone." Joy repeated, pulling the stone out of her pocket. It grew brightly once again. "Can I use it to get home?"

The woman nodded. "Yes, child. You can go home whenever you wish. I know your grandma's probably worried sick about you."

Joy frowned. "But if I go home, can I come back?"

The woman sighed. "While your grandmother and mother would prefer to raise you strictly in the human realm, this is your home, too, by birthright. I welcome you back anytime if they allow it. However, after you get back home, this place may feel like a dream. Eventually, it may feel like nothing at all."

Joy frowned. "I don't want to forget. I want to make sure I come back."

Asha took a bracelet off of her wrist and clasped it on Joy's. "Maybe having something from here will help you remember this world."

The green and purple gemstones sparkled as Joy waved her arm about. "It's pretty. I feel like I've seen this bracelet before."

Asha raised an eyebrow. "That's good to hear. Maybe all isn't forgotten, after all. You are always welcome here, my child."

And with that Joy looked down at the moonstone that grew warm in her hands. "How do I go home?"

"The larger stone is recharging it. The closer you get, the quicker it will charge."

Joy took a step toward the large rock while holding her moonstone in her hand. As Joy moved to the center stone, her moonstone shone brighter. Soon the light engulfed her, and once it faded she found herself back in the basement of her grandmother's restaurant, surrounded by three unhappy adults.

"Joy!" Mama screamed, pulling her into an embrace "What happened. I'm so glad you are safe! What was all that light?"

Joy blinked at her mother, struggling to gain her eyesight back after being blinded by the light.

"This basement gives me the creeps," Aunty said.

"Did you do that?" mama asked grandma. She lowered her voice to a whisper. "With your magic?"

Joy looked around the room until she found Grandma, leaning against the wall in the corner. There were wrinkles on her forehead. When Joy looked at her, she looked down at her feet.

"I did nothing," Grandma said. "but neglected to hide my basement key."

"But what was that light?" Aunty asked.

"It was nothing. Look, you guys make sure the other kids aren't destroying the restaurant. I'll take her up." Grandma stepped forward and shooed mama and aunty away with her hands. "You can go. I'll talk to Joy."

Mama and aunty hesitated, but the queen had spoken. Joy listened to the stairs squeak as they walked up and the jingle of the keys as the door unlocked. Once the door was shut behind them, Joy exploded with questions.

"They don't remember any of it?" Joy said once they were out of the basement. "They forgot all about that world? How could you keep a place like that to yourself?"

"It's not easy," Grandma said. "But it's for the best."

"Will I remember?"

Grandma's lips pressed together in a tight line. She said nothing.

"I want to go back," Joy said. "You had the chance to choose which world you wanted. I deserve that chance too, even if I choose the magical one."

"For now, I need you to keep that world a secret," Grandma said. "I'll take you back someday but only if you tell no one. You are too young to choose anything. The fact that I decided to hop from world to world is the reason my family is split up now. I don't want that for you. I want you together with the people who love you. Love is its own type of magic."

Joy scratched her head as she looked around the empty basement. "Where does the food come from?"

Grandma grinned as she lifted her hand and materialized a plate of food just like her sister has created tea. She held the plate in one hand.

"Mama and auntie know you do magic?"

"They do," said Grandma. "They just don't remember where the magic comes from." Grandma held out her free hand. "Now where's my rock?"

Joy placed the moonstone in Grandma's hand.

"Run upstairs. I'll be up soon. I need to have a chat with my mother."

"You're going back?" Joy asked. "Can I come?"

The look on Grandma's face was enough to tell Joy that the answer was no. Joy nodded and raced up the stairs, crashing into Keisha as soon as she ran out of the door.

"Ow," Keisha stumbled back.

"Were you just standing here with your ear pressed to the wood?"

"Of course!" Keisha was eager to learn what happened. "Was there anything in the basement?'

Joy hesitated. Grandma asked her not to tell. On the other hand, she wanted Keisha to know she'd been right all along.

"There *was* something!" Keisha exclaimed. "I can see it on your face!"

"Not the something you wanted." Joy lied.

Keisha put her hands on her hip. "Oh yeah?"

"Yup," Joy said, the lie coming more naturally. "It was just a kitchen. With a few cooks working hard." She shrugged. "Nothing exciting."

They started to walk toward their table. Justus sat and watched them approach with concern etched on his face. "That was not smart," he said as soon as the girls sat down.

Keisha looked disappointed. "I know you both think I'm crazy, but I just have a feeling there is more to the basement. I remember there being no kitchen down there at the time. Beyond that, I can't remember what I saw. It's like part of my memory is missing." she fiddled with the bracelet on her wrists.

Joy's eyes grew wide as she looked at Keisha's bracelet. Its green and purple gemstones matched the bracelet on her own wrist. She looked down at her own, as if to make sure she wasn't imagining it.

Keisha followed Joy's gaze and gasped when she noticed the matching jewelry. "Where did you get that?"

"I'm... not sure." Joy lied.

"Mine makes me think of the beach." Keisha laughed nervously. "Isn't that funny?"

Justus looked from bracelet to bracelet, unease on his face as he tried to make sense of it. Keisha looked uncertain as well.

Joy knew grandma expected her to forget just like her mama, Auntie, and Keisha had. She doubted Grandma had any true plans of taking her back there. But Grandma was wrong. Keisha had mentioned the beach. Once you stumble into a world like that you may not remember, but you can never fully forget. Joy wanted Keisha to know she wasn't crazy after all.

"You guys," Joy lowered her voice. "Please don't freak out, but there's a place I need to tell you both about."

Keisha raised an eyebrow. "Oh?"

Joy knew she was opening Pandora's box by telling them about the Adaeze Kingdom, but she couldn't keep it to herself. She wouldn't allow herself to simply forget.

Joy took a deep breath before she said "I found something in the basement."

There were adventures ahead for all three of them, and maybe the grown-ups as well.

ABOUT THE AUTHOR

K. R. S. McEntire is from the generation that dashed through platform 9 ¾, fell in love with sparkly vampires, and volunteered as tribute in the reaping. She remembers how magical it felt to follow wardrobes into unimaginable worlds, and she hopes to bring that same joy to the next generation. Her earliest introduction to swords, dragons, and mythical kingdoms was playing RPG games alongside her father, and she's glad that writing allows her to build her own epic worlds. She runs the Facebook page Diverse Books With Magic, where she promotes diversity in speculative fiction. McEntire lives in Indianapolis with her husband and sons. Her YA dystopian series The Eden Saga can be purchased on Amazon. Find on social media @krsmcentire.

krsmcentire.com

A Trip to Sunma

BY JESSICA CAGE

On a warm summer day, the place to be for the kids of the south Chicago neighborhood was the park. No, it wasn't the best. The bars were rusted, the swings only had two functioning seats, and the seesaw hadn't seed nor sawed in over two years. But this was where kids could be free. Without teachers scolding or parents nagging. The neighborhood hummed with the enthusiasm of children just beginning their ten-week vacation from alarm clocks and mothers eager to wake them for a day of class.

Every child across the city ran through the streets, headed to their outdoor headquarters while excitedly conversing about their newly found freedom. On the first day of summer, ten weeks felt like ten months, and there was nothing anyone could do to ruin their vibe.

While the rest of the children headed for the monkey bars and rope tire swings, there was one who felt much more comfortable in his own backyard.

Ameer, a brown eyed, curly head, twelve-year-old, sat among the rose bushes in his mother's garden, lost in his own thoughts and imagined worlds. For him, summer meant one thing: continued exploration of his own imagination. Sixth grade had been the worst year. His best friend moved clear across the country, leaving him alone in the middle of the first quarter. Which meant Ameer either had to make new friends or get used to being by himself. He chose solidarity. Besides, with the increasingly difficult course work from his homeroom teacher, he didn't have time for friends. At least that's what he told himself.

He wasn't entirely alone. He had one pal, someone who would never up and leave him alone. Someone who loved his favorite foods, watched anime with him, and who was currently licking his face to bring him back from the depths of his own winding thoughts.

"Oh, gross! Jack, stop it!" Ameer laughed as he pushed the dog's face away from him.

The dog, a beautiful Shiba Inu, was a gift from his grandmother on his fifth birthday. For seven years, through the power of Ameer's imagination, they explored far off galaxies, battled alien colonizers, and saved countless lives. They were a superhero pair that the world never knew it needed.

Often his mother would ask him if he wanted to join the other kids in the neighborhood. She gave her blessing for him to run up to the park and stand in line for the swings, but Ameer was happy in his own world, where he controlled the rules.

He lay back beneath the clear sky and smiled as the warm blanket of sunlight fell across him. The rays of the sun bouncing from his tan skin slowly worked to bring out his summer bronze. Before he danced out the backdoor singing the theme song from his latest anime obsession, his mother lathered him with sunscreen despite his grandmother's dispute because, 'black boys didn't need sunblock'.

Once again, Jack licked Ameer's cheek, and the boy laughed as he wiped his face and his dog frowned, disgusted by the taste of the sunscreen lotion. Jack blew raspberries and tried to get the taste out of his mouth.

"Come on, Jack." Ameer hopped up from the ground and

patted his dog's head. "I'll see if I can sneak us a popsicle. I'm sure you'll like the taste of that a lot more than SPF 30."

Jack barked in agreement and followed the boy, who headed for the porch that led up to the back door of his home. But Ameer stopped in his tracks when he heard a soft crackling sound coming around the side of the garage. When he looked back, he saw Jack's ears perk up.

"You heard that too?" Ameer asked and Jack's short tail shook. "Think we should check it out?"

Jack lifted his head as if to say he was ready for duty and Ameer nodded, abandoning his task of retrieving sweet treats for the pair.

"Looks like we have something to investigate, buddy." Ameer narrowed his eyes and with Jack right behind him, he crept across the backyard. As he neared the garage, he dropped into a crawl to be sure no one saw him. He crawled until he reached the wall, then pressed his back against the side of the garage as he did his ninja scoot up to the edge to peer around the side of it.

He expected to see squirrels or the neighbor's cat who often tried to get into their garage so it could sleep underneath his mother's car. But Ameer found something that looked like it was pulled from his own imagination.

On the side of their garage, hidden by the overgrown bushes and trees, an opening appeared. The crackling sound belonged to a ring of light that stretched until it looked like a doorway. A moment later, two figures moved through the opening. Ameer blinked twice as he tried to make sense of what he saw.

They were blobs! Like the slime monster from the Ghostbusters movie his mother insisted he watch. Ameer's eyes widened as he watched two sloppy figures made of colorful swirls of slime slide forward, leaving a trail of gunk behind them. He held his breath, because as they moved away from the door, their forms morphed. Where there were no legs, two appeared, and with each step, the rainbow blobs became men.

Ameer's eyes widened as he realized he knew the men who

took form in front of him. One of them was his neighbor George, a grumpy old guy who chased the kids from his front lawn regularly, and the other was Mr Bacon, the principal from his school! As Mr. Bacon, a chubby man with curly hair and a penguin's waddle, walked away, Ameer was met with the horrible realization that his principal was an alien. How was it that he never knew? He had never liked the guy, but that was because he always smelled like boiled eggs and sardines. There was nothing to like about that.

Ameer covered his mouth, knowing it would be bad if he let the gasp slip through his lips. The alien invaders would realize he saw, and there was no way he could get away from them if that happened. The last thing he wanted was to become an alien captive to be experimented on. He pressed his back against the side of the garage, trying to flatten himself as much as possible. His mother would be upset about all the dirt he was collecting in his hair, but he couldn't risk being seen.

The two men spoke in a language he didn't understand. A series of whistles and clicks as they headed down the alley and turned the corner. He listened as their voices changed to mimic human tones. He expected some insight on what they were doing but all they talked about was going fishing. Once they were out of sight, Ameer continued his investigation. He tiptoed carefully, approaching the opening. He had to be nimble just in case another appeared, and he needed to get away.

When he looked through the doorway, he gasped, forgetting his rule about not making noise. On the other side of the opening, he saw something that gave his imagined world a run for its money. Fields of blue grass with trees that had feathers instead of leaves. He felt the breeze of the air against his skin and smelled the sweet aroma of cherries.

Ameer peered closer, trying to see as much as he could before the door closed. But as he leaned forward, he heard something unsettling. A deep rumble of what he imagined being a beast with horns and sharp teeth.

He backed away because suddenly popsicles sounded a lot better than exploring strange portals to dangerous new worlds. Besides, if anything else came through the door, he couldn't be sure it wouldn't try to bite his head off.

Just as he turned, the neighbor's cat jumped down in front of him. It hissed viciously at him. Jack, always ready to protect his friend, moved into action. The dog barked, chasing after the cat who ran behind Ameer's legs.

"Jack, no!" Ameer cried out, realizing what was about to happen, but it was too late.

Jack charged forward, knocking into Ameer and exactly as he feared, he stumbled, tripped over the terrifying cat, and fell through the portal.

Ameer never thought he would hope to feel the impact of concrete against his back. But as he fell back, watching Jack chase the crazy cat who hissed at him, all he could think about was how the risk of breaking his tailbone was a much better option than falling into an alien world. Unfortunately for him, his tailbone was safe.

The soft crackling noise he heard before became thunderous as he passed through the opening of light. The world around him changed to something foreign. Suddenly everything was much too bright, and his ears burned. He cried out and reached for his home, hoping to pull himself back, but it was no use. The opening dropped him ten feet above the ground. Even if it hadn't closed, there was no way he was going to reach it without at least a trampoline and a good running start.

His mind felt heavy, and his chest burned, and the overly bright world disappeared. Because his body wasn't used to shifting through space in time, Ameer passed out. He didn't even wake when he hit solid ground, though he could feel the ache in his muscles from it. It was the cool breeze and the cherry scented air that finally woke him from a dream about flying through space with Jack. That and a hand nudging at his back.

"Hey," the bold voice said, nudging him harder.. "You there, wake up."

Ameer groaned. "Is it time for school?"

"School?" the voice asked.

Ameer rolled over onto his back and opened his eyes to what he thought would be his mother. Some days she sounded a lot more like a gruffy bear if she woke him before her coffee. Instead, as he opened his eyes, he found a large pair of green eyes surrounded by orange and yellow fur looking down at him. His heart raced as he realized this was not his mother waking him to tell him summer was over and he had to go back to the torturous halls of his middle school.

"Hello," the beast spoke.

Ameer gasped and scooted across the ground, putting as much space between him and the creature as he could. When he had enough room, he scrambled to get to his feet and started running.

"Hold on, wait. Where are you going?" The beast yelled as he followed him.

"No, no, nooo." Ameer screamed as he pushed his legs as fast as he could muster, but came to a stop when the clear field he landed in turned into a thick line of trees.

"Are you done now?" The monster who stood three times Ameer's height crossed his thick arms over his chest. "That was cute. You could be pretty fast if you trained a little."

"Get away from me!" Ameer yelled. "I will not let you eat me."

"Let me guess, you're not from around here?" the monster laughed. "Well, that much is obvious. Just look at you. So scrawny and barely any protective layering over your soft inner workings."

"Soft inner workings? What?" Ameer looked around, finally taking in the world around him. It wasn't just this monster that stood in front of him. It was the trees that grew feathers instead of leaves, the grass that felt more like bubbles, and that strange cherry scented air. "What are you? Where am I?"

"I'm Felix and considering you're the one that looks so strange, I think I should ask the questions." The beast sat down in front of Ameer and peered at him with those large green eyes. "Nope, I don't think you're from around here. Besides, I saw you fall out of the sky. Where do you come from? What do you want with our people? Are you here to experiment on us?"

"I don't want anything!" Ameer denied Felix's accusation. "I saw those strange men come through the wall and I tried to see where they were coming from. I just wanted to investigate. It wasn't my plan to come here! All I want to do is go home!"

"I hate to be the one to tell you this because you already look like you're going to puke, but I think you're stuck here now."

"Stuck here? I can't be stuck here. I need to go home!"

"I don't know how you're going to do that." Felix stood. "You know, you might want to find a good place to hide. I'm one of the nice guys, but there are people here who... well, if they see you, they may want a snack." He sniffed the air and smiled. "Yeah, you're human. One of them earthlings. I can smell it on you. There are people here who like to have human kids as a treat, and I have to admit you smell appetizing."

"You can't eat me!" Ameer screamed.

"I just said I'm one of the good guys." Felix frowned. "You're not too good with the listening skills, are you?"

"You still haven't told me where this place is. What world is this? It's clearly not Earth."

"Ah, there you go buddy, figuring things out." Felix laughed. "No, this isn't earth. This is Sunma. A world filled with creatures, big and small. And some who eat children."

"Got it. There are monsters who eat children." Ameer threw his hands in the air and huffed. "How many times are you going to say it? I don't want to be eaten. I just want to go home. Like I said, I didn't mean to come here. If it wasn't for Jack, I wouldn't be in your world."

"Jack, who is Jack?" Felix frowned. "Did Jack come here too?"

"Jack is my dog. He was trying to protect me from the neighbor's evil cat, but I got knocked through the portal."

"So, you're telling me you fell into our world because the dog pushed you?" Felix said with a snicker.

"Yes." Ameer frowned as the monster continued to laugh, his yellow and orange fur shaking with each hearty chuckle. "It's not funny."

"Yes, it is, boy. I can't wait to tell the others. That is classic." He turned his back on Ameer and waved. "Well, good luck whoever you are."

"What?" Ameer stood there in shock. "You're just going to leave me here? You aren't even going to help me?"

"Nope!" Felix's large body bounced as he walked away.

Ameer couldn't help it. The moment Felix turned away, his eyes started to water. The monsters no was the final straw and tears began to slip down his cheeks, a sob building in his throat. Ameer bowed his head and cried.

"Wait, wait, wait!" Felix shouted, startling Ameer into looking up at him through blurry eyes. "What is that? What are you doing?"

"I'm," Ameer sniffled, wiping a hand across his snotty nose. "I'm crying."

"Why are you doing that?" Felix grimaced, his body shaking with discomfort.

"Because I'm scared!" Ameer shouted, a new round of tears rolling down his cheeks. "You said I'll get eaten and left me. I just want to go home and you won't help me."

"Yes, yes," Felix said, waving a dismissive hand, "Why does this crying make me... care?"

Ameer frowned, confused at the question. "You said you're one of the nice guys?"

Felix laughed. "I said I'm nice, not suicidal!"

"That's exactly what I expect from someone who calls themselves a nice guy." Ameer challenged the monster, angry now. "Nice guys help those who are in need!"

"I am a nice guy, but I didn't sign up for this. You're making me feel things!" Felix shook his head, frustrated. "I saw something falling from the sky and thought, hey this might be a free meal. Then I get here and there's you. This earthling with no name. I don't eat humans. I don't care what anyone says, you're too salty."

"I want to go home." Ameer repeated.

"You keep saying that." Felix sighed. "Do you know what we would have to go through to get you back home?"

"No, I don't know, but I guess it's gonna be tough." Ameer nodded his head and puffed out his chest. "Yeah, it's gonna be difficult, maybe even impossible, but it's not something that I think nice guys would back down from. Me and Jack never did."

"You and Jack, the dog that pushed you through the opening?" Felix laughed.

"Yes, he's the one that I have adventures with."

"Again, we're talking about a dog." Felix pointed to his palm as if the dog was in his hand. "I don't know a lot about Earth, but I know that a dog is an animal that doesn't communicate with humans. And you want me to believe that you've gone on dangerous adventures with him?"

"A dog would do a lot more for me than you would, apparently." Ameer stuck his tongue out.

"Do you want my help or not, kid?"

"I do." Ameer lifted his chin. "I want to go home."

"Fine, then we're gonna need to get you a disguise. You can't walk around looking like that." Felix leaned in and sniffed Ameer again. "And we're gonna need to find something to cover up that stench of yours, too."

"I don't stink." Ameer sniffed his own armpit. "Much."

"Maybe not to you, but you're a human who is on the brink of a hormonal change. In my world, that smell is like laying out a free buffet. People from miles around will smell that if the wind picks up your stench."

"Can you not refer to my smell as a stench? It's offensive."

"Fine, odor, aroma, whatever you want to call it. We need to cover it up." Felix said, emphasizing his point by covering his nose.

"Whatever." Ameer rolled his eyes. "Do what you must. As long as I get to go home."

Felix took his time carefully crafting a disguise for Ameer. He ushered him into the line of trees, pushing them deeper as he plucked feathers from the limbs. As he collected the feathers, he tied them together and with more care than Ameer thought possible before layering him up with the conjoined feathers. Eventually the boy was covered head to toe in the feather. Some even stuck out his shoes like lampshades to cover his human sneakers.

"You don't exactly look like anything from our world, but people are idiots and will think you're just a species they've never encountered before." Felix said as he scratched his chin. "Now for your smell..."

He landed on a combination of mud and berries from a nearby bush. He mashed them together into a paste, which he then forced Ameer to smear over any exposed part of his body.

"Nope, I can still smell you."

"What?" Ameer looked at Felix in horror as the monster handed him more paste. "It's already everywhere!" He groaned. "I even got some in my underwear."

"I know what you need." Felix walked away and when he returned, he held a handful of bugs.

"What are you going to do with that?"

"These are stink bugs. We mix these into that paste, and no one will want to come anywhere near you."

"Oh no," Ameer protested, but it was too late. Felix quickly mushed the bugs between his hands and started rubbing their smashed bodies over the boy's face and hair.

"My mom will not like this." Ameer groaned.

"She'll get over it." Felix shrugged and continued his work. "Alright, that ought to be good enough. Unless it rains and washes all of this away and then, well, you'll be on your own."

"What do you mean, I'll be on my own?"

"Hey, the worse they will do to you is eat you. For me, it will be some serious trouble if I get caught harboring fugitives."

"I'm not a fugitive. I didn't break any laws." Ameer protested. "And how is getting eaten the better option here?"

"Oh, no?" Felix said with a scoff. "You're just an illegal space traveler who likely brought in foreign objects that will harm our world. There are sanctions in place, laws that we must respect, documentation that has to be filed when anything, especially something living, comes into our world. And here you are, a human with no papers, covered in mud and bug guts, and making me break the law with you."

"That still doesn't explain how me getting eaten is the better option."

Felix shrugged, "It'd either be that or being trapped here in prison forever for breaking the law. What would you choose?"

"I'd choose to return home." Ameer snapped, irritated beyond belief. He'd have called Felix a coward, but there was no point in having a go at him. Besides, he didn't want to risk angering his ticket home. Ameer took a deep breath to calm himself. His uncle always told him the best way to deal with a difficult situation was with a calm heart and a rational mind. "Let's focus on what to do now, okay? Instead of the worst case scenario. What's the next part of the plan? The sooner I get out of here, the sooner I'm no longer a fugitive and you don't have to continue breaking the law."

"We need to get you to the hive. It's where all of our space travelers are."

"In the sky?"

"No, that was just where the portal dropped you. I should really file a form about how reckless they were to leave that open like that."

"Why didn't it drop me at the hive?"

"Oh, well, travelers have technology that allows them to leave from, well, anywhere. They upgraded a few years ago, but prior to that, all transports had to launch from their headquarters. The hive."

"So, you're saying we have to walk into the headquarters of the people who would eat me if they found me?"

"You got that right." Felix flashed a grin full of spiked teeth that made Ameer's stomach turn. "It's the only way you're getting out of here."

"Do you have a different plan, maybe?" Ameer pondered. "Maybe we can find the suit the travelers use?"

"Right, because those are just lying around, completely unattended to." Felix laughed, then paused as he pondered a new thought. "I could always take you home and keep you as a pet, but then you seriously would have to do something about that smell of yours."

"I'm nobody's pet." Ameer stomped his foot. "Where's this hive?"

"You know, I'm helping you out and I don't even know your name." Felix spoke as he carried Ameer under his arm towards the nearby city.

"You stuffed me into your armpit and now you want to ask my name?" Ameer scoffed. "That's backwards, don't you think?"

"Look, you move too slow. I couldn't risk losing precious time because those little legs of yours can't keep up." Felix explained his reasoning. "We don't have a large window of opportunity to get this done. Besides, I think a little monster sweat may help further disguise your identity."

"Right." Ameer said, annoyed. "Because your armpit smells so much better than I do."

"So, what's your name?" Felix ignored his implied insult.

"My name is Ameer."

"Nice name." Felix said, a smile to his voice. "I like that name, it's solid."

"Thanks, I guess."

"It's nice to meet you, Ameer."

"I'd say the same but, it will be nicer when I'm freed from the sweat pit beneath your shoulder." Ameer stuck out his tongue then spit when he got a mouthful of armpit hair.

While he was disgusted with his position beneath the monster's armpit, Ameer took the moment to look around this new world. He spent so much time imagining new worlds and now here he was in one for real. And it was nothing like he thought it would be.

Ameer expected advanced technology beyond his wildest dreams. He'd always imagined mechanical streets and gritty air. He pictured civilizations torn to pieces by greedy alien forces that he would need to save the people from. But this world was pleasant. No monster overlord destroying the world. It looked like the countryside. He saw animals running in the distance and they all looked happy, free, and safe. Where was the danger? Where were the people for him and Jack to save?

Yes, the grass was different, and the trees looked weird, but ultimately it was nothing more than a farm side. He still couldn't get over how the air smelled like cherries. As a gust of wind picked up and spread the scent more, Ameer thought of his grandmother. She loved cherries, and would even bake cherry pies for the winter. It was never really his thing, he liked chocolate cake more. But at that moment all he wanted was to sit across the table from his grandmother having a slice of cherry pie.

As Felix continued to carry him, the look of the world changed. Structured buildings replaced the strange nature. In the distance, he could see ones that reached up into the sky and flying vehicles that hovered around the tops. There were floating buildings and odd creatures flying between them. Weird sounds and stomach turning odors hit him from every angle. This was the alien world Ameer had always imagined.

With the change in scenery came something else, sounds. Not only did he hear the hum of machinery, but the unsettling sounds of monsters. In the distance, he could hear grumbles, growls, and terrifying roars. He even heard more of the clicking and squeaking chatter he first heard from the monsters who came to his world. Suddenly, Ameer wanted nothing more than to return to the peaceful countryside. When they reached the city's edge, Felix put Ameer down.

"Okay kid. From here on out, you do not speak. You don't make eye contact with anyone, you keep your head down. Let me handle everything." Felix instructed him. "Got it?"

"What if someone tries to talk to me?" Ameer asked. "Wouldn't it be rude not to speak back?"

"Trust me, you won't understand them if they did."

"What do you mean?" He asked.

"I mean, not everyone here speaks your language. Now just do what I say." Ameer went to protest, annoyed about being bossed around, when Felix bent over to look him in the eye. "I get that you don't like how I go about things and want to debate my every decision, but this is not the time. This is about survival. We're gonna need to make it past a lot of people on our way. That's going to seem simple at first, but when we get closer, it's going to get a lot more difficult. People pay much more attention to outsiders the closer you get to the hive. So again, do me a favor, keep quiet, eyes down, and do as I say."

"Okay." Ameer nodded. He wanted to be brave. He wanted to believe that he could take on any monster here, but he was smart enough to know that this was not the time to let his imagination run away from him.

He followed Felix as closely as he could as they moved through the streets, avoiding the main roads and taking ways that would bring the least attention to them. But taking the back alleys meant coming face to face with some of the strangest creatures. Some of them were simple enough, bulky with boils and horns. While others looked like they were ripped out of the nightmares of the most elite anime creators.

He kept his eyes lowered as Felix told him, but now and then, he would peek up and see a snarling face. Most of them looked at Felix and not the unexplained monster that trailed behind him. It was like they were afraid of him, or at the very least; they didn't trust him. Ameer wondered what Felix could have done to receive that type of reception.

"Alright kid, we're close." Felix pointed to the tall cone shaped building ahead. "That's the hive. We need to make it inside and then head for the basement. It's where they keep the backup space jammers. We want those."

"How do you know this?"

"There's food available." Felix pointed to the building behind Ameer, ignoring his question. "Maybe we should get a snack before we risk getting our head cut off."

"I don't think I want to eat anything from here." Ameer frowned.

"Fine, skip your last meal. Trust me, you'll regret it."

"Tell me how you know where everything is," Ameer said, not ready to give up on getting answers. "You're avoiding my question."

"You won't like my answer, kid." Felix said, not looking at him.

Ameer frowned, "look, I know I'm not from here, but things aren't adding up. No one else here speaks my language, but you do. And you know so much about Earth and pets, and hormonal changes. How? And all of them," he pointed to the alley they'd come from, "they're afraid of you, I think."

""They have these frozen treats you might like." Felix said, ignoring him. "I'll grab us a couple." He moved to go to the building.

"Tell me!" Ameer grabbed his arm to stop him from leaving, his grip was weak, but it was enough to have Felix turn around and snarl at him.

With a yelp, Ameer let go and scrambled away from Felix, his heart pounding in his chest.

Felix's snarling expression faded away, replaced with one of horror. "Crap, I'm sorry." He reached for Ameer as if to try and help him up, but the boy moved away from him.

"No, don't touch me." Ameer snapped, his voice shaking. "You're not a nice guy. You're mean and you're a liar."

"You want to know why I know so much?" Felix said, sounding exhausted. He pointed to the hive. "I used to work there. That's how I know so much."

"Wait, you were one of them?" Ameer gasped. "You're one of the human eaters?"

"I was. I'm reformed now." Felix rubbed the back of his neck, uncomfortable.. "I was a traveler. For a long time but I stopped. It just didn't feel right anymore."

"Right." Ameer said skeptically. "And now you're just a normal monster guy?"

"Look, none of that matters." He said, raising his hands in a placating manner.. "What matters is getting you into that building so we can get you home. You don't want to be here, and I don't want you to be here, so let's get this over with. Just make sure you keep that disguise intact."

"Leave me alone." Ameer stepped away from Felix, ready to run away, until he realized he had nowhere to go.

"What happened to you wanting to get home so badly?" Felix snapped, his patience running thin. "Don't you want to see your family? Or your dog?" He laughed unkindly, "and I'm sure you can't wait to tell your friends about this exciting adventure."

Ameer dropped his head, "I don't really have that many friends."

"You don't?" Felix asked, his tone softening.

"I had a friend, a best friend," Ameer replied, "but he moved away. And I just haven't really made any new ones yet."

"Yet," Felix nudged Ameer with a smile. "That's the key word. You haven't made any new friends yet. Which means you will. We just need to get you back home so you can make those new friends."

"You sound like my mom."

"Well then, your mom is very smart." Felix nodded. "So, can we get you home now?"

"Right." Ameer held out his arms and checked his disguise. "Still good?"

"Um, sure, yeah."

"Doesn't sound like you're sure."

"Well maybe, hold on." Felix stepped away, then returned with a string of plants, then draped them over his head. "We'll call it an accessory, but it works."

"An access—" Ameer stopped talking as the pungent smell filled his nose. He gagged. "Oh no, that smells like something that came out of Jack!"

"Then it's perfect." Felix clapped. "Alright kid, let's get this over with."

It was surprisingly easy to get to the front door of the hive. Felix made small talk with almost every person they passed. If Ameer hadn't known better, he'd think it was just another normal day in the guy's life. But even though Felix made their efforts easy, Ameer was afraid.

The closer they got, the faster his heart raced. He kept telling himself to calm down because he was afraid the increased sweat would cause his disguise to fail. Science wasn't his favorite subject, but he knew that sweat meant the release of pheromones. And even with the plant that smells like dog poop wrapped around his neck, he couldn't be sure that none of the surrounding monsters would be able to smell past it.

At the door was a lanky being with blue skin and a large horn sticking out of their chest. They held what looked like a holographic keyboard and tapped their fingers along the translucent surface as they approached.

"Felix?" They looked up with white eyes that held no iris.

"Hey moon face! How are you?" Felix greeted them.

"I'm surprised to see you here." They responded with a smile that was eerily human. "What brings you by? Rumor has it you quit and told the council that they could kiss your big furry butt."

"Yes, I was a bit dramatic, but we all have our days, right?" Felix chuckled.

"I'd say that was more than a bit dramatic, but whatever you say. What are you here for?" They continued tapping on their keyboard.

"I just left a few things in my locker. Thought I should come by and get them instead of leaving it to someone else." He raised a playful eyebrow, "unless I'm on the no show list?"

"Not as far as I see. Doesn't appear they thought you were a threat." The one he called moon face smiled again. "I'll give you a temporary badge that won't get you anywhere but to your locker and back."

"Sure, unless Janno has already emptied my things out." Felix held his hand out, waiting for the temporary pass.

"He might hate your guts, but he's not going to go against protocol. All your things are safe in your locker for, let me see... six more days." They nodded as they placed a small black card in Felix's hand. "Yep, standard protocol."

"Great. I'll go get them and get out of your hair. Thanks, moon face." Felix saluted as he walked past them.

"Are you ever gonna stop calling me that?" they asked, then frowned at Ameer, who followed Felix as if noticing him for the first time.

"The second your eyes stop reminding me of the moon."

"New friend?" They pointed to Ameer, still in his disguise, and frowned. "Smells funny."

"More like a pet." Felix nodded. "I'll clean him up when I get home."

"Oh, it's... odd."

"Well, you know me, I gravitate towards the odd." Felix turned, and the two headed through the massive doors of the hive.

"Who is that?" Ameer whispered his question.

"An old friend who lets me slide when I break the rules a bit." Felix answered. "Now zip it before you get us caught. Pets don't talk, remember."

"Right." Ameer mimed zipping his lips.

Felix was casual, yet quick with his movements. He made a straight dash for what looked like locker rooms and outside of the door he waved at someone Ameer assumed was another unusual monster friend. The two had a small talk, but he didn't pay attention to it. He was far too busy looking around at all the weird machines and floating devices. It was like being inside a robot.

"To the basement, we go." Felix said.

"But your badge."

"Weren't you paying attention, kid?" Felix held up a silver card, not like the one he had before.

"You stole that thing's card?"

"Borrowed." Felix corrected. "He'll get it back, eventually."

Felix picked up his speed as he led Ameer through three doors, each time swiping the card to unlock them. Behind the third door was a set of stairs that led down into the basement. Ameer could feel his heart racing once again, this time not because he was afraid, but because he knew he'd be home soon.

"Back here." Felix pointed to a machine covered in heavy fabric. He pulled the cloth away and revealed what looked like an old arcade game with about one hundred buttons on it. "Just gotta plug her in and-," Felix found the plug and connected it to a power source. The screen lit up, and he shouted, "Bingo!"

He got to work configuring the dials and tapping the screen to get the settings just right.

"There, we're locked in. Took a bit to figure out where you came from, but I think this is close, give or take a few blocks."

"What do you think you're doing?" A deep and grating voice sounded from a figure outlined in the doorway's light.

"Janno." Felix huffed. "I knew this was way too easy."

A monster uglier than anything else he'd seen in the strange world approached them. He had gray skin and eyes that protruded from the side of his head like a lizard. His teeth were so large that his thin lips barely covered them and yellow sludge dripped from his mouth, creating a small puddle at his feet that quickly evaporated. Ameer gasped and stepped behind Felix. The furry monster would protect him. He hoped.

"You know, I was just wondering if these old things still worked."

"You aren't allowed down here." Janno grunted. "You shouldn't be here at all."

"I must have misunderstood." Felix turned to Ameer and pointed to a large button on the machine. He whispered, "When that button turns orange, press it, and run. As soon as the opening is clear, you need to get through it. It won't stay open for long."

"You're a disgrace, Felix." Janno called his attention and ignored the fact that he spoke to his pet.

"I've been called worse." Felix stepped closer to Janno. "Come on, you can do better than that."

"I'm not getting into your games. What are you doing down here with that-," he peered around Felix and frowned as he tried to understand what creature stood behind the monster. "What is that?"

"Um, a social experiment?" Felix chuckled. "It doesn't really matter. Does it?"

"Time for you to go." Janno reached for Felix, who surprised both the monster and the kid he protected when he punched him in the face.

The gray skinned monster fell back and crashed against another one of the covered machines.

"You're going to regret that." He returned to his feet and growled.

"I'm sure I will." Felix beckoned Janno with his hand, daring the monster to engage in combat. And Janno accepted the offer.

Ameer watched as the two monsters battled, often looking back to the button to make sure he pressed it as soon as it changed. And it did, just as the gray monster kicked Felix into the wall and Janno looked ready to kill him.

"Press the button!" Felix called and Janno turned to look at Ameer.

Ameer did what he was told. He hit the button. Ten feet away from him, the crackling sound of energy sounded off and a moment later, the door of light opened. Ameer knew what he had to do. He ran for the opening, but three steps into his fastest run, he tripped over a cord and fell. When he fell, some of the mud paste, the feathers, and poop scent fell from his face.

Janno sniffed the air, then said with all disgust, "A human!"

"Kid, run!" Felix urged Ameer to get back up and make it to the door right before he tackled Janno.

"First you let those kids free and ruin our mission, and now you're sending the ones we captured back home?" Janno pushed Felix away and snarled. "You really are a disgrace!"

"You let kids free?" Ameer stopped and asked Felix, who now stood between him and Janno.

"I told you, I'm one of the nice ones. Those kids, they started crying. I couldn't take it." Felix explained. "It made me *feel things*! I don't like hurting people."

"I'm-," Ameer started. He wanted to apologize for the way he treated him, but Felix held his hand up.

"You must go. Now!" Felix pointed to the doorway. "It won't stay open for long. This is your only chance to go home. Make some new friends, kid."

Ameer nodded and ran the rest of the way to the door. He looked back just as Janno knocked Felix to the ground. The gray monster turned to run after Ameer, but he was too late. Ameer stepped through the doorway and fell away from the strange world filled with even stranger creatures. The last thing he saw was Janno's outstretched hand before the portal snapped shut.

Ameer could hear the murmurs of children approaching. Some sounded afraid, some sounded excited. He opened his eyes to see the tops of trees, the kind that had leaves and no strange feathers. The wave of relief washed over him, he made it home. He lay on the ground in the alley just behind his home.

A moment later, he felt the familiar pull of a wet tongue against his cheek. Jack. He sat up and met the curious yet confused face of his dog before he looked around and realized that all the neighborhood kids hovered around him.

"Dude, where did you come from?" The excited voice of a boy called out, taking Ameer's attention from Jack, who once again blew raspberries. The taste of alien mud and bug guts was no better than the SPF 30.

"You wouldn't believe me if I told you." Ameer looked up to see the outstretched hand of a girl with large afro puffs and the image of aliens dancing on her shirt.

"Try me." The girl's grin stretched across her face. "We were heading to the park when you appeared out of nowhere! You coming with?"

"No," Ameer looked back over his shoulder at the back of his garage. "I better get home."

"I'll come with you." The girl announced without receiving any invitation.

As Ameer headed home, preparing to explain to his mother why mud and other strange substances caked his hair, he told his new friend of how he tripped and fell into an alien world called Sunma.

Two weeks later, Ameer, Jack and his new friend, Tasahni played in his backyard. Jack ate a coconut popsicle while Tasahni laughed at the strange faces the dog made. Ameer smiled, happy that he'd made a new friend. He was so caught up in his new found happiness that he almost didn't hear it. But he'd never forget that noise as the sound of crackling energy tickled his eardrum.

ABOUT THE AUTHOR

Jessica Cage is an International Award Winning, USA Today Bestselling Author, and dedicated mother to one amazing son. She brings stories with strong characters of color in fantasy because representation matters in all mediums. Connect with her on social media @jcageauthor

www.jessicacage.com

The Guardian's Twin

BY KISH KNIGHT

It was the third Saturday in a row that she had come, but it was clear that Shayla didn't want her here. Large raindrops slapped the ground around her, turning the mud beneath her feet to mush. She ignored the pelting drops, and the squelching of mud, as she slipped through the gates of the cemetery. It wasn't the first time it had happened; in fact, every time she came to her twin sister's tomb, a sudden downpour began the moment she got within one foot of the gates. It didn't stop until she was well inside the graveyard.

If she didn't know better, she would think that Shayla was trying to keep her away.

As she approached the massive tomb, wreaths decorating its top, a figure leapt, as if from nowhere, out of the sky. He landed in a light crouch on top of the tomb, his back to Kayla, and slowly stood. From his frame, he was around her age, maybe twelve like her. Glancing first left, then right, the boy turned around to face her, his eyes locking with hers. A strong wind blew across the graveyard. A light frown rested on the boy's face before melting away.

He was staring at her, unmoving, eyes as brown and clear as colored glass.

"I've been calling you," he said, his expression intense.

"Huh?" Not the smartest thing, but it was all she could think of.

She must have heard him wrong. There was no way she would have forgotten someone like him. He stood tall, silhouetted against the sky, his hair close-cropped. Though he appeared relaxed, she could sense alertness radiating from him, as if he was ready for a battle. Lean cocoa skin showed below his black T-shirt. He seemed light on his feet, catlike.

How did he jump from the sky like that?

Taking advantage of the way he gazed around the cemetery, surveying everything, she studied him closely. Nope, she didn't know him. Suddenly his gaze snapped back to her, amused.

"Interesting place for you to be hanging out," he commented, a hint of a smile on his face.

His small smile unnerved Kayla. Why was he acting so familiar with her? Instinctively her guard rose; he was a stranger in a graveyard after all. Best not to engage with him.

"Did you go to Aquaris?" The boy watched her closely, clearly waiting for her response. She would be glad to, if she knew what he was talking about.

She frowned. "Aquaris? I'm sorry, I don't know what-,"

"Anyway," he continued, interrupting her, "we're back from our Shrines." He turned away, but then looked back over his shoulder, tossing something in her direction. "Here. You can have it back."

Despite herself, she reached out and caught the item. It was a necklace decorated with strange symbols. Without another word, he leapt from the tomb and headed away through the graves. Knowing that she hadn't even blinked once as she'd watched him, her eyes widened as he just disappeared. As soon as he was gone, she shoved the necklace into her pocket and walked, quickly, towards the gate.

She would visit her sister's grave another time; right now, there were too many strange characters lurking about.

Back at home, she headed for Shayla's room. After her sister's death, no one had touched anything inside. Even now, months after the funeral, the room still sat untouched.

Nerves shot through her as she opened the door gingerly. It was still strange seeing her sister's neat room sitting quiet and lonely, as if Shayla hadn't ever been inside.

Her eyes strayed to the floor. There was a box peeking from beneath the bed. "Weird," she muttered. She'd never noticed it before.

Stepping into the room, she walked gingerly towards the bed before kneeling down. With a simple tug, she pulled at the box. It was heavy. "What's in here, Shay?" she murmured. Recently, she'd started talking aloud as if Shayla was still there. It made her feel less sad. She only did it when she was alone, though; she wanted her parents to think that she was okay.

But really, she felt out of place and lonely without her sister.

It took her a few seconds to drag the box out. It was an ordinary cardboard box, but something didn't feel right about it. Carefully folding back the flaps, she looked inside.

Inside was a shiny black box. The top lid was covered with bronze symbols etched into the sleek surface. Gingerly, she lifted it out from the cardboard.

The second she placed it on the floor, she opened the lid eagerly. "Strange..."

The sight of worn black leather greeted her. Pulling out the material slowly, she realized it was a shirt and pants. Still nestled in the glossy black box, was a metal chestplate with silver trim along the edges.

It looked like armor.

"I don't remember Shayla having anything like this," she murmured, trying to remember if her sister had been in any school plays. That was the only reason she could think why her sister would have this costume. Like the leather shirt and pants, she lifted the chestplate out and placed it on the floor. The last thing in the box was a belt buckle. This she was familiar with, since Shayla would wear the buckle a lot. In fact, their parents used to joke that Shayla would sleep with it if she could.

Frowning, she struggled to remember. Unlike her, Shayla had always had an incredible memory; her sister had even been able to remember things that had happened when they were really young. Kayla, on the other hand, could barely remember the previous week.

Looking closely at the buckle, she noticed a small hole in the metal. Several stamped designs circled it. Her eyes widened as she remembered something. She had seen that design before, on the necklace that the strange boy had given her.

Quickly, she pulled it out of her pocket and turned it until she found the matching design. Set in its middle, a tiny post stuck straight out. "Maybe a key?"

The two pieces joined together as if they were made for each other. A small jolt shot through the metal, making her gasp. At her feet, the chestplate seemed to glow a little.

"Wow..." Whatever this costume was for was clearly something exciting. A pang of longing shot through her. She wished that her sister had confided in her about it.

That was the thing with having an identical twin: they'd shared everything up until around age eleven. After that, they'd grown apart. They were still best friends, but recently, she'd sensed that her sister had been hiding things. Clearly, this strange costume was one of them.

Before she could stop herself, she undressed and pulled on the leather outfit. The chestplate was a little difficult to strap on, being half-metal, and half-bindings. The pants, she discovered, had a belt that the buckle slid onto perfectly, and when she secured the belt in place, the entire outfit fit like a glove. The necklace still stuck out of the buckle, and so she pulled it off and slid it onto her neck. Outfit complete, she strode to the mirror, pulling her braided hair behind her.

A fierce warrior seemed to look back.

Again, she wondered what the costume was for, when suddenly a loud crack of thunder rumbled overhead. Eyes flickering to the window, she saw that the rain had gotten heavier. Water beat in through the window, several drops spattering the floor.

"Great."

Wanting to wipe up the water before the floor got too wet, she grabbed a towel and moved to the window. But as her hand got near the drops, the water seemed to come alive, splashing upward onto her clothing. The droplets bounced off the leather, sending more splashes into the air. Stunned, her eyes widened. There suddenly seemed to be a lot more water than the few drops from the floor.

Yanking her hand away, she noticed the water settling back onto the floor as she did so. Her heart pounded. *It's like it moved when my hand moved.*

Then, out of the corner of her eye, tucked up against the wall, she saw something that hadn't been there before. A tiny red feather, so small that if she hadn't already been on high alert from the water, she'd likely not have seen it. Bending, she scooped it up. Fingering the little bit of fluff, she frowned.

Shay, she thought nervously, *what is all this? Crazy water, now feathers?*

A brisk rap came at the far window, making her jump in fright.

She whirled around and was shocked to see the boy from the graveyard at the window, staring at her. As she watched, he lifted his hand and tapped on the glass again. Surprisingly, he was wearing the same black leather outfit as her.

Quickly, she slipped the little feather into her pocket. Then, moving to the window, she eyed him warily, wondering about the matching costumes.

"Look, I don't know who you are, or what you want, but I'll call the police. Please leave."

The boy laughed. Speaking through the window, he said, "Shayla. You're funny as always."

He thinks that I'm Shayla, she realized suddenly. Earlier, she'd been confused, but now she understood: it was mistaken identity. The boy didn't know that Shayla had an identical twin.

Then he spoke again. "Sorry to track you down like this, but the Boundary's open, and you weren't responding."

He looked so serious that she only stared at him. Somehow, this boy knew her sister.

"Shayla," he said, "are you okay?"

There was no denying it....Shayla'd had a secret life. A frown crossed her face. Twelve years as Shayla's identical twin, and she clearly knew nothing about her sister. First the armored costume, now this boy.

"Um, yes?"

The boy shook his head. "Never mind. We need to go to the Shrine. Now. Come on."

Her brows shot up. Who was this guy that he just expected Shayla to go somewhere with him like that? The Shrine?

"Um, I'm grounded," she said, trying to stall.

With a careless shrug, he just looked at her. "Say you're volunteering again."

This caught her by surprise. Shayla had been a youth volunteer for the past two years.

Now, she had to know more.

"All right," she nodded slowly, "let's go. But only because you said it was important." She added the last part to sound tough, but even to her ears, it hadn't.

Laughter drifted through the glass. "Just hurry."

Luckily, the window could slide open all the way, and she wasted no time climbing out of it. Outside, the rain beat down, soaking her. Frowning, she noticed the boy wasn't wet at all. Lifting her hands, she covered her head from the rain. Then, her jaw dropped as the rain started to fall *around* her, not *onto* her.

"Let's use the temporal," the boy said, pulling something from his pocket.

Temporal? But she didn't say it aloud. Instead, she nodded.

It was a decision she regretted immediately as he used the narrow object to draw a large circle in the air. As soon as he ended the circle, the area filled with a frothy, bubbling, lavender liquid that churned constantly.

This time, she couldn't help the gasp that slipped her lips. "Is that the temporal?" she whispered.

In answer, the boy grabbed her hand and stepped into the bubbling lavender froth, pulling her along with him.

Stepping out of the temporal, the first thing she noticed was the sky. Though still blue, it was brighter than what she was used to. In fact, everything around them was more vibrant than the rainy world she'd left behind.

They stood in a small clearing that was ringed with thick forest all around. A path of flat stones led through the space, and each stone emitted a soft glow along the rocky ground. In her pocket, the little feather trembled, and she pulled it out warily.

The boy had already walked several steps away. Now he turned, clearly surprised that she was still standing where they'd entered. "Since you've been gone, several of the Maraudi have entered the human world. The crystal showed that they came through your Boundary door. Come on. We need to find out what's happened at the door, we need to round up the Maraudi, bring them back, and fix whatever went wrong."

The words were clear, but he might as well have been speaking gibberish since none of it made sense.

"There's no way that they should have slipped through, not unless your Boundary door is unlocked." Impatiently, he beckoned her forward with a frown. "Hurry."

But she remained next to the bubbling froth. "Stop. Who ARE you? What's your name?"

He laughed. "Tajil. Now, stop playing. You-," He froze as his gaze fell on the feather she held. "Where did you get that?"

"The feather?" she said.

He glanced at her sharply. "We need to leave. Quickly." He reached for her arm, but she jerked away. Surprise crossed his face, shadowed by suspicion. He took a step back, body tense. "What's happened to you?"

She held the feather out. "This worries you? Why?" He didn't respond, so she moved closer and held up the red bit of fluff. Above them, a bird shrieked loudly and instinctively, she turned to stare. A bright red bird, almost as large as a bear, circled in the air. She gasped in shock, then almost jumped out of her skin when Tajil's voice came from behind her.

"Duck."

She had no idea how he had moved so swiftly and quietly, but she had no time to think of it before they both dropped heavily and quickly to the ground as the bird swooped low over them. A waft of hot air brushed against her skin as the bird passed her head.

With another loud squawk, the bird flew straight up and was gone.

They got to their feet, Kayla's trembling slightly.

"What would have happened if it had touched us?" she asked shakily.

He shook his head grimly. "We both know the answer to that. The feather was a warning. The tamon bird appearing is a sign that something is wrong. Where did you get it?" He took the feather and turned it over in his fingers.

Brows going sky-high, she just stared. "Warning for what?"

"Maybe your memory is gone," Tajil said thoughtfully, staring at her. But she noticed that he had stepped back again, keeping some distance between them. "Some of the Maraudi can do that. But why you, why your Boundary at Aquaris?"

"Aquaris?"

"Seeing the bird proves that Maraudi have been escaping through the door. That feather you're carrying probably summoned it to us."

It was her moment to find out exactly what her sister had been involved in. "Maybe," she said slyly, "but how do we know about the Maraudi again? How do they steal the memories?"

His eyes narrowed instantly. Without warning, a soft glow formed around his palms, and he reached toward her. "Give me your hand."

She shook her head hastily. "You know what? It's probably just a misunderstanding. Let's talk later," she mumbled, suddenly nervous at the sight of his glowing hands. "I should go."

Kayla stepped backwards only to be stopped by Tajil grabbing her shoulder, the glow somehow warm through the leather.

"Shayla, this is important, stop messing around. This isn't funny anymore. If you're joking, stop. If not, give me your palm so that I can let the magic read you. The crystal will sort this out."

He stared at her, and she stared back, not sure what to say.

"Whatever's happening with you may have something to do with the Boundary being breached." He frowned then, still holding onto Kayla's shoulder. "But who would want to steal a Paladin's memories?" He shook his head, "It doesn't matter. Let's get the crystal...,"

Afraid of what would happen if she was found out, Kayla started to protest. But as he reached out to the nearest tree and placed his hand against it, an incredible glow illuminated both of them. Light spread over the trunk until it completely encircled the tree.

Shocked, she could only stare. Where his hand lay against the tree trunk, a puff of smoke rose. At that, Tajil lifted his head. As she watched, the fog began to twist and bend itself into different forms.

Raising his hand toward the cloud, Tajil curved his hand around the shape. Slowly, the smoke became round and solid.

"Once the crystal is ready, it can scan you to see what's happened to you and if you're okay."

The glow, which had been illuminating the area, began shrinking, growing tight around the smoky sphere. Slowly, the glow became solid before her eyes. *He's actually making the magic crystal,* she realized. Everything that she'd seen so far had been nothing short of astonishing, but this was simply too much.

No longer apprehensive, she moved to his side, now amazed by what she was seeing. The forming crystal was beautiful, even in its smoky state. It was streaked with a prism of colors, and still had a soft glow. With one finger, she gingerly stroked the smoky sphere. The red feather, still in her hand, trembled once and then wafted from her grasp.

"Don't let it touch-,"

The warning came too late. As the feather settled on the smoky figure, the cloud imploded and dissipated. The little sphere was gone. Tajil looked frustrated.

Knowing that she'd messed up, all she could ask was, "Was that the crystal, or....?" From the look he gave her, she knew it was the wrong thing to say.

A guarded expression slid over his face. "It's like you're seeing everything for the first time."

She made a face, beginning to get annoyed with the surreal events. "Um, maybe I am?"

"Look, this is serious, Shayla-,"

Something in her snapped. "I know!" she hissed through gritted teeth, nerves on edge, anger starting to simmer below the surface. "But I don't know what's going on!"

His frown grew as his stance became defensive. "You're serious." It wasn't a question. "Akbiani sic oli mantu?" he said suddenly. His expectant gaze met her own.

"I-," she started, not having a clue what to say to the strange language.

At that, Tajil's jaw clenched tightly. He pursed his lips. "It means 'are you okay?'"

"Fine," she said edgily. When he said nothing, she spoke again. "Look, I think we got off on the wrong foot-,"

Wordlessly, Tajil shook his head. They stared at each other for several seconds without speaking.

Suddenly, a wild wind began to whip around them. Overhead, the leaves on the trees ripped from the branches and began swirling in the air. Her braids buffeted and flapped.

The only thing that wasn't moving was Tajil. It was completely clear that he was causing the small windstorm.

During it all, he stood unbothered. But she wasn't fooled into thinking that he was relaxed. His body language reminded her of earlier in the cemetery; he was alert, ready for a fight.

Shay, she thought suddenly, *what to do?*

"Tell the truth," he said, voice eerily calm. "You're not Shayla. Who are you?"

Words failed her, as she cycled through several thoughts at once. None seemed to be right for the possible danger that she was in. An angry boy who could control wind and create crystals out of thin air wasn't something she was equipped to deal with.

As the wind continued to rage around her, she felt a slight tremor beneath her feet and glanced down. "I-,"

Suddenly, a loud BOOM sounded and with it, a section of the rock at her feet rose from the ground, forming a wall. Fear gripped her as she realized that she was in danger. Leaping backward out of the way, she slammed against something hard. Rock formed all around her body, trapping her up to the waist. Realizing that she couldn't move, she thought quickly. Flinging a balled fist behind herself, she felt her fist connect with something or someone.

There was an annoyed grunt and suddenly, the rocks tightened around her. Her heart pounded as pain shot through her legs. She was terrified.

"Let her go," Tajil snapped. "Now, Chilles."

There was an annoyed sigh, before the rocks dropped away and settled back into the ground. She spun to face her attacker. It was a boy around their age with braided hair. A frown covered his face, and he casually bounced a stone in one hand. His eyes never left her face.

The newcomer narrowed his eyes. "All right, mate. Who are you? There's no way that you're Shayla. You don't know our language, you don't know the crystal, and you don't know what a Paladin is...."

"Well....um..." Just her luck, she was facing yet another magical person. This boy was clearly able to move rocks with his mind. Her chances of escaping this were growing slimmer by the minute. Words stuck in her throat as she faced him.

"Wait!"

A fourth voice broke the tension. Another person stepped into view from behind the second boy, and Kayla found herself surrounded. A girl now blocked the way to the lavender froth. She had light brown skin, and a long black ponytail.

Both newcomers were dressed in the black leather.

"Made it just in time, Alyssa," said the one called Chilles. The girl didn't acknowledge him. She simply pinned Kayla in place with a glare.

She wasn't any friendlier than her friends, then. When she spoke again, it was in a steely voice. "Who. Are. You?"

Defiantly, Kayla set her jaw and shot her a glare. "*Kayla*. Shayla's twin sister. Since you supposedly knew her, didn't she tell any of you that she had an identical twin?"

"No, she didn't. Where is she now?" Chilles asked, voice unfriendly.

Her eyes closed as the words rose in her throat, fighting to get around the lump that had suddenly formed. Tears slid down her cheeks as she remembered being told the terrible news. "Dead," she whispered, opening her eyes.

"What? How?" Tajil asked sharply.

She took a deep breath. "She got sick."

Several long seconds passed as the trio said nothing. Every so often, one would shake their head and glance at one of the others. After a while of this, Kayla was certain that they were communicating telepathically. They were silent for so long, there was no way they couldn't be communicating somehow. So, she continued waiting, realizing that some sort of decision was being made.

Chilles was the first to break the silence. "Is it possible? That a Paladin can die of a human sickness?" Disbelief filled his tone.

"We're still human." Alyssa voiced through a frown. "But you say she had a feather?"

"Her sister still has it." Turning to Kayla, Tajil said, "Where did you get the red feather?"

"In my sister's room," she replied, noticing the anger that had slid onto Chilles's face.

Chilles released a long breath. "Sounds like she ran into trouble on one of her missions. Maybe a rogue Maraudi tagged her with the feather. It could have caused her sickness."

"And once she....died," Alyssa mumbled, "then her Boundary was just open-"

Tajil nodded, the barest of movements. "-with all the Maraudi flocking through to this world," he finished. His eyes flickered back to Kayla. "Take us there."

"Take you where?"

It was Chilles that answered. "To Shayla's resting place. So that we can know."

It was raining in the graveyard as they entered.

Paying the light raindrops no mind, Kayla made her way through the tombs, keeping her eyes focused on her sister's. Shayla's three 'friends' followed her silently. In fact, neither had said a word since they arrived back through the temporal. The temporal had taken them right to the graveyard once she'd told Tajil 'the spot where we met this morning'.

He'd stared at her for the longest while but said nothing. Then the whoosh of the bubbling froth had signaled the opening of the temporal, and then they'd arrived at the cemetery.

Finally reaching the tomb, she stopped. "Here," she said softly.

Alyssa took a deep breath. After taking a step forward, so did Chilles. Tajil remained in place, standing with his head tilted slightly. "She's here," Alyssa whispered, voice incredulous.

Tajil glanced at Kayla. "I understand now."

"Understand what?"

"Why I felt Shayla here earlier today. When I landed on the....tomb, it was because I felt her there. I was confused, but then I turned and saw you standing there. My mind knew something was off, but my eyes said that you were Shayla." He shook his head, frowning. Only the hitch in his voice gave away his sadness.

As one, the three knelt in front of the tomb, among the flowers. Tajil began to speak, and they all closed their eyes. When the other two voices joined him, weaving into one, Kayla realized that they were praying.

The prayer was unlike any she'd ever heard before. Unfamiliar and ancient-sounding, the words flowed together like a song, grief wrapping each word. Mesmerized, she kneeled and closed her eyes too.

Since she didn't understand the words, she let her mind wander. After a while, she realized that the praying had stopped.

Her eyes opened to find herself alone. Looking around hastily, she saw the three walking off, already several feet away.

"Wait!"

Running in a graveyard wasn't the easiest thing, she soon realized, weaving her way between headstones and tombs. Plus, the soil was still soggy from the rain earlier, and mud made the ground slippery but she kept going, desperate to catch up to them. They were the only connection she had to her sister's secret life. Even though Shayla hadn't shared that life with her, Kayla still wanted to know all about it. Unshed tears filled her eyes as she realized that if she let them leave, that part of her sister's life would be hidden forever. "Wait! I want to go with you!"

"No. You're not one of us."

She wasn't even sure which of them had said it, since the voice was so flat and dejected. Neither had any of them turned around; they'd all just kept walking.

"What are you?" she asked, exasperated and desperate.

A sigh, then they stopped and turned.

"Paladins," Tajil stated, sadness in his voice. "Guardians of the four Boundaries between the OtherWorld and the human world, who keep ancient magical creatures from crossing over. Our existence ensures the protection and survival of humans, or of those without magic. The OtherWorld is filled with magical creatures called Maraudi, who like to hurt humans."

She frowned at his matter-of-fact demeanor. "You say it so exact, like you're reading from a book or something."

He gave a shrug. "It is what it is....and I'm giving you an explanation that you can understand. What if I told you that magic runs through us, and that I can hear the whisper of the wind shifting miles away? What if I told you that I feel things with my magic first, and with my fingers second? What if I told you that I can remember every moment of my life, from the moment I was born until now? And that I'm responsible for everything that happens within my Boundary, and that I'm a Paladin first and a boy second? And that I have spent nights tracking lost Maraudi when they break through my Boundary, and then spent hours using my magic to repair the break? And that I sleep only to replenish my magic? And that it's hard, but it is the best thing in my life. Would you understand that instead, Kayla?"

She shook her head. "No. But what does that have to do with my sister?"

"She was one of us, a protector of your world. Paladin of the door at Aquaris, the north Boundary. She was a partner, a friend and....you're wearing her clothes." He said the last bit as if that explained everything. "Now that she's ....gone, it seems that the

Maraudi have been sneaking in through her door. Who knows how many are already here. We need to find and stop them."

She frowned. "How? Shayla and I were born together. How could she be one of you?"

"We were all born into human families, but Paladins are born of magic. Our human bodies are simply vessels for our powers. The best explanation might be nature spirits, or elementals, who inhabit human bodies in order to take care of the earthly world. Without being born into bodies, we'd just be spirits, unable to touch the invaders. Shayla was just like us."

"But our bodies were the same, maybe I'm like you too?"

Tajil shook his head, "Only one can hold that power. And that isn't you."

"Please let me go with you," Kayla pleaded.

"No."

Now she felt more alone. "I can help. Earlier today, I put on Shayla's necklace and I think I used magic to move raindrops around."

"That was because of the necklace." Tajil said, voice tense. "Shayla had real power, with or without it."

"Ok, fine. But why can't I go?"

"Because you're not one of us. You are not her."

Frustrated, Kayla started to say more, but stopped as the atmosphere around them changed. Before, an innocent drizzle had been falling, but now the drops grew cold and icy. The air seemed to grow thicker, and tension crackled in every inch of it.

A loud rumbling filled the air. Hastily, she looked around for the cause of the sound, and her eyes fell on two dog-like creatures huddled several yards away. They were growling.

Though they were 'dog-like' in body, the similarities ended there. They had huge mouths, many teeth and large glowing eyes. In those eyes, a ferocious glare shone back at her as she watched. Even worse were the large fiery wings that sprouted from the 'dogs' backs.

She gasped.

A few feet ahead of her, Tajil sighed loudly.

"Great," Chilles muttered, "with the dogs, come the elves." With that, he turned and raced to her side, gripping her wrist in one quick motion. He pulled her forward to the others. "Stick close to me," he said urgently. "They're from the OtherWorld, and really nasty."

"Elves?" Shock didn't cover how she felt. There was so much happening, she was getting lost in the incredulousness of it all. Her brain clung to the most recent thing. "Did you just say elves?"

"Yeah, mate, I did," he murmured, his eyes focused on the approaching dogs. "Now, do as I say-,"

"No," she replied, making her voice as tough as she could. She was sick of being shut out of their 'big' secret life. They needed to tell her what was going on. "Not until you tell me what those dogs are."

"C'mon, mate," Chilles groaned, "not the time. Those doggies over there are more dangerous than they look. You probably want to run over and pet them, make them your best friend, or whatever girls do. But this isn't that type of party, mate."

Her jaw dropped, face growing hot. His comment was a clear insult. Alyssa just shook her head and rolled her eyes.

Just ignore him, Kayla told herself.

As angrily as she could, she glared at him. Her best evil eye was aimed his way, but Chilles ignored her. With Tajil, he was facing the dogs, apparently sizing them up.

"Look," Alyssa said quickly, "they're not dogs. They're creatures called pogyls, and they eat everything in sight, including people. Normally, you'll find them hanging out with elves in the OtherWorld. Sometimes the elves send them out to cause trouble and fight. And no, before you ask, the elves aren't cute and friendly like in books. They're mean, awful, and dangerous-,"

Both dogs suddenly disappeared into thin air. Alyssa gasped.

"And sometimes pogyls are a warning-," Tajil's eyes widened. "Elf! Look out!"

Kayla felt a shove at her back that sent her sprawling. Instincts reacting swiftly, she rolled onto her stomach and came face to face with the horrific sight of a disheveled girl. Her long black hair seemed dirty, and her eyes were almost yellow and feral. She was dressed in many pieces of worn material. The horrific girl seemed slightly goblin-like and wild. *'This is an elf?'*

The most frightening thing were the sparks that flew as she moved her hands. It was clearly magic, but it didn't look like the good kind to Kayla.

The elf stood, hands raised, sparks ready to slice and burn.

"Hate you!" she screamed, eyes glaring. "Hate you!"

Both Tajil and Chilles were frozen in place, eyes on the sparking magic. One spark landed on a nearby wreath and the flowers burst into flames, petals wilting to nothing.

"You lock us inside OtherWorld!" As she shrieked, her arms whipped toward Kayla, sparks popping.

Rolling away from the whirl of sparks, Kayla barely escaped being struck. A swarm of sparks slammed into the ground, erupting into huge flames in several places.

With a mighty heave, Tajil flung his arms out and a burst of wind whipped forth, blowing some of the flames out. Rushing to the far side, Chilles lifted his arms in a fast upward motion. A wall of rocks followed his direction, rumbling upward and around, cutting off the remainder of the flames.

The elf growled, but Tajil tackled her, the two of them tumbling to the ground. They wrestled as he tried to pin the creature who seemed slippery as an eel.

Finally, the elf wriggled out of Tajil's grasp and struggled to her feet. In an instant, the sky was awash with fiery missiles, right over the two Paladins. Only hesitating a second, Kayla unsnapped the metal chestplate and raced forward, trying to protect them.

Too late, her brain pointed out that the shield was too small to cover them all, and the fiery missiles began to fall towards them.

"Don't forget about the power of Inferno!" Alyssa's voice screamed.

They all turned to see Alyssa leap into the air, pitching forward towards the elf. Surprisingly, the fiery sparks twisted mid-air and flew into Alyssa instead. Instantly, her body was engulfed with fire.

Slamming into the startled elf, Alyssa held the creature in place until the fire caught hold of it. As the flames spread across the elf, Alyssa jumped back and began to draw the fire away, working it until she shaped it into a fiery ball with the elf trapped at the center of it.

Springing to her side, Chilles whipped out the temporal and opened the lavender froth. Without a second's hesitation, Tajil opened his mouth and blew out a great breath, sending the fire ball hurtling into the temporal.

The froth disappeared, closing the portal.

Catching Kayla's eye, Alyssa said, "The froth will put out the flames before she gets back to the OtherWorld."

Only then did Kayla release the breath she didn't know she'd been holding. "So that's what you guys do."

"Yep." Tajil nodded.

She was surprised when Chilles clapped her on the back. "I'm impressed, mate. You were willing to risk your life for us? Maybe we should bring you along."

"Trust me, I didn't think it through." She shook her head.

Chilles motioned his friends over. "More could be hiding."

Alyssa shook her head quickly. "No time. Shayla's door needs to be closed now." After a quick glance at Kayla, she added, "It's our job to stop the Maraudi from popping up in your world. You see how dangerous they are."

"We're going to the Water Shrine." Tajil faced her. "But it's hard for a human to get there."

Kayla frowned. "How do you get there?"

"Don't worry." Chilles winked at her. "You can travel with me, but you'll have to hug me really tight."

"Ugh! Nope," she glared at him.

Alyssa smiled. "Come on. I'll take you."

Though she wasn't at all certain what they meant by 'travel' and 'take', Kayla hurried to the other girl's side. Anything was better than the hug Chilles wanted.

At that, all three of the Paladins knelt. Awkwardly, she watched them, still confused.

"Do you remember playing piggyback when you were a kid?" Alyssa asked.

"Yeah....,"

"Well, that's what we're going to do. Get on my back."

Kayla's brows shot up and she glanced at Tajil quickly. He nodded. With a deep breath, she got onto Alyssa's back. It was all crazy, but somehow, she believed their wild story about the Paladins and Shayla. Any way that she could be connected to her sister again, she was willing to try.

"Where is the Shrine?" she asked.

This time, Tajil answered. "Up there," he replied, pointing towards the sky. Her gaze followed his finger, and she saw a tiny glint of something among the clouds. Higher up, there was an even tinier glint.

"Ok, that's crazy. Then how do you get there?"

The Paladins were still kneeling as Chilles said, "You see those shiny bits up there? What you're looking at, mate, are steps."

"Steps? But how do you get onto them?"

"Y'all ready?" Tajil asked quickly, and beneath her, Kayla felt Alyssa take a deep breath.

A mere second before the Paladins moved, did it finally hit her: they intended to jump. With a massive spring, the three Paladins leaped as one into the air, hurtling upward. The wind whipped her hair around and whistled past her ears as she clung to Alyssa's back..

Then finally, with a BOOM!, they landed on the hard surface nestled among the clouds. It was a step, just as Chilles had said, made of a pale white, translucent material.

"Oh my goodness," she gasped, unintentionally gripping

Alyssa tighter, afraid she'd fall. "We're like, a hundred feet in the air!"

Chilles caught her eye and winked again. "Not done yet. This is only the first step."

Instantly, her mind flashed back to when she had first met Tajil in the graveyard. Back then, she'd thought it 'seemed' like he had dropped from the sky. Now she realized the truth: he had.

There was a whole other world above the clouds.

It was stunning. On one side of the steps, everything was a series of hills and valleys and trees. The steps were high, but hilltops rose higher into the sky. It was all bathed in silvery light. The moon hung high in the sky and threw out the bright light that covered everything.

On the other side of the steps, there was a vast ocean that stretched wide before them.

"So where are we exactly?" she asked a few seconds after sliding from Alyssa's back.

"At Aquaris, the north Boundary. Your sister was the guardian here. It's where her door is located," Tajil said. "I'm guardian of the south, Ozorin, Alyssa guards Inferno to the east, and Chilles guards The Shales in the west."

"Each of our Boundaries represent the element that we have the strongest abilities in, water for Aquaris, air for Ozorin, fire for Inferno, and earth for The Shales," added Alyssa.

They had begun walking, and now Kayla discovered that they were heading toward the ocean.

"Um, just so you know, I can't swim," she pointed out.

Tajil laughed. "Not surprised. Chilles, do your stuff."

With a grin, Chilles stretched one hand before them. A loud rumbling started and as she watched, enormous stones rose through the water, forming a bridge for them to cross.

Despite her earlier irritation with him, she smiled. "For once, you're being useful."

The three Paladins laughed, and after a moment, she joined in. It was a small thing, but at the moment, she felt like she fit in. It was the first time she'd felt that way since her sister had died.

A large stone temple sat out in the middle of the water, and walking on Chilles's makeshift bridge, they headed right to it.

"The door will be in here," Tajil said.

"Obviously," she mumbled.

"I'll keep that in mind the next time you have questions," he said, raising one eyebrow.

Water lapped at their feet, and she smiled at the excitement of walking across the ocean. The door to the temple was a plain opening in the stone wall, and one at a time, they entered.

Inside the temple, the floor glowed.

She dropped her eyes. The floor was made of rectangular stone slabs, except for a circular ring cut into the stone.

The ring was broad and made of wedge-shaped pieces, lighter in color than the rest. Every so often in the pattern, there was a darker stone. Slowly circling the ring, she noticed symbols cut into the smooth surfaces. They were the same symbols from the box below Shayla's bed. Lifting her eyes, she noticed that matching stones hung in the air above, forming a circular opening.

But within the stones, a long jagged tear hung in the air, and inside the tear, she could see another landscape, this one dark and gloomy. Tajil walked right up to the tear and began inspecting it with a frown. It was opening wider as they watched.

"Is this the door?" she asked.

"Yes." Alyssa touched a stone. "The Maraudi live on the other side."

"How do we close that tear?" Kayla whispered anxiously, barely containing her nerves. She wasn't ready for another elf battle.

"Good question," Alyssa murmured. "We aren't prepared for this. This hasn't happened before."

Chilles shook his head. "It's only a matter of time before more Maraudi come along and try to get out."

Kayla pointed. "Look."

One of the darker stones now glowed with a dull light. "The stones seem important. Maybe we could remove them?"

Alyssa and Chilles looked at Tajil, as if seeking his thoughts on her idea. At his quick nod, they began pulling stones away from the ring. They worked quickly until they had the side of the dark stone exposed. Staring at it, Kayla's spirits slid downwards. The stone was huge.

She groaned. "We'll never get this out."

Tajil turned to Chilles. "Your earth powers can get it out."

"Maybe." Kneeling next to the stone, Chilles rolled up one sleeve. Leaning over the rock, he touched it. The stone trembled but didn't budge.

"Heads up!" Alyssa called suddenly, seconds before sending a blast of fire through the tear. "There are Maraudi inside, racing this way. We need to hurry and fix this before they get out!"

Following her gaze, Kayla could see several strange creatures inside the dark gloomy world, running towards them. Immediately, Chilles slapped his hands together, and the stones in the air drew closer together, making the tear smaller.

Just then was a loud crash. Maraudi were throwing themselves at the much smaller tear, trying to force it back open. Stones began falling from the air ring.

"Time to move, guys." Kayla jerked Tajil's arm hastily.

Tajil reached into his pocket. "Hate to say it, but it's not looking good." He yanked the temporal out of his shirt.

"You're one of the great Paladins of the World," Alyssa said. "You're not allowed to say that."

"I'm thinking of how to fix the door. We were supposed to close it, not destroy it."

"Well, whatever you're doing, do it quickly," Kayla added.

"A force field!" he said quickly. "A force field of Paladin magic around the door would save it."

Arms out, he grabbed a stone and let his glow spread over it. Instantly, a faint ring of light encircled the door. The banging from the other side stopped.

"There, that should hold it. Now, let's hit the road." He opened the lavender froth and they raced through.

They arrived back in the clearing, wet and tired. Even after what they'd been through, Kayla had found the Boundary beautiful and already missed the silvery moonlit sky stretching on above them.

It had been dangerous, but the Paladins had saved the day.

"What now?" she asked.

"We wait until a new water Paladin is assigned to Aquaris," Tajil shrugged. All three guardians looked sad. "Then I'll remove the force field. It will be a new experience with a new partner." He offered her a small smile. "Come on, we'll take you home."

But Kayla didn't feel like returning to her plain old world. The Paladins would be going off on adventures and visiting the magical Shrines. Things her sister had probably done before she died. Kayla wanted to be a part of their adventures... to have the chance to see endless new worlds.

ABOUT THE AUTHOR

Kish Knight is an urban fantasy author who is "just another book character". Her forever goal is to create fun, escapist novels with characters of color or otherwise. She writes for adult, young adult, and middle grade readers. To become a new friend and reader, join her online and say "HI"! Find her on social media at @kishknightauthor or @kish.knight.

www.kishknight.com

BY KEN KWAME

The earthy colors of the world around me slowly came into focus. I closed my throat to the invading cool air before ultimately deciding it was supposed to go that way. The underbrush beneath my webbed feet crunched as I stretched. My tail swished back and forth until it hit into dry tree bark and chipped some of it away. My tongue moved lazily out of my mouth, brushing against a set of sharp teeth, including a pair of long fangs.

I was born.

There was nothing but white all around. As Celine passed through it, the white mist took on solid form, symbols that moved too quickly for her to make them out. It gave her form, too, constructing the body she would need to walk through this new place.

Celine stepped out from the mist onto dirt and sparse grass. She was on a hill that overlooked a carpet of treetops. Behind her, the glowing mist had returned to its original form: a rocky wall covered with nsibidi symbols—proto-writing native to southern

Nigeria and Cameroon. This, she'd been told, was the only reliable doorway to and from this place.

Her heart sped up as she took in the landscape. She'd seen images of it before, but now that she was here, she grinned like a child in a playpen.

It was a lush, wooded landscape that stretched out so far that she couldn't even guess where it ended. That wasn't the otherworldly thing about it, though. There were loops of wooded ground that rose high into the sky, and even loops of glistening blue ocean in the distance.

She was glad she'd convinced Emem to let her come.

Suddenly, Celine had to take a step forward to keep from falling. At first, she thought there had been a small earthquake, but she was quickly distracted before she could give it more thought.

"It's beautiful, isn't it?"

Celine turned to her right. A leopard stood a couple yards away. This leopard was twice as big as any normal one and boasted an impressive pair of horns.

"Hello, Ikang," Celine said with a smile. She searched for words for a moment before adding, "It's an honor to meet you."

Ikang stepped forward and lowered her massive head toward Celine. "The honor is all mine. Emem has told me about your love of animals."

Emem Ekoyi was the one who discovered this parallel world and the very first human in perhaps centuries to set foot in it. In fact, he and his team were developing the technology needed to enter this place, which they called the Forest.

He and his team designed avatars for traversing this world. Her real body was resting on a recliner in Emem's lab, wearing a headset that projected her consciousness into the Forest. Celine made sense of it by likening it to virtual world technology, except this other world was anything but virtual.

"He's told me a lot about you, too," Celine answered. She started to lift her hand but stopped. "May I?"

Ikang chuckled and gave a quick nod. So, Celine raised her hand and placed it against Ikang's chest.

The musculature underneath was exactly as it should be. Of course, no leopard on Earth had horns like Ikang had. Without even being asked, Ikang graciously lowered her giant head to let Celine touch them.

"Incredible," she breathed.

These horns were quite similar to those of *Kobus kob*, an antelope species, though much bigger. They curved majestically and felt so real to her fingers that she could not convince herself that she was dreaming.

Dr. Celine Musa was a zoologist. Emem had asked her to partner with his team in documenting the creatures of the Forest, which he'd nicknamed nsibeasts. Apparently, most of them were chimeras of at least two animals. Celine couldn't be content studying screens or 3D projections, though. She wanted to travel the Forest herself.

Ikang slowly raised her head away from Celine's reach. "Are you ready?" she asked.

"I am still overwhelmed by all this," Celine answered, "but let's go."

Ikang blinked and turned, brushing against Celine. "Stay close to me."

As Ikang led Celine downhill, she laughed to herself at the fact that she had studied Ikang's body before even looking at her own.

What remarkable technology. Or perhaps juju? Both? This avatar not only felt real but captured everything from her long dreadlocks to her deep black skin and even the scar in the palm of her hand from when she was a child.

"So, you are from the same place Emem is from?" Ikang asked as they neared the trees below. "Nigeria, is it?"

"Yes," Celine answered as she slipped her hands into the spacious pockets of the clothes her avatar wore. It was a simple white shirt and pants with matching sneakers. She fished out the digital tablet that would allow her to take notes.

She needed it sooner than she thought, too. Her mouth fell open when a gigantic bird burst forth from the canopy. Based on the dark, earthy plumage, it was probably a thrush of some kind. But Celine gasped when she noticed that it didn't have a beak. In fact, its entire head looked rodentlike, probably a grasscutter's head. It was hard to tell, though, because it was moving so fast.

Celine wished Emem and his team had figured out how to send a camera to the Forest, but this technology was still so very new.

"You look pleased," Ikang said. She blinked her amber eyes. Celine heard just the hint of a laugh in her voice, but it was hard to confirm it since that feline face didn't show it.

Celine nodded and followed Ikang into the woody area below.

I took in another breath, trying to get used to the scents. The trees. The earth. Other things I couldn't identify yet.

I let out an excited chirp as I tried to figure out how I was supposed to get my body moving. Was I to move one foot at a time? Two, maybe? All four? The earth rustled in response to my shifting toes.

Something moved just at the edge of my field of vision, and I turned towards it. It was big with massive front teeth and dark spots all over its fur. Before I could blink, It lunged at me with its mouth open wide.

Somehow, I leapt, but not fast enough. Teeth sank into my flesh, and I let out a squeal of agony. I kicked as hard as I could, but it wouldn't let go.

The Forest was full of these strange, fascinating creatures. When Celine had asked Emem why he'd called them nsibeasts, he said that it was because of how they'd been created all those centuries ago.

On Emem's first trip to the Forest, he'd learned that ancient people had used nsibidi to channel juju into the creation of these, well, beasts. Celine had found it hard to believe. She'd spent her entire career learning about how every living thing had evolved naturally. Yet here she was walking among beings that had no right existing.

She'd seen a snake with a hawk-like beak, an ant with fangs instead of mandibles, and a lion with the tusks of an elephant. All of them were much larger than their counterparts on Earth. It was like someone had played mix-and-match with these creatures. Celine could barely wrap her zoological mind around it all.

Some of the nsibeasts they passed watched her and her horned leopard escort. Many ignored her or pretended to. As she walked, she typed away on the tablet, adding as much detail as she could.

Ikang had Celine stop walking as a clan of giant hyenas walked past. Most of them had the usual tawny fur and black spots of the spotted hyena, but one was covered with what looked like black feathers. Some had horns, others had long bushy tails, and one even had a large dorsal fin like a fish. They chattered among themselves, giving her side-glances like they were gossiping about her.

"Do they live in this wooded area?" Celine asked.

"No. They pass through sometimes, though. They live in the grasslands outside the woods."

Containing her scientific excitement, Celine entered the details of this clan, adding that maybe they should change the name of the Forest if there's more to this world than woodlands.

Celine let out a small scream and nearly stumbled back as something snapped at her ankle, missing by only a few centimeters. Ikang sprang into action, letting out a roar that vibrated

Celine's very core. Lavender flames danced along her fur in warning.

The nsibeast at Celine's feet glowed a bright blue and instantly grew to many times its size. Celine found herself staring through wide eyes at a giant squirrel with a scorpion's tail. It squealed at Ikang, brandishing its tail. Celine shrieked and dropped the tablet, stumbling into a nearby tree.

Luckily, though, the squirrel turned and escaped into the trees, chattering as it went. Ikang roared at it one last time before turning back to Celine.

"Are you alright?" Ikang asked.

Celine let out a slow, steadying breath. "Yes." She picked up the tablet with shaking hands and let out another. "Yes. I'm fine."

"Good." Ikang growled softly, her ears twitching. "This was a bad idea, Celine. I know you are curious about us, but it is not safe for you here. We should leave."

Celine wanted to protest, but she could think of no argument after what had just happened. The first time Emem had come to the Forest, he was attacked by a nsibeast. Back on Earth, his real body's heart had stopped and if it hadn't been for his connection to Ikang, he wouldn't have survived both here or on Earth.

"Okay," she said. "Thank you."

"Good," Ikang answered through her snarl. "Come. Back to the doorway." She kept a steady eye on Celine, her ears at the alert.

Celine clutched the tablet. Emem had told her that some of the nsibeasts were hostile towards humans, but she was still disappointed that her trip had to end so soon. Ikang bared her fangs and tensed as though preparing to pounce. Then, she started forward slowly, and Celine followed, keeping a hand on Ikang's flank.

Celine kept her eyes and ears trained on her surroundings, too, both to watch out for any hostile nsibeasts and to continue her observation. When she'd returned to the comfort and safety of the lab, she would continue her research there, but her observations wouldn't be nearly as thorough.

Suddenly, a question popped in her mind.

"Your connection to Emem, what's it like? I mean, how does it feel?"

The tension in those massive muscles decreased a bit. "It is hard to describe," Ikang answered. "I can sense him. Even though we are in different worlds. I know, for example, that he misses me, as I miss him. But until the relationship between nsibeasts and humans improves, it's best to limit the human presence here."

Celine let out a slow sigh through her nose. She let herself wonder for a moment what it would be like to receive such a bond but let the thought slip away.

The nsibeasts mostly kept their distance during their walk back. A pair of giant butterfly wings twitched in the canopy above. Celine couldn't figure out what the rest of the nsibeast looked like, but there were definitely two beady eyes staring down at her. Maybe even glaring. The impossibly long legs of a brown spider shook a tree as it turned away after watching them pass.

"A zoologist's dream come true, and I have to leave it all behind," Celine muttered.

There was a sudden high-pitched cry somewhere in the Forest. It must have been coming from just the opposite side of a particularly large tree trunk. Celine and Ikang's heads swung towards the sound and stopped walking.

"What's happening?" Celine asked Ikang, leaning closer to her.

Ikang blinked, her face in an even deeper snarl. "A fight. Someone is losing. Badly." The tension in her muscles had returned.

Then, Celine said, "We should help. Shouldn't we?"

"If I go to interfere, then you will be vulnerable, Celine. I'm sorry. We should go."

She'd barely finished saying this when the ground shifted beneath their feet. It was slight at first but quickly grew violent, making it almost impossible to stand. Ikang growled, looking around frantically as Celine struggled to keep herself upright.

The other nearby nsibeasts were chattering and screaming. The ones that could fly took to the sky while the others hung on to whatever they could to keep themselves from being flung all about.

A giant spotted rat burst from behind the tree where the fight had been going on. It had a single long gash on its left side. Could it have been one of the nsibeasts that had been fighting?

The earthquake then tossed Celine to the ground like she was a piece of trash. Not even Ikang, with her claws, could keep steady. Leaves were being shaken from the trees and even some nsibeasts were falling from their perches.

"Hold on!" Ikang yelled.

The ground continued to slap Celine about, forcing her to close her eyes and pull herself into a fetal position to protect herself against the dirt and the pain. Then, she snapped her eyes open as she realized there were cracks forming beneath her. She screamed as the opened up beneath her, and she fell through. As Celine was smacked on all sides by the falling dirt and, Ikang called her name.

And then there was nothing but pain and darkness.

The shaking ground shocked not only me but my attacker. It let me go. Or rather tossed me into a nearby tree. All the breath left me, and the convulsing tree slapped me to the ground.

I wanted to move, to go anywhere but here, but every time I tried to get to my feet, agony shot through me.

Then, the ground broke open and swallowed me whole. I tried to grab hold of something, anything, but I just kept falling, hitting against sharp rock and cascading dirt.

When I crashed into solid ground, I started coughing almost as violently as the earth had been shaking. It was dark down here. I could barely breathe. But what scared me most was that I wasn't alone.

Something else was breathing down here. And moving. Not knowing what else to do, I froze. Maybe whatever it was wouldn't notice me if I just lay still.

Celine groaned. Her skin felt like it had been flayed and her bones ached. She knew that this wasn't her real body, but the pain told her otherwise.

This cave was a low one. Even as she sat, her hands could touch the ceiling. In the darkness, all she could feel was dirt, stone, and the occasional root sticking out of the walls.

That is, until she found one glimmer of hope just a short distance away from where she'd fallen.

"The tablet!" she practically screamed.

Somehow, she'd managed to keep hold of the digital tablet until she crashed into this cave. It was covered in dirt but seemed intact. She brushed it off and turned on the screen.

The dim light practically poured out into this cramped space. And Celine jumped at the sudden movement in the corner of her eye. She turned the tablet's light toward the far side of the cave, revealing a creature that shrieked and kicked at the dirt as though trying to push itself into the wall. She recognized that scream. It was the same nsibeast that had been losing the fight right before the earthquake.

It was a giant toad. A tree toad, by the looks of it. Though, of course, it was much bigger, about the size of a cheetah. Unlike normal toads, it had a long scaly tail like a crocodile's and bore a mouth of mammalian teeth. Celine thought she saw incisors and molars, but it was hard to tell in the low light.

She had no doubt that, if it tried, it could have killed her easily. But there were deep gashes all over its body. It watched her with saucer-like eyes, shivering as though it were cold.

She took a deep breath. Then another. Despite her best efforts, her heart still thumped violently in her chest, though. "It's okay," she soothed. Slowly, she placed the tablet on the ground, screen facing up.

It wasn't okay, though. They were trapped here. And this poor nsibeast was covered in scratches and bite-marks. Every time she moved even slightly, it hissed and tried to push itself into the wall again. It was like a frightened puppy, and she didn't want to accidentally set it off.

"I won't hurt you," Celine said softly. She focused on breathing slowly.

As the toothed toad-croc's own rattling breathing slowed, Celine looked around. Maybe this chamber had belonged to some kind of burrowing nsibeast. Maybe the toad-croc's? Its feet didn't look suited for burrowing, but did anything about this world make sense? In any case, there was no way out. The opening must have collapsed in the earthquake.

The cave suddenly shifted, sending a shower of dirt down on them. Celine covered her nose and mouth so it wouldn't get into her airways, but the toad-croc thrashed and coughed.

When the dust settled, she brushed off the tablet, allowing light to fill the cave again. Her only hope was for Ikang to save them. Somehow. Dig them out, maybe. Before the cave collapsed on them both.

The roof shifted again, and the toad-croc squealed.

"It's okay," Celine repeated gently. "You know, I should thank you. I think that having someone else to focus on is helping me stay calm. And you should try to stay calm, too. We need to conserve our air."

Swallowing her fear, she inched forward, stopping every time the nsibeast hissed or jerked. She imagined Ikang would scold her for taking this risk but didn't care.

Eventually, she reached the nsibeast. Its wounds looked even worse up close. Something had bitten deep into its hind leg. Some of the scratches had even managed to penetrate its scale-armored tail. Its big circular eyes were trained on her, but it didn't seem to have the strength to move, anymore.

"There," she said, putting a hand on its shoulder. "See? I won't hurt you, sha. Who did this to you? Poor thing."

As she petted it, its breathing slowed. "I know you don't understand me, but I won't leave you. I promise. Not that I have a choice."

Celine hunkered down beside it, keeping her hand on it. Its rough skin wasn't as warm as Ikang's had been, but she hadn't expected it to be since both toads and crocodiles were cold-blooded.

"You're brave, you know that?" she said as its eyes fluttered closed. "Keep fighting. Help is coming."

Celine kept an eye on the rise and fall of its belly to make sure it kept breathing. It coughed every now and then, but did nothing more for a while, even when the roof shifted yet again, sending even more dirt down on them.

"Good," Celine continued, "stay calm. Stay—"

And the strange, babbling thing vanished. Just like that. Its warmth, its touch, both gone. Even the glowing thing in the center of this place had vanished.

As if that wasn't enough, the cave suddenly dumped all the dirt in its ceiling, smothering me.

I couldn't scream through the cloud of dust, but I knew that no one would have heard me, anyway.

"—calm."

Celine found her skin and lungs free of dust. Her hands were resting on the arm of a reclining chair. She snapped her eyes open. She was in the lab she'd left Emem in. The computers and monitors checking on both her vital signs and the happenings of the

Forest beeped gently. The smooth metal of the headset pressed into her temples.

"Where is it?" she demanded.

To her right, Emem looked at her with wide eyes from where he stood before a computer.

"Where's what?" he asked.

"The nsibeast!" Celine answered. "It's still stuck there." She gave him a rundown of where she had been with the toad-croc. "We have to go save it."

There was a monitor to Celine's left with Ikang's distorted image. She seemed to have returned to the place where Celine had entered the Forest, the only place where the barrier between worlds was narrow enough for communication.

"It must be young," Ikang said. "Like a newborn. It hasn't learned how to take its tiny form, to heal itself." She growled. "To think someone would attack one so young."

"Send me back!" Celine yelled. "Now!"

Emem lifted his hands as though to protect himself from her. "No, it's not safe," he answered. "What if another earthquake happens? Or a nsibeast attacks? Let Ikang take care of this. If something happens, I might not be able to save you in time. We barely managed to bring you back with the tablet's signal. It's entirely experimental. And—"

Celine growled as fiercely as Ikang ever had. She reached over and pressed the button to activate the headset.

"Stop!" Emem shouted, but he was too late. She hadn't even had time to return to a seated position before feeling herself being pulled from this reality.

Celine stumbled through the door between worlds, only barely managing not to fall forward and tumble down the hill.

"You stupid human," Ikang snapped to her right. "You can't save it. You must know that. It's too deep underground. We can't reach it in time. And going down into the woods just puts you in danger of attack." Her feline face was twisted into a snarl, her canines bared.

Celine righted herself. "Ikang, it's a baby. Alone and terrified. I have to help it, o!"

Ikang just stared at her.

"I go with or without you," Celine said, starting down the hill. She picked her way over the grass and loose stone, ignoring Ikang's growls.

"Fine," Ikang snapped. "Get on." She headed to Celine's side and knelt so she could climb on.

As Ikang ran, downhill and through the forest, Celine held so tight to Ikang's fur that her hands hurt. Every time Ikang's feet hit the ground, it felt like her brain was crashing against her skull. Still, she suffered through it as the trees whipped past and nsibeasts jumped out of the way like pedestrians before a runaway car.

Much quicker than the first time, they arrived at the scene where Celine had fallen through the earth. It was a mess. Fallen branches were scattered everywhere and the ground looked like it had been churned by a ladle.

Celine jumped off and started clawing at the large clumps of earth. Beside her, Ikang started scratching at the ground, too. But it was too slow. Celine was afraid they were too late.

The strange thing was close again. Close, but far. I could feel its presence somehow. Its warmth. It was like it was calling out to me.

My chest was burning, though. As was every scratch and cut. I felt sleepy. Maybe if I just closed my eyes, all the pain would go away.

Sleep.

Celine gasped and froze. The thought that had popped into her mind was as fleeting as it was foreign. Along with it was a sensation not unlike crying.

"No," she murmured. "No! Don't go!" She started digging more frantically, even as dirt and tiny stones dug painfully into the skin under her fingernails.

"Celine?" Ikang said, no longer digging.

Sleep.

"It's dying," Celine shrieked, her eyes growing moist. "It's dying!"

Ikang rested a massive paw on Celine's hand. "Then we won't reach it in time, my friend. I am sorry."

Celine shoved the paw away. "No! Keep digging."

Why?

"Because you deserve to live!" Celine yelled to the pathetically shallow hole she and Ikang had managed to dig. "Don't die!"

The foreign emotions in my head were like a hook that had lodged inside me, pulling me towards the surface. I didn't want to sleep anymore.

And there was nothing but warmth and light.

Celine let out a tiny cry as a ray of light shot forth from the ground and hit her on the forehead. It grew until it became a column of white. There was a pattern in the light that Celine could have sworn was the nsibidi symbol meaning 'hook.' The dirt disintegrated like sublimating ice, leaving a perfectly cylindrical hole that descended diagonally into the darkness.

Without missing a beat, Celine jumped in and slid down until she got to the bottom and rolled to a stop. When she lifted her head, the toad-croc's wet brown eyes blinked at her. There was a layer of dirt over its green skin.

"You came back for me," it said weakly. It sounded like a preteen. A hoarse preteen.

She knew what that meant. Emem had told her about the time he and Ikang had bonded. It had given Ikang the ability to speak and the same thing had happened here.

"Of course I did," she answered. "How could I not?"

She pushed herself off the ground and up into a crouch and placed a hand on its big toady head. It closed its eyes and made a tiny whistling sound. Under her hand, it glowed white, slowly shrinking and changing shape. Within a few seconds, it had become a tadpole about the size of a housecat with tiny front and hind legs. Its crocodile tail had shrunk, too, though it was still much bigger than any hatchling croc's.

Celine smiled at it and scooped it up as Ikang slid down the hole behind her.

"It's safe," Ikang said.

"Yes. Thank you." Celine cradled the sleeping nsibeast against her chest.

"No," Ikang replied. "I do not think I deserve those thanks. This was all you." She stepped forward and nuzzled Celine's cheek. "Now that you're bonded, I suppose you won't want to return to your world until this little one is completely healed."

Celine smiled. "Definitely not."

Ikang licked Celine's cheek before turning towards the surface "Then come, brave, reckless human. Let's tell *my* human what's happened and then find a safe place for you both to rest."

Ikang started climbing up towards the surface, allowing Celine to hold on to her tail for support. After a few minutes, they emerged into the light, the tadpole-croc snuggled against Celine's chest. Again, Ikang led the way towards the hill where the doorway stood.

Warm.

Celine smiled down at the nsibeast and rested her hand on its head.

"You will have to come up a name for it when it awakens," Ikang said, her tail swaying gently, "just as Emem did for me."

Celine nodded. "I think maybe Akin. It's Yoruba for 'strength.'" The little one's tail swished as though giving approval in its sleep. Celine couldn't help but smile.

Ikang's ear swiveled a little and she let out a low laugh. "I think that is a fitting name, my friend."

ABOUT THE AUTHOR

Ken Kwame is a strong believer in expanding his horizons, which he does by studying languages, keeping active, and watching endless YouTube videos about science and art. He lives in St Andrew, Jamaica, where you just might find him practising his skateboarding.

The Green Man Falls

BY FRANCESCA MCMAHON

CELEBRATIONS' END

Festivities in the *Ar Dachaidh* were always extraordinary. However, it was only on the day of the Spring Equinox did the whole land celebrate. Cernunnos, the Lord of All Wild Things, and his beloved wife, Danu, mother of the Earth, were always the leaders of the feast. It was, after all, their day. The day that they would be reborn.

As the sun above them reached its peak, Cernunnos took his beloved's hand and they began their walk to the weeping willow that lay in the center of their land. Its vines falling all around them, the flowers of its leaves blooming, creating an effect of floating blossoms as they stepped through the curtains and to its center.

It was time.

An orchestra of bird songs filled the air when Cernunnos and Danu stood before the tree trunk, followed by the backing vocals of the other animals' howls and hoots. The loudest of the two being Fey and Gaian, Cernunnos's companions. As the animals sang, the waters of the lake lay still and undisturbed, reflecting the world around them in a perfect mirror image. Unlike the human world, the land of the Gods was untouched by the plague of mankind's existence. Everything here was left wild and untamed. As it should be.

As the fractured light of the sun split through the vines of the willow tree, lighting their skin in its golden and rainbow shimmer, the rebirth began.

Cernunnos watched as Danu's skin withered and wrinkled like the winter leaves on the forest floor, until the holes in her skin grew large enough that they turned to dust. And Danu with it. Then, like a flower coming to bloom, her new body grew out from her fallen form and sprouted into an array of colors and smells, her luscious green-flowered hair falling across her body of yellow, pink, and red flowers and beautifully grown grass skin.

Rebirth was always a painful process. The feeling of your body falling apart can be unnerving even for an immortal, but as he took in Danu's breathtaking new form, he reminded himself that it was a necessary one. It was the only way for their strength to be renewed and for the thread of life that lived within them to regrow. The pain, after all, was only temporary.

Wincing as his antlers shed themselves from his head, Cernunnos took a breath; he was ready to be reborn.

Then something different happened.

After shedding his furred skin, just like his snake, Gaian, Cernunnos expected his fresh coat to follow soon after. He wondered if it would be the same dark brown fur as before or if his coat would change, but he never received that answer. As the sun passed overhead, its light no longer with them, he found himself still connected to his rotting body.

Where new skin from sap and chlorophyll should have arisen on his torso and arms, a crisp and dry brown stayed behind. Where the new fur on his goat legs should have grown, the old continued to fall away in clumps, leaving his legs bare and sore. Even his new growing antlers were not as they should be, the muscle split and chapped as if they were dying as they extended.

Cernunnos had never been one to panic. He always considered blind panic to be a human emotion and, like Ar Dachaidh had always been intended, this world was not the same as the mortal plane. Here, Gods ruled with a level head. He would seek out his old friend, Dian Cecht, one of the eldest healing gods, to gain answers and a cure.

As his hand brushed against the peeling skin of his chest, he turned to his wife, intending to tell her not to worry, he would have their answers soon. In doing so, he caught the look of horror in her eyes.

The once bright green that could reflect the land of their home back to him if he looked deeply enough had dulled to a sickly algae color. Even the flowers of her hair had dulled, matching her expression, their blossom fading with her worry.

"What is it, my love?" He asked, reaching out to her. Cernunnos could never stand seeing her afraid; it was why he had sealed off their world from the mortals in the first place.

"Husband," Danu said, her voice, though even, held the barest whisper of worry. It was as if she were trying not to frighten the surrounding land. "Where are the birds?"

"Why they-" he began, ready to placate her worries with a simple wave of his hand, but as he called out to his creatures, he received no answer from the birds.

Frowning, he stepped out from beneath the willow tree's protection and onto the lush green fields past them. As the sun beamed down on his skin, prickling the sore flesh with its heat, he walked further out into the land, his woodland creatures at his side, searching with him.

Beyond the buzzing of the bees and the chirps of crickets, or even the stomping feet of the herds in the distance. He could hear nothing. No tweets. No sing-song. Nothing.

He felt Danu appear at his side, her soft fingers resting just below his back, as if she were afraid to touch him. Anxiety rolled off her in waves, a scent that carried across the wind and beyond their domain. Signaling to the Gods and creatures of this world that something was wrong.

With a shaky breath, Cernunnos turned to Danu and spoke aloud what they both now knew to be true.

"They're gone."

SOMETHING LOST

First it was the birds, who once filled the world with song. Next came the insects.

There was no warning of their disappearance either. One day they were there, crickets chirping in the grass, butterflies and bees pollinating the flowers and bushes, even the spiders creating their webs to keep them all in balance. Then, in the blink of an eye... they were gone, leaving silence in their place.

It had been a week since the Equinox, or a day if you were going by mortal realm time. Whatever way it was looked at, something was falling apart within Ar Dachaidh and Cernunnos had no idea why.

He sat at the water's edge, his goat-furred legs dipping into the cool water to soothe the ache there. As his creatures disappeared around him, he too suffered more. The fur on his legs had become matted, clumps of it falling out often, leaving ugly blemishes and scarring skin as it fell away. With each passing day, he felt weaker.

Cernunnos had been to see the healer, Dian Cecht, in his part of the world the day after the ceremony. He'd hoped that, in seeing the healer, he would regain his strength and new body and be able to go in search of his creatures. He was their protector, after all, they needed him.

As he laid on a bed as soft as feathers, Dian Cecht's hands above him, the Gods eyes closed as he worked to find the answer, Cerunnos had felt hopeful. Until the God had collapsed at his feet.

"This... this has never happened before, my Lord," Dian

Cecht had said, looking down at his hands in betrayal before turning to look at him. "It was as if something was fighting back against me."

They'd tried another two times after that, with each as unsuccessful as the last and with less reason or logic than when they started. Cernunnos had left soon after and, as his animals continued to disappear in the days that followed, he felt more lost than ever.

"You mustn't be so hard on yourself, my love," a calming voice said, the words drifting around him like pollen spores. Cernunnos looked up to find Danu smiling down at him. "We are all doing the best we can. Have patience and hope. They will return to you."

She sat down beside him and placed a hand on his thigh. Instantly, he felt stronger. The power of the earth coursed through his veins as she pushed her energy into him, allowing Cernunnos the chance to breathe easier.

"Thank you," he whispered. "Do not waste too much of your power on me. With what is happening, I do not want you to be without your strength if you must protect yourself."

Danu pressed a gentle kiss to his cheek, her lips soft like rose petals. "I will be fine; it is you I worry for." She moved her hand away from his thigh and, as he had expected, loose fur fell to the ground. "You are getting worse by the day."

Cernunnos didn't look at her. Instead, he looked around their home. The lush fields of grass where the hares played, the distant meadow where Fey and Gaian, his deer and snake, spent most of their time with their own kind. Even the river where he currently lived, with the fish and frogs that lived within its depths, swimming casually at its base. It was all perfect and yet...

The balance of their home had been destroyed. With the birds and insects gone, there was nothing to keep the land from fading. Even now he could see the flowers across the way becoming brittle, their petals having gone unpollinated for some time.

Whatever had caused his sickness and the kidnap of his creatures, it wasn't only affecting him anymore. It was now going after his wife. If his animals did not return, her land and, one day, herself, would fade. The land needed the animals, and the animals needed the land. One could not live without the other. And he could not live without her.

"I am fine, I promise you." He lied, hating himself for doing so. "I just need to find my creatures and return them home. That way, we will both be safe."

"You must rest," Danu countered, her voice rising an octave. Cernunnos turned to his wife and found her staring up at him, eyes narrowed. It looked as if she were trying to read his mind. "You cannot help anyone if you are not yourself."

Sighing, Cernunnos picked up a flat stone and threw it across the river, skipping it atop the water in a near perfect line. He watched as it sank to the bottom, scaring away the fish below as they swam to somewhere undisturbed.

"How can I rest when I know my people are out there?" He said, his words more curt than he intended.

Pushing himself up and onto his feet, Cerunnous turned away from his home and looked into the distance behind them. He could feel Danu standing beside him, but all he could focus on was the land ahead of him. Ar Dachaidh spread further than even a Gods eye could see. He could make out, just about, Brigid's volcano, the lake of *Caer Ibormeith*, the library of *Ecne*, and even the mills of *Sucellos*. All the Gods of Ar Dachaidh had their own domain where they could hone their abilities in their chosen craft or retire into what they knew best.

He would need to pass through most of their lands to seek the trail for his missing creatures. It would be long and tiresome work but, for his animals and his wife, he would do it.

"I will find them," he started, looking at Danu. "One way or-"

"My lord!" A voice called out, panicked.

Turning away from each other, Cernunnos and Danu looked at the newcomer.

"Bhradain? What are you doing here?" Danu asked, stepping away from Cernunnos. "You should be at Morrigan's side."

Bowing his head, Bhradain struggled to catch his breath. The kelpie was looking worse for wear, which was saying something for a creature of death. While most kelpie's appeared like the monsters they were, Bhradain was Morrigan's favorite creature. She had gifted him with the ability to shift into a more living horse appearance. But instead of his beautiful dark brown mane and body that he wore so often, his form had faded to the green of algae and his eyes, once brown, had turned pure white.

"I know, Your Majesty," Bhradain began, his voice hoarse to the ears, "but I have been without her for a long time now. She passed a mission onto me to guide my brothers and sisters into continuing our work as she dealt with something that even I am not privy to."

Cernunnos and Danu looked at each other, surprised at this. While it was true they had not seen Morrigan in many years, that was rarely something to be concerned about. As a God of war and foresight, she was often in the mortal plane, using her gifts often to guide man in the direction they must go. If they choose to listen to her is up to them in the end.

Yet, to hear that her own companion had not seen her, that was most troubling.

"What is wrong, Bhradain?"

The kelpie shivered slightly, the muscles of his body twitching with nerves.

"Morrigan appeared before me, warning me that it was here. It had made its way into Ar Dachaidh."

Cernunnos stepped closer to the kelpie, searching its eyes for answers. "What do you mean?"

Bhradain shook his head, "her connection with me was spotty at best, her words did not come through clearly. I didn't hear what *it* was. All I know is that something is wrong in Ar Dachaidh."

"How do you know this, Bhradain?" Danu asked, resting a

hand on his muscular neck, an attempt at a calming gesture. "What have you seen?"

The kelpie didn't look at Danu. Instead, he continued to hold Cernunnos's gaze, his bright white eyes filled with worry. "My lord, it's Fey and Gaian."

Fear seized Cernunnos's heart at those names: his two most loyal companions. Fey, one of the first deer, connected to all those born on Earth. Cernunnos's first antlers had been a gift to Fey, creating the cycle of growth and renewal among male deer. And Gaian, a horned snake, who had been by his side since the beginning. He was Cernunnos' symbol of life, death, and rebirth.

"What happened?" He demanded, getting up close and personal with the kelpie.

Bhradain shrunk back, afraid, but told his story all the same.

"They've... they've gone, my Lord." He began, eyes not meeting Cernunnos. "I caught sight of them heading towards the Withering Woods after I had delivered another soul to the land of the dead." Bhradain frowned, "they were acting strange. I called out to them, loud enough that they couldn't have not heard me, and yet they disappeared among the trees without a single glance in my direction.

"I went to follow them into the Woods but, as I traveled further, *this* happened." Lifting his hoof, he awkwardly gestured to his newly formed skeletal body. Only small pieces of flesh remained, most of which was around his head, giving him a grimacing appearance. "So, I turned tail and ran. I don't know what's wrong with that place, but something is."

"And you are sure it was them?" Cernunnos asked, turning away from the horse and looking into the distance.

He would not be able to see the Withering Wood from here, the land there being the furthest point of Ar Dachaidh. Nearby it laid the land of the dead, where all human souls were brought when they passed. This distant plane was the opposite of what Cernunnos represented. It was a land of death and despair while he was the symbol of new life and growth, though as he looked down at himself, taking in his molting fur and scaly skin, he didn't look like he did anymore.

"I am sure of it, my Lord," Bhradain said, lowering his head. "I could guide you there myself, if you so wish."

Cernunnos could feel the change in the air the moment it happened. Turning towards his wife, he found her with her eyes closed and a hand over her heart. She looked defeated, almost, as if she knew whatever she would say would not dissuade him. And she would be right.

With a breath, she opened her eyes and locked onto his, holding his gaze tightly. "Come back home, Cernunnos, or so help me-"

She didn't finish her thought, instead she pulled him tightly into an embrace. Her arms wrapped around him, holding him close as she pushed the warmth of her magic into his body, rejuvenating him as much as she could. Cernunnos smiled into her neck, love in his heart.

"I will always return to you."

As he and Danu embraced, he plucked a rotting leaf from his arm and crushed it within his fist and allowed the dust to sprinkle to the ground.

At least, I hope so, he thought.

***

DEATH: SHE GROWS NEAR

It took longer than it should have to travel from Cernunnos' domain to the Withering Woods. He knew Danu's magic had been sustaining him; he just hadn't realized the extent of it. As he walked on, his pace—once fast to allow him to travel the great distance of Ar Dachaidh—had fallen flat. Now each step sent a shooting pain through his legs, as if needles were beneath his feet. The more he walked, the more drained he felt. Without Danu's support, he needed to rest more than usual.

Even Bhradain seemed to be losing his patience with their slow pace, though he worked to hide it as best he could. Which, for a being of chaos and death, wasn't particularly well.

"My Lord, please, allow me to take us there. It will—"

"No," Cernunnos croaked, "I am perfectly capable of traveling there by my own means. I do not need your pity."

"It is not pity, My Lord," Bhradain said, coming to stand in front of him, his pure white eyes meeting his. "I just wish to help. You are not in your usual state of strength. Please."

Cernunnos was ready to refuse once again, even pushing past the kelpie to continue walking, when another crack in his horns appeared.

The snap echoed around them until the chipped piece fell from his crown to the muddy ground. As it hit, the broken bone turned into a small spout, reaching out to the sun for nourishment until it slowly withered and died. Turning to dust before the God's very eyes.

Cernunnos stood stunned. Even Bhradain, a kelpie well known for his inability to keep his thoughts to himself, stayed silent for a time. Thankfully, just like the humans he studied, he could not keep quiet for long.

"My Lord..." Bhradain stepped forward, his white eyes looking over Cernunnos's body. "Maybe I should return you to your domain. I can continue this journey for—"

The look Cernunnos threw at him made the kelpie skitter backwards in fear. Bhradain wouldn't understand the insult in his words. He spent so much time around death that he likely saw no reason for Cernunnos to push forward. Monsters, such as he, hung on the fence of mortality and immortality; he was neither God nor animal. Of course, he would push for Cernunnos to return home, to fade until death took over. That is what creatures of Death did.

A God like Cernunnos, however? He was his own life force. The power of the Ar Dachaidh ran through him just as he ran through it. If he was failing to sustain himself, what did this mean for this world? He had to gain answers. Even if it meant admitting weakness.

Reigning in his pride, Cernunnos held back a sigh and turned to the kelpie, who, to his surprise, had been waiting patiently for his command. Kelpie's had never been a fan of his; a God of life and living things was always going to be in conflict with death, though they each held respect for one another in some ways. They were, of course, both part of the cycle of life.

"Take me to the Withering Woods. As soon as you can—"

Before Cernunnos could even finish his words, Bhradain was on his knees, gesturing for the God to climb aboard his back. With only a moment of hesitation, Cernunnos sat astride the horse.

Being atop the kelpie was a unique experience. Cernunnos was used to the role of being in control but, as his legs tightened around the kelpie's skeletal body, he knew he would rue this relinquishment the moment Bhradain spoke.

"Hold on, Boss," Bhradain said, snickering at an inside joke of his as he leaped forward in a sprint. He then made an about-turn and charged towards the small nearby puddle... And dived in.

Around them, a tunnel of water swallowed the two of them whole. Surprisingly, the waters were warm and inviting, keeping him calm. It felt as if he were being lulled into letting go. He understood now why most mortals succumbed easily to the kelpies' tricks. The warmth and the sparkling light that sprinkled into the rushing waters made the death trap feel pleasant.

Tunnels of water appeared left, right, upwards, downwards, and kelpies could be seen in almost all of them. As chaos creatures, their transportation matched their style as the speeding monsters would cut through their tunnel into others so fast and so close to them that Cernunnos was shocked there had been no head-on collisions.

During one such incident, Bhradain nickered angrily at the she-kelpie that shot past them, a mortal man on its back. They were unconscious in the beast's grasp, only small bubbles of air escaping their mouth until there were no more. Cernunnos turned away in shame. He could not help the man. It was not his place to do so.

Death has her reasons, he thought, shaking away the sadness that threatened to overwhelm him before taking a breath.

Just then, his chest went tight, surprising him. Pressing a hand against his sternum, blinking his eyes, Cernunnos tried to catch his breath. But that just made things worse.

A feeling of lightheadedness took over him, bringing glittering dots across his vision as the building pressure in his chest took over. Panicked and confused, Cernunnos kicked Bhradain's side, urging him to go faster. Tension built in Cernunnos's head as if it were about to explode.

The world around him started to fade at the edges and his grip on Bhradain's mane loosened until they burst out from the water and back into the open air.

Cernunnos's body went slack, leading to him falling from Bhradain's back and hitting the ground hard as he desperately gasped for air.

Heaving, Cernunnos tried to dislodge the water that had made its way into his body, but only found himself struggling to catch his breath more. His vision was blurry, black dots spotting across the images of the world around him. He could barely make out where he was, let alone what was happening.

The panicked whinnies of Bhradain could be heard behind him, but all Cernunnos could do was vomit up water onto the ground beneath him, covering his hands in the clear liquid.

Eventually, as his sight and breath came back to him, he laid himself down on the watered mud and rested his head. His chest hurt badly, as if he'd been stabbed in the heart and lungs repeatedly. A groaning wheeze left him whenever he attempted to breathe in or out.

Then, the skeletal green face of Bhradain appeared above him and Cernunnos had to stop himself from gasping in horror. He knew the stories in the mortal world that, if you looked upon the kelpie when you felt close to death, you were already dead. Cernunnos closed his eyes.

Gods do not die, he told himself as he opened his eyes and refocused on the kelpie and forced himself to sit up. *This is no premonition.*

"My Lord, what happened?" Bhradain nickered, his tail flickering.

Cernunnos took a shaky breath and pushed himself to stand.

"I-I do not know."

Looking around, Cernunnos took in their new environment. It wasn't the Withering Woods, that much he knew, but they were close. All around them hung the images of winter, as he had expected of the land at the end of time, but the air around them felt... off. The trees hung empty, their bark dark and cracked, the branches curling above them, pointing in their direction. Beneath him, under his feet, the grass lay short and cold, prickling against his soles. Ahead, just past the empty tree branches, lay a darkened arch that was surrounded by vines. That was where the off sensation was coming from. Cernunnos could feel something within its darkness calling to him.

He went to step towards it when Bhradain let out a snort.

"Was it my fault? I can't think of any God that has ever had a problem traveling through the water before. Maybe the puddle was too small?" The kelpie paused. "No, that can't be it. Did you eat beforehand? Eating before water travel can give you cramps."

"That is a myth among mortals, Bhradain," Cernunnos said, his voice strained and sore.

"Right, yes, of course. A mortal told me that as I carried his spirit to the afterlife, said he couldn't die on a full stomach in the water. That was just a myth. He was rather hysterical when I told him he was already dead."

Cernunnos had no idea how to respond to that. He'd never been comfortable hearing the stories of his mortal's demise, even if he knew all human life must come to an end for new life to continue.

"I am sorry, my Lord." Bhradain said then, head bowed. "I should have been more careful bringing you here."

"There is nothing you could have done, Bhradain." He patted the kelpie's skeletal skin. "If I do not know what is happening to me, how could you? How could any such being know?"

"Then allow Death to answer that for you," an unknown voice said, echoing around the two beings. Its voice was soft and gravelly, allowing for the echo to last longer than what would be normal.

Cernunnos didn't recognize the speaker, and he'd had enough of whatever game was being played against him.

"Show yourself!" he bellowed, putting as much weight behind his words as any fading God could. "I am the Lord of all Wild Things; I demand your presence."

To his surprise, the being obeyed.

From the darkened thicket ahead of them, a mist spread out, engulfing the land. The high rising cloud swallowed bushes, grass, and tree trunks. Not even Cernunnos and Bhradain went unaffected, the waters of the mist latching to the small hairs on their body, wetting them.

Then... the mists receded. Only a small blanket of fog stayed, floating atop the grass. When it disappeared, the remaining greenery of the land went with it. In place of many of the bushes lay tombstones of all sizes and color.

"Welcome to the Grave of the Withering Woods, My Lord," the voice spoke again as a figure stepped out from the darkness.

Cernunnos's eyes narrowed on the figure while Bhradain skittered backwards in fear. Even creatures of death feared this one.

"Banshee," Cernunnos hissed.

The woman, whose skin was as white as the sun, bowed her head, her long dark hair falling around her face, framing her like a portrait. As she raised her eyes to his, she smiled sadly.

"We have much to discuss," she whispered.

THE WITHERING WOODS

"Why are you here?" Cernunnos demanded, having no time for the Banshee's games. They were creatures of death, just like kelpies, but their prophecies spared no being. Any could hear her screams. It was why even gods feared the Banshee. "Your realm does not belong in the heart of nature."

"That is something we can agree on, My Lord." The Banshee said, smiling that same sad smile, as if everything she was doing and experiencing pained her.

Cernunnos could understand, to an extent, her misery. The Banshee's gifts were a curse and a blessing. They would guide Death to their victims and receive her thanks and kindness, but were hated among mortals and immortals alike for the role they played. He understood that, yes, but if her screams were ever to be directed at him, she would come to understand genuine pain. Gods do not die. And he would make sure it stayed that way.

"Answer my question." Cernunnos snapped.

The Banshee didn't flinch, only sighing as she turned away from him and walked towards the darkness behind her. He didn't await her permission or guidance, instead charging into the shadows after her, forcing himself through to the other side, even as he felt the pull of... *something* tugging at his mind.

When he reached the light, Cernunnos almost turned to return to the darkness.

What had once been the entrance to the Woods, a beautiful arch made of tree branches and vines, had been swallowed by a smog so dark and thick that Cernunnos couldn't even see the entrance anymore. He stepped towards the smog and pushed his hand against it. As he drew back, a waft of the black smoke came with it. Stumbling backward, coughing hard, he struggled to catch his breath.

As tears came to his eyes, whether from the smog itself or what it meant, he wasn't sure. All he knew, as he watched the smog billowing in front of him, trapped behind some invisible force, was that his home was in trouble.

"How... how can this be?" He asked, his voice smaller than he'd ever heard it.

The Banshee appeared beside him at his question. The fear laced in her eyes alone terrified him.

"Something is infecting this world." She laid a hand on her chest, rubbing the emptiness there. "I can't feel what it is or even know what is doing it. All I know is, the more they tug their way through, the more of this," she gestured to the thick dark smog before them, "we will see.

"I have tried for many days to get through and see what it has done, yet even I, a harbinger of death, a being that must be wherever death will soon follow, cannot enter this place." She laid a hand against the smog patches, but it pushed her away with a shock of electricity. "I have tried for many days to find a way within. I have watched as animals from all over flocked to it, drawn inside its barriers, for reasons I do not understand. But it still does not let me in."

She turned to Cernunnos, her eyes solid black and soulless. Or at least, that is how they appeared. All creatures, even those whose only purpose was to help reap the spirits of others, had a soul. Some just knew how to hide them better.

"Yet you," she began, her voice devoid of emotion. "A God older than existence itself, one tied to the strength of Ar Dachaidh, has just passed further through the barrier than I ever could."

Cernunnos frowned at her and turned towards the archway, the cascade of blackness hurting his eyes from how little he could see through it. He reached his fingers out once more and, unlike the Banshee, his touch passed right through the smog.

"What does that mean?" Cernunnos asked, though he knew the answer. He just didn't want to be right.

"Only you, the eldest of gods, may pass through." The Banshee whispered, her cool hand resting against his shoulder.

"Whatever is causing this..." her voice turned tight, rage building within it. "This sickness... it is calling to you."

Cernunnos sighed heavily before tugging at his horns. More cracks had formed just standing near the poisonous air and so, nervous, he picked at the decaying bone and let it drop to the ground. As he decided on his course of action, Bhradain arrived from the darkness behind him.

"Mother Earth, warn a kelpie before you vanish into emptiness..." He snorted, his white eyes blinking, adjusting to the light. When he caught a whiff of the smog, he skittered backwards, hacking. "What in Danu's name is that?"

Rolling his shoulders, stretching, the Lord of the Wild prepared himself. He knew what he was planning was ludicrous. Madness even. For a moment, he wondered if whatever had been keeping him from being reborn had intended for him to come here. A land where Death can't even reach, but a fading God can. Cernunnos wondered if his creatures inside were even alive.

Trick or not, he thought, eyes falling on the smog. *I will not allow innocent creatures to suffer.*

"That is where my people are." Cernunnos said, resigning himself. "And it is where I must go to save them."

"You can't be—"

Bhradain never got to finish his sentence. The God wondered if maybe he should have waited, heard out the kelpie even. Maybe he'd have stopped him from making such a reckless decision. Cernunnos would never know.

Taking a deep breath, he plunged himself into the smog and faded into its blackness. The Wood had been waiting for him. And he was ready for it.

It Takes Hard Work And...

Cernunnos had been the Lord of Wild Things since his creation. He was made to protect the wild places of the Earth. To help them grow, spread, and seep into the Earth's core. It was how he met his wife and love, Danu, the very Earth itself. They balanced and healed one another. She held and protected his creatures while he provided them to help her world grow strong. He'd even created Ar Dachaidh for them and their people to keep them safe from the failings of the mortal world.

A God of the Wild was not meant to be killed by it. Yet, here he was.

The surrounding smog was thick and pitch black, making it hard to see even an inch in front of his face. He'd known the Withering Woods well beforehand, but his knowledge would only go so far. Throughout the smog, he would catch glances of the surrounding Woods. From the naked trees oozing black liquid down their trunks, swallowing birds and rodents whole, to the fresh water stream that burned an acidic green. Even the grass beneath his feet had wilted under the toxic pressure of the smog, acid, and gunk.

Everything that had once been wilderness and natural had been poisoned. This land may have been a perpetual autumn, but there had still been life within here. Or, at least, there should have been.

No living creature could survive this, Cernunnos thought, struggling to hold his breath. If he thought being underwater was bad, he dreaded to think what would happen if he inhaled the air here.

As he stumbled further in, placing a hand over his mouth and nose to keep himself calm, as his eyes adjusted to the thick cover, Cernunnos saw them under a wilted weeping willow.

Rushing forward, he came to Fey and Gaian's side, and felt tears spring to his eyes. Fey's antlers, just like his, had cracked and splintered—they were now barely half the size they were before he went missing. Black liquid covered his legs, snout, and antlers, and the weight of it kept him stuck to the ground. Gaian beside him was no better. The smog had affected him the most, choking him where he laid. But it was his eyes and reptilian skin that concerned Cernunnos. As a slithering creature, he must have passed through the stream to get here, and now almost all his scales had been burned off and his eyes... they were as empty as Balor's blind one.

Here, Cernunnos took a chance.

He exhaled and inhaled. "My friends, what has happened?"

Fey bucked slightly at his words, as if he had not sensed his approach. While Gaian curled into a ball. The noise was too much for him.

"We were drawn in..." Fey began, before choking on the liquid that covered him. "And we could not escape."

The deer could say no more, and Cernunnos couldn't blame him. He had only spoken once, and he could already feel his lungs tightening at the attempt. There was only so much time he'd have left before he wouldn't make it back out.

The mortal realm, My Lord, Gaian said, his words told through telepathy. It was too hard for him to speak aloud. *It is seeping through.*

How? Cernunnos questioned, unbelieving.

Even in his mind, he could feel Gaian's struggle as he continued. *The seal...* he said, his white eyes on his. *It is weakened.*

Fear gripped at Cernunnos's heart. It couldn't be true. He had worked to make Ar Dachaidh a world stronger and separate from all others. It had been made to be the protector. Yet, Gaian had never lied to him before and would have no reason to do so now.

Cernunnos knew this must be true, but even so, he could hardly consider the possibility. Ar Dachaidh has always been the dominant realm. One that shadows the mortal world, mirroring it through a better lens. Showing how the grass is, in fact, greener on the other side.

Then Cernunnos looked at himself. His decaying body, the loss in his speed, his near inability to survive basic travel. Especially in this almost dying Woods, he could feel himself fading. He was the source of nature itself, Lord of the Wild Things. The Woods should bend to his will, not try to force him under theirs. Where he once would have been able to use his life force to fight against the power of a dying wild, he felt the poison pushing back stronger against him. Pulling him into it instead.

Nothing we can do, Lord, Gaian hissed, his body shivering.

Cernunnos looked at his companions and then turned to look behind him. The smog had pooled around them, making it hard to see what he had trudged through to get here. But he knew, could feel, that his animals were in danger.

Cernunnos closed his eyes and brought his hands to his sternum. Taking a breath, trying not to choke, he dug deep inside himself for what he needed.

It should feel warm, loving, and dangerous. Just like the Wild.

He thought of his times with Gaian and Fey when they would explore Ar Dachaidh, playing games and seeking new animals that had crossed over to their realm to provide them a new home. Then he thought of Danu. Light of his life. Owner of his heart. His love. He knew she would be mad, but he would make it up to her. One day.

Deep down in his center, he felt it. His life spiral.

The smog closed in on him, as if it knew what he was trying to do. But he fought back against it.

"Creatures of the wood! Run, run as fast as you can."

And then the light exploded from his chest.

SACRIFICE

The Life Force of a deity was the strongest power of all. Named the Spiral of Life, it was a never-ending energy that, no matter how long you pulled at it, would never end. It could give life, it could take life, and it would sustain all those blessed by it. The force of the Wild was stronger than anything. No matter how ruined a land became, the Wild would heal it. Cernunnos had to believe that. So, when he dug deep into his core, pulling at the spiral's edge within him, he knew what he would be doing.

He just didn't know how painful it would be.

As the shield burst from him, he could feel his spiral's thread of protection tighten around his heart, cutting him as he unwound it. The poison in this land was pushing back hard, trying to force him to retreat and allow the smog to consume them all. He kept his eyes tightly closed to stop himself from screaming as he fought back. The only sign that what he was doing was working came from the sound of the birds as their wings flapped sluggishly away. Cernunnos could only hope that the other animals were following suit.

But Gaian and Fey had not moved.

Opening his eyes briefly, he took in his two companions who lay at his side, heads bowed towards him. With the smog and poison that laid waste to the land pushed back, the black sludge that had covered Fey receded and the scales of Gaian's skin had returned. Still, they did not leave.

"Go, my friends," Cernunnos commanded as he felt another stab to his heart from the poison. "We only have so much—"

It is then that he felt it. The thread of their own spirals of life pushing into his own, helping him to sustain the pressure of the dying land. Theirs wasn't as strong as his. Their immortal forms were limited compared to a deity. They would die if they kept helping. And he couldn't have them die for him.

Pushing back, Cernunnos held onto the fading light of his own, praying he would have enough for a few more seconds.

My Lord! Gaian's panicked voice came into his mind. *You will die if you go on like this.*

Cernunnos felt another stab to his heart as the tears grew wider. Gritting his teeth, he pushed back, giving as much of his life to hold back the smog. If he gave enough power, maybe, just maybe, the seal that held this land away from the mortal realm would heal. Even if only just a little.

"Gods do not die"... He ground out, scrunching his eyes tighter.

"But a God can fade," a woman's voice said, echoing around the Lord of the Wild's shivering body.

The Banshee had made it through the barrier and to Cernunnos's side. Though he couldn't see her, barely able to summon the strength to open his aching eyes, he could sense the aura of death.

"Is... it... done?" Cernunnos asked through his teeth.

"Your creatures are safe, my Lord. Now, the choice is yours on what must happen next."

As soon as Death had arrived, it disappeared, and the strain of what Cernunnos had been holding back attacked him with added fervor. Whatever had cut through the barrier and allowed this poison to seep through to Ar Dachaidh was far stronger than Cernunnos expected. His life, and that of Ar Dachaidh, were connected. Whatever was weakening the split between the realms was siphoning the life force from them both.

Cernunnos could not allow his home to be destroyed.

The spiral tightened again against his heart, and he could only feel a small piece of the thread left. Fear seeped into his very bones. He had existed for millenia—his spiral shouldn't have deteriorated this quickly. If he pulled anymore, he was unsure what would become of him.

Without help, he and his home would be lost.

As the smog began closing in on him and his companions, he thought of what an old friend had once said to him.

"Mortal heroes, whether they be descendants of our lineage or mere believers, can be our greatest strength when we are in need."

His spiral had only one more piece to unravel before only the center remained. If he was going to do this, he could only hope that whoever came to his aid would know what they were doing and be willing to sacrifice for him as he had for this world.

"Hear me, Descendants of our Line," Cernunnos bellowed, tying his words to the last curve of his life spiral. "Darkness is falling upon us and we are in need of new heroes to fight it. Those brave of mind and strong of heart will be tried and tested to see whether they are worthy of coming to my aid."

Cernunnos shivered as the spiral's curl was pulled from his chest, and he finally opened his eyes. As the cloud of smog charged towards him and he took his last breath of fresh air, he finished his decree.

"The Lord of the Wild Things needs you once more."

ABOUT THE AUTHOR

Francesca McMahon was born in Oxford, England, to a Scottish father and an Essex mother. They gained a B.A. in Creative Writing at Edge Hill University and was shortlisted for the university's Dame Janet Suzman Playwriting Award in 2019. Since graduating, Francesca has worked consistently in publishing while working on her writing of fantasy, horror and romance fiction, as well as various tabletop RPGs and screenplays. As a queer person, their work is dedicated to the LGBTQIA+ community, and she hopes that they will all find a home in her imaginary worlds.

https://francescamcmahon.com/

The Beams of Faelleria

BY RYAN J. SCHROEDER

Wendall Stumpmeier gazed out at his so-called competition. The gym was packed with spectators donning the school colors, and he knew they could only be there for one thing. To watch Wendall perform. He was only a freshman, but he was about to prove himself worthy of the accolades and admiration of the entire school body. He had trained hard for this moment, getting himself into peak condition. He would soon be leading his school to state and holding the trophy he, and he alone, had earned high over his head as he was carried through the hallways. The cheers would be deafening. Girls would flock to him, boys would want to be him, teachers would bow to his greatness. This was his moment. It was time for—

A wadded-up piece of paper hit Wendall in the face, catching him off guard and bringing him back to the reality of the almost empty school gymnasium. There was not as much of an appetite for science fairs as there was for sports.

Roger Drummond, flanked by his two henchmen, Todd Cross and Max Dolan, smirked. "Whoops."

Todd and Max chuckled.

Wendall's face burned with rage. He didn't dare say anything though. Roger was a god in this school, and Todd and Max were too, based on their association with him. Meanwhile, Wendall was one science fair victory away from getting his name broadcast during the daily school news announcements right after the first period bell. For many students at Virginia Everson High School, it would be the first time they had ever heard of Wendall Stumpmeier. Some days he wished he was more like his sister.

"Hey, what does this do, Stumpy?" Todd asked, reaching for one of the wires coming out of Wendall's science experiment.

Wendall hated when they called him that. Stumpy, the nickname Roger and his crew bestowed upon him on Wendall's first day at middle school. Roger, Todd, and Max thought it was so clever. Kids who could barely read or solve the simplest math problems weren't known for their abilities to come up with creative put downs.

"Don't touch that," Wendall said sternly. He stopped working on the code he was programming on his laptop.

Todd yanked his hand away from the wire as if he had just been zapped. Roger, Todd, and Max laughed.

"Tell us what you've got here, Stumpy."

Wendall wasn't sure they were really interested, but he couldn't pass up an opportunity to discuss his project. Even if the three boys didn't care, it would give him a chance to practice for when the judges arrived.

"Ok, well, what do you guys know about Star Trek?"

Wendall wasn't entirely sure, but he thought he may have heard time literally grind to a halt.

"Have you heard of Ansel Truscott?" Wendall asked, trying a different approach.

The boys rolled their eyes.

"Of course. He's only the richest man alive," Max scoffed.

"And his girlfriend is hot," Roger added.

"He also happens to be a brilliant scientist, but sure, those other things are important too. So, you know how he is going to build a hyper loop that will get people from one place to another," Wendall snapped his fingers, "Like that?"

The boys stared at him blankly.

"Well...," he pointed at the project. "This builds on that idea." Wendall wanted to say it improved on it but he didn't want to sound like he was bragging.

"And what happens if you win?"

"Then I get a place in his summer internship program. I would actually get to work with Mr. Truscott at his company Tomorrow Today." Wendall hiked up his pants and puffed out his chest.

"You made a high school science fair project that costs millions of dollars so you could spend your summer working for free?" Roger asked, sounding like he was about to start laughing.

"No, of course not. That would be... This only cost me $20. I already had the glue."

"What a dork."

The other boys started snickering.

"It works though!" Wendall said, scrambling to keep their attention now.

"Yeah, right, Stumpy." Roger scoffed, smirking at his friends. "I don't believe you."

"It does, I swear."

"Yeah?" Roger smiled, "Okay, can you get me into the girls' locker room?"

Wendall cringed. He wanted to do something good for all of society with his project, not spur on the unfortunate fantasies of teenage jocks.

"No, but I can get this apple from here to there." Wendall pointed at the table his project rested on to the table on the other side of the aisle. While his back was turned, Todd began fiddling with the wires again.

"And I can get that same apple from this table to... that trash can." Roger picked up the apple and tossed it in the bin by the door, about forty yards away. Roger gave Todd and Max high fives.

"Did I just win the science fair, boys?"

The three friends walked away laughing. Wendall's shoulders slumped.

He hadn't noticed that Todd had pulled out a wire until it was too late. The damage the fire caused to the gymnasium when Wendall's experiment exploded was going to cost much more than $20. Even if Wendall did still have some leftover glue at home.

Linaria Penrose was reading. Which was not unusual for Linaria. She was always reading. It gave the impression she wasn't paying attention to the lecture her professor was giving the class, but she was. She just didn't think the professor was right.

The professor underlined the word, "human" with what was left of the worn down piece of chalk. Then he drew an equal sign and next to that wrote, "danger." This too, he underlined. Then, thinking maybe he wasn't getting his point across well enough, decided to also draw a box around, "danger." He tapped the two words for further emphasis then dropped his chalk into the tray next to the few remnants of other pieces. He slapped his hands together in a poor attempt to clean them. The arms of his cloak were faded from the white dust. He turned to face the students in the one-room school, his wings brushing against the tray. The sunlight from the lone window caught the lenses of his glasses, revealing greasy smudges.

"There is nothing more dangerous to our way of life than humans. And who can tell us why that is?"

"Because they stole from us," Brigidand Burp said. He was dressed in overalls and a plaid shirt. His feet were bare and covered in dirt.

"That's correct. And who can tell us what they stole?"

"Our way of life," Hextor Grimp replied. Hextor was dressed in a similar fashion as his counterpart.

Linaria sighed dramatically. The professor ignored her.

"That's right. We used to be friends with the humans. And then they stole from us. We gave them everything they needed, taught them our ways, our culture, showed them how to fly, provided them with fairy dust, but that wasn't good enough, was it?"

Linaria's classmates all agreed with the professor's retelling of what happened. Linaria knew it not to be true however. She knew it was all a big misunderstanding.

"Why, if I ever see a human, I'll—"

"Squash 'em!"

"You bet!"

Cheers went up around the room.

"You'd be too busy cowering behind the nearest stump, your teeth chattering would chisel a toothpick before you even got a word in, yeah?" Linaria said, not bothering to look up from the book to see what kind of reaction her comment would warrant. She could feel everyone's eyes on her in response. It was enough to make her skin crawl and her wings stiffen against her linen dress.

"Now, now, Linaria. No need to stir up trouble with that kind of talk," the professor said.

Linaria rolled her eyes at the professor, then turned to Brigidand. "I think you are only afraid of what you do not know. And you, Brigidand Burp, do not know humans."

"And you do? Ha! There haven't been humans here in years. All you know about them you read in your stupid books." Brigidand crossed his arms.

"Books aren't stupid." Linaria snapped hers shut and glared at Brigidand, daring him to say another word.

"Books are only as good as the people who write them. And no one who writes about humans has lived long enough to tell the tale," Brigidand retorted.

"Now, now children. Let's calm down," the professor said.

Linaria's hand shot up. She was no longer the passive observer now that Brigidand had raised her hackles.

"Yes?" The teacher sighed. This one was sure to lead him to early retirement.

"Excuse me *professor*, but Brigidand Burp was saying how terrible humans are. And I don't think he can say that without having met a human."

"And you can say that they aren't terrible, Toadflax?" Brigidand accused.

Linaria bristled at the name.

The professor shot Brigidand a look that made the fairy slump back on his bench seat. "There's no need for name calling." He turned back to Linaria with a soft, if frustrated, expression. "He's right though, you know. You have no proof that humans are good."

"Well, they helped us with the location displacer. They wouldn't have done that if they wanted to harm us, would they?"

The location displacer, or The Beams as it was informally referred to, was the only thing keeping humans from entering the fairy world, while still allowing fairies free passage. It was three white orbs on top of three stone pillars that rose twenty feet in the air with electricity flowing between. As long as the electricity moved, the entrance to the fairy kingdom of Faelleria moved too. They were a genius feat of engineering.

"You know that is a lie, Linaria. Humans did not help us construct The Beams. A classroom is no place for your, or your father's, outlandish theories!"

Linaria glared at the professor, who returned it in kind.

She wanted to argue with him but knew that would get her nowhere. Just like it hadn't for her father. Her father had explained to Linaria in great detail how the humans helped raise The Beams. He had tried to teach this history to others but to no avail. It was the fact that he was the lone dissenting voice in a pool of contradictory ones that made him a pariah in the fairy kingdom.

Linaria buried her face in her book, hoping that her cheeks, burning with rage, would not set the pages on fire.

———

It was two weeks later after the fire destroyed the gym, and Roger Drummond and his crew were still tormenting Wendall. He had just returned to school having served what he felt was an undeserved suspension.

"You better run! You cost us state!"

Wendall Stumpmeier ran as fast as his overweight physique could carry him. His stout legs ached as his raggedy shoes slapped against the pavement. The sound of the boys on their bikes chasing behind him got louder with each step.

"We're going to get you!" The boys peddled faster.

Wendall hated being the target of bullies, but with a name like Wendall Stumpmeier, he was born into it. This time, however, it wasn't because of his name. They were blaming him for his science experiment burning the gym and causing them to forfeit the big basketball game against their crosstown rivals, the Spooner Rails. Wendall knew the experiment was perfect when he set it up. The boys must've done something when they came to his table. Wendall saw Todd eying the wires.

He had been told they would be waiting for him outside the school when the last bell rang. Afraid, Wendall had waited until he saw his favorite teacher leaving the building and followed them out. As naturally as he could, Wendall asked about a subject from class as if he had been waiting all day to discuss it further.

After the two of them had exited and Wendall was sure he was safe, until the next day at least, he had stopped in to the corner store to buy a comic book. He left the store, casually flipping through his fresh purchase when he heard the boys' shouts. He gripped the comic book, crushing the soft pages, and ran.

Wendall rounded the end of the block to the baseball diamond. Beyond that was the forest. If he could get to the forest, he figured he'd be safe. There was no bike path, so they would have to follow him by foot. Wendall spent enough time playing by himself in those woods that he knew exactly where he could hide. Pushing himself to go faster, he tried to ignore the burning in his lungs and aching in his stomach.

Wendall didn't dare turn around to see how close they were to him. His shoes skidded in the dry, chalky dirt as he wrapped his fingers around the chain link fence and flung himself toward the woods.

"We're going to kill you, Stumpy!"

Wendall ran from home plate to second base, making a beeline for center field. He knew there was a gap in the fence that led to the forest. It was one of three in the outfield, put there to make it easier to fetch baseballs that went over. Wendall wasn't athletic, but he was a body to throw out in right field.

Wendall could see center field getting closer, and then, he tripped. The base had been removed where second usually laid, but the post and the hole the post sat in remained. Roger and his crew laughed. Wendall felt his face redden in embarrassment and his pulse quicken in fright. Wendall struggled back to his feet. He pulled his saggy pants higher up his waist. His legs were dead. Wendall couldn't remember the last time he had run this long or hard, or the last time he had ever run. It wasn't something he did voluntarily or for fun.

The boys got closer, but so did the woods. Wendall got to center field and pushed his girthy frame through the tight opening to the forest.

He paused for a moment to look back. The boys were careening through the short grass of the outfield. It wouldn't be long before they too had gotten to the gap. Wendall groaned. Wendall advanced through the brush. The grass here wasn't as short as it was in the baseball field. It hid branches, rocks, and other things Wendall didn't want to think about. He heard the boys get to the gap.

"Leave the bikes," Roger shouted.

Wendall breathed a little easier. It wasn't much, but it was something. If they weren't on their bikes, they would be at a similar disadvantage as he was, weaving through the branches at shoulder height and struggling over the fallen trees.

"We're coming for you, Stumpy. You can't hide from us!"

Wendall tripped again. He braced himself against the dirt ground. Pain ripped through his palms as they slammed over sharpened sticks. He bit his tongue to keep from crying out. No reason to make it easier for them to find him. He forced himself back up, ignoring the sting of pain, and scanned the area in front of him. He furrowed his brow. Something wasn't right. This was not the way the woods in this spot were usually laid out. He turned back again. He could see Roger and the others about twenty yards from him.

Wendall started running again. He'd figure out where he was later, for now he just needed to get away. Of course, he managed to trip again, this time on a tree root, which sent him tumbling. He tried to brace himself, but he didn't find level ground. Instead, Wendall rolled over and over down a steep hill and slammed against a tree trunk. Wind knocked out of him, he considered just lying there, but he couldn't risk being found. He scampered behind the trunk just as the boys got to the top of the hill.

"You see him?" one of the boys asked.

"You down there, Stumpy?"

"We're coming to find you!"

Wendall peered around the tree. He saw the boys talking, but he couldn't make out what they were saying. He watched as Roger started to make his way down the hill, with Todd and Max staying behind. Roger started to slide and braced himself against a tree, stopping himself from sliding down to where Wendall remained out of sight. Roger scanned for a different way down the hill. He took another step and caught himself a second time

"I guess it's your lucky day, Stumpy," Roger shouted. "We'll catch up with you again tomorrow. Same time. We'll wait for you outside your classroom though."

Todd and Max laughed. Their laughter followed them until it had almost disappeared. Wendall stayed where he was, too afraid to move in case it was a trick. It was only when his heart had stopped pounding that he finally relaxed.

Linaria walked past The Beams every day after school. Unfortunately, so did Brigidand and Hextor. Linaria was able to avoid the two fairy boys most days. This was not one of those.

"Hey, Linaria, if you love humans so much, why don't you marry one?"

"Maybe I will," Linaria retorted, tossing her golden hair for good measure.

That gave Brigidand and Hextor momentary pause. They hadn't given much thought as to what to say if Linaria answered that she would in fact be willing to marry a human. In response, they decided to pick up rocks along the path and throw them at her. Eventually that grew tiresome as Linaria either dodged the projectiles or batted them effortlessly with her wings back at the two nuisances, so they began throwing rocks at the birds flying overhead.

"Oh! I hit one!" Brigidand shouted.

"Whoa!" Hextor was equally excited.

They had traveled this rocky terrain every day for years and had never successfully hit a bird, despite what they liked to tell anyone who was within ear shot.

Their excitement was short lived as they watched the bird, partially stunned, fall out of the sky and slam against one of the orbs. Its body then slid down the side into the electric field. The shock of the electricity hitting its feathered figure was enough to jolt the bird back to consciousness. The bird flapped its wings hard against the orb and kicked out its legs to give itself some distance, knocking the sphere slightly off kilter. The change in balance was enough to alter the course of the electricity between the orbs. Instead of their intended target, the blue currents shot into the sky.

"Imagine that. I didn't know birds were that strong," Linaria said, intrigued.

Brigidand and Hextor weren't as indifferent to the danger. Their eyes went wide and their mouths dropped open. Linaria wasn't surprised to hear the cowards yell "run" before they turned and bolted, leaving her behind.

Finally, she thought, *some peace and quiet.*

Eventually feeling safe enough, Wendall poked his head around the tree to check the boys had left him alone before getting to his feet. His backpack, which had gotten tossed during his fall, laid ripped open beside him. His books and other school supplies were strewn in every direction. He sighed. He'd better clean everything up and get home before his parents, or his sister, wondered about him.

He went to bend and grab his bag when stars appeared in his vision. Stumbling, Wendall slid his body against the craggy tree trunk he had hidden behind and rested against it. He grimaced as pain raced through his body. He was going to have to remember that if the opportunity presented itself again in his life, he should not tumble down any embankments. He felt the familiarity of tears starting to well up in his eyes. And then the unfamiliar feeling of sinking.

Wendall started to panic. This was unusual. He had to have a concussion. He couldn't possibly be sinking into... the tree?

Wendall wiggled his body to move it away from the trunk. But he was stuck. He strained harder, but that just sucked him deeper into the bole. He stretched out his arm, his fingers fumbling, then snatching onto the arm of his backpack.

Wendall started to scream. His body from his neck down was completely enveloped by the trunk. Then his face.

And that's when the screaming stopped.

***

And that's when the screaming began.

"What's that?" Brigidand asked, stopping in his tracks.

"It's coming from the forest," Hextor said, his wings quivering with fear.

"We're going to get into so much trouble."

"*You're* going to get into so much trouble, yeah? I didn't do anything." Linaria retorted.

"I saw *you* throw the rock, didn't you see that, Hextor?"

"Yep, I definitely saw it. Rock throwing is a thing I've never done before in my life. Never saw the appeal. Too dirty."

"Why you—"

But before Linaria could say what she really felt about the two fairy boys, there was a rustling in the forest. Linaria, curious, stepped closer.

A hand shot out from the shadows, making her jump back in surprise. Another hand appeared and pushed aside the bushes in front of them. Then, out of the bush, came the face of a boy. His rounded ears gave away that he wasn't a fairy.

Brigidand and Hextor's eyes opened wide in horror.

"Human!" They both shouted before turning tail and running for home. This time, they didn't stop to look back.

"I told you you'd cower," Linaria yelled after them.

It was only when she realized she was alone with a human that she wondered if maybe she too should cower. After all, everything she knew about humans she'd read in a book. And sometimes books were wrong.

But before Linaria could make a decision, Wendall stepped out from the forest. His head was down, and he was brushing the leaves from his dusty brown hair. He raised his eyes and saw Linaria standing before him. Wendall stopped brushing his hair, and instead gave it a quick comb through with his fingertips. He straightened his posture, gave a timid smile and raised his hand in a tentative greeting. He opened his mouth as if to speak. Then his eyes drifted to Linaria's wings, and both the smile and the wave faded as his eyes rolled into the back of his head. His body hit the ground with a solid thud.

Wendall fainted.

"So, humans?" Linaria said, stepping closer to the unconscious boy and looking him over. "Not scary. Good to know."

<hr>

Wendall blinked a couple times, then opened his eyes. He was on his back looking up into a blue, cloudless sky.

"I must've tumbled down that hill and hit my head," Wendall said to what he thought was only himself.

"What hill, mate?" Linaria's head was suddenly hovering over his, her sparkling blue eyes looking directly into his hazel ones.

Wendall scrambled to a seated position.

"Who? What? Where?"

"And how, yeah? I'm Linaria Penrose. I'm a fairy. You're in Faelleria. And a couple of dumb boys knocked that big orb over there out of place. Now, you're probably asking yourself, is this real? It is. I can punch you if you'd like to prove that you're awake." Linaria clenched her fist and smiled helpfully.

Wendall shook his head. "I want to get back home."

"Not sure I can help you with that. You see that electricity there, shooting in the sky? Well, that's what allowed you in. It's supposed to be hitting those other two orbs, but when it isn't..." Linaria shrugged and gestured toward Wendall, "I guess this happens."

"This hasn't happened before?"

"Nope. You're the first human here in ages, mate."

"Wendall."

"Bless you."

"No, that's my name. I'm Wendall. Wendall Stumpmeier."

"Ahhh, that's a good name. It fits you." Linaria had no idea whether either of those things were true as she had never met a Wendall Stumpmeier before.

The two of them stared at each other. They both were filled with questions but were unsure of where to start.

"I should take you to my house to see my da'. He'll know what to do," Linaria broke the silence. "And, if I know anything about those two knuckleheads who knocked The Beams, we better get going sooner than later. I'm sure they've already started forming a posse. And, well, I assume from what I've read in books and stuff, a posse never leads to anything good."

<hr>

Linaria's concerns were valid, because at that very moment at the Burps' house, the two fairy boys were relating what had caused them to sprint all the way home, even after they had lost sight of the orbs on the horizon.

"You should've seen 'im, pa. He was likely 10 feet tall!"

"And he had these... things coming out from his head!" Hextor held his hands, fingers outstretched, next to the side of his head.

"Humans with horns?" Ma asked.

"It was only a matter of time," Pa sighed.

"What are we going to do, pa?" Ma asked.

"I'll tell you what we're going to do." Pa pushed himself back from the table, stood up from his chair, and picked up his pitchfork and a lit lantern. Both were next to the door for circumstances such as this. Or for farming and providing light. Whichever need was more convenient in the moment.

<hr>

Linaria bombarded Wendall with all kinds of questions that Wendall wondered if anyone had ever had a conversation with her. He knew a lot of the answers, since he was conveniently a human, but he was also distracted by being in this strange world and eager to ask questions of his own. They passed by few houses, and those they did were built into the bases of giant mushrooms, or tree trunks, or hillsides.

They arrived at a tree that looked like something out of a Victorian stage play, withered and curled, and straining under the weight of branches that bore no leaves. Linaria quickly ushered him inside.

Wendall was surprised to find that the inside was quite spacious, aided by some type of magic he imagined, although he was unsure if fairies knew magic. He had been with Linaria and had yet to see her fly despite the presence of wings.

"Da', you in here?"

"Yes, Linny."

They followed the sound to two long leather boots sticking out from under what Wendall believed to be a sink.

"Da' I have a surprise for you."

"I'm quite busy, dear. Can it wa—"

"Da' it's a human!"

Linaria's father slammed his head on the bottom of the basin, forgetting for the moment where he was. He slid out, rubbing the crown. Then leapt to his feet at the site of Wendall.

"By Sir Grunyon's beard! It can't be. It's impossible." He lowered his glasses to get a better look at the boy in front of him.

"Give him a spin, yeah?" Linaria encouraged.

Wendall, though confused, did as he was asked and spun around.

"No wings, da'."

"No wings!" Linaria's father cried with a grin.

"And you were right. Humans are nice."

"Was there ever any doubting me?" He said with a twinkle in his eye. Then his gaze grew serious. "Does anyone else know?"

"Well, about that..."

Suddenly there was a loud knock at the door.

"We know he's in there!" A voice yelled from outside. The deep baritone belonged to Blister Burp, Brigidand's father.

"We know you can shut your big—"

Linaria's father shot her a look, and she stopped talking.

"Blister," he started, his voice calming. "It's alright, the human has done no harm. You can leave."

"No harm yet, Franzen. Send him out, and we'll ignore your daughter's transgression."

"My—" Linaria started, too angry to finish her sentence. "It was Brigidand and—"

Linaria's father shot her another look that clamped her up again. Linaria folded her arms and screwed up her mouth.

"All I want is to get back home." Wendall whispered, afraid.

"And that's all we want too, boy. But you see, no one knows how to fix The Beams..." Blister started.

"That Linaria destroyed," someone shouted. Linaria was sure it was Brigidand.

Blister continued, "That Linaria destroyed, yes. Which means more of your kind are coming. And we're going to need a bargaining chip when they do."

Linaria whispered, "Da', don't you have a book about the history of The Beams? Do you think it says anything in there about fixing it?"

"I do! I think it included a blueprint if I'm not mistaken. You go find it. It's on the top right bookshelf. I'll keep them distracted."

Linaria scrambled over to the bookshelf and drew her finger over the spine of several leather-bound volumes.

"Aha!" Linaria's finger landed on exactly what she was looking for, "The Beams: For Fairies." It was one of the few books Linaria had yet to consume, although it was one of many on her To Be Read list.

She pulled it out and slipped it into Wendall's backpack as the first ax blow splintered the door frame.

Approximately twenty fairies filtered into the room, led by Blister Burp. There were easily a hundred more outside.

"Posses never lead to anything good," Linaria said.

Linaria pushed the greasy canvas flap aside. She checked her peripherals and then slipped quickly inside. The flap fell closed behind her. The air inside the tent was hot and still, and it smelled slightly like pickles. A kerosene lamp sat atop a plump wooden barrel that rested against a pole in the center of the hastily thrown together tent.

She scanned the inside and found no other fairies, only Wendall. Wendall was curled up in a ball pressed into the far back corner of a steel cage. The cage was originally designed to catch large wild animals. Linaria knew that to most fairies there was no difference between animals and humans.

Wendall could sense someone was there. He didn't bother checking who.

"Leave me alone. I just want to go home."

"Oh, buck up. It's me, Linaria. I'll get you out of here before you can say ballywalligan."

"Ballywalligan?"

"It's gibberish, but it's oh so much fun to say. Also, I'm going to need a little more time than that."

Wendall unfurled himself and scooted over to where Linaria stood outside his cage. "I didn't think you'd come for me."

"And why not?" Linaria crossed her arms. "I'm not like those other fairies. I can see there's good in you, Wendall Stumpmeier."

"I just... After they took me away..."

"You can't keep Linaria down, mate."

"But how did you... and your father..."

Linaria quickly explained how she had slipped out during the tribunal. She wasn't sure what would happen to her father, but she was sure none of it would matter if they could prove Wendall was a good human. She figured they could do that by fixing The Beams, but the only way for that to work was to free Wendall.

Linaria could see the drying tears on Wendall's cheeks. She reached through the bars and took his hand in hers. Linaria smiled at him reassuringly as she gave him a pat. "Now, let's see how to get you out of this thing, shall we?"

Linaria examined the cage as if she knew exactly what she was searching for, but in reality, she had no idea what she needed to do to get Wendall out. She rubbed her chin and made a lot of soft noises while tilting her head this way, then that. Suddenly, she snapped her fingers. "Sometimes the simplest solution is the most obvious," she said.

"You've figured out how to set me loose? But how?"

"Fairy dust, of course."

Linaria shook some fairy dust from her wings. She sprinkled it on the lock. She said, "Ballywalligan," for her own amusement, and then voila, Wendall was free. "Now let's get you home, yeah?" she said.

"Wait, you've had magic fairy dust this whole time?"

Linaria shrugged.

"Why don't you just use that to fix The Beams?"

"Did you read the book?"

Wendall stared at her blankly.

"Ok, so The Beams were created by both fairies and humans. You need both in order to fix them."

"So, why didn't they just have me do that instead of sticking me in this cage?"

"Who knows why anyone does anything? People get scared, and they don't think rationally, you know? They probably also figured you weren't going to be able to fix it before it would be too late, mate."

"Well, let's prove them wrong."

"I like your spirit."

They reached The Beams as night arrived. It didn't look well guarded, which was good for them. Still, they decided to wait it out to be sure. Linaria kept a lookout while Wendall flipped through the book for answers.

He read and skimmed, read and skimmed, taking in as much as he could. Wendall flipped to the back cover and then tossed the book aside.

"So..."

"It tells me what *you're* supposed to do. But then it says, see 'The Beams: For Dummies' edition for the humans' role. There isn't an answer in here for us."

Linaria opened her mouth to say something encouraging, but before she could, two hands reached out and snatched her and Wendall from the ground.

"Thought you'd come back to let your friends in, eh?" Blister accused.

Wendall kicked out, tears pooling in his eyes. "I just want to get home. I don't see why you won't let me do that."

"Because we know your true intentions. We let you go home, you'll tell the whole lot how to find us. And then it's good-bye to our way of life. You'll force your way down our throats so fast we won't be able to breathe," Blister growled.

"Humans and fairies used to live in harmony, did they not?" Franzen stepped out from the crowd.

"Da'!"

"Yes, Franzen, and we all know where that got us," Blister pointed out.

Wendall was shocked when he witnessed about a hundred fairies earlier at Linaria's house, but he now saw the group had possibly doubled in size, all there to view the spectacle. They cheered on Blister.

Which Wendall did not think bode well for his chances to get home.

"Listen here, yeah?" Linaria shouted. "The way I see it, we have two options. Option one, we wait it out for the humans to arrive, or option two, we let my mate Wendall here try to fix The Beams. The worst that could happen in both instances is we all die. But wouldn't you rather die having tried to do something than waiting for the fight to come to us?"

"I'd rather not die at all," An older fairy yelled from the back of the crowd. "Is there an option where the worst that happens is we just get, like, an infection or something?"

"Well, yeah, there is." Linaria said with a smile. "Wendall fixes The Beams, goes home, and we all live happily ever after."

"Oh, I like that! Let's do that."

A charge rose up from the crowd. Everyone heartily agreed that it was much better to not die.

"Ok, mate. It's your time to shine."

Wendall gulped.

———

Wendall and Linaria stood at the base of one of the pillars and looked up at the errant electricity.

"So, what do I do?" Linaria asked.

Wendall had a general idea of Linaria's role, but he wasn't too clear on the specifics of how it worked.

"You take your... dust, fairy dust and sort of... sprinkle it."

"Sprinkle it?"

"Yeah, just sprinkle it. Sort of." Wendall made a sprinkling motion with his fingers.

"Sounds a bit crazy, but ok, mate. I trust you, yeah?"

Linaria produced the dust from her wings and as she was about to sprinkle it, Wendall shouted, "Wait! Not on the ground. On the pillar."

"Ah, yep, that makes much more sense." Linaria winked.

Linaria sprinkled some fairy dust on the pillar and rubbed it in, "For good luck."

It took only a second before a panel appeared on the side.

"By Sir Grunyon's beard," Linaria's father whispered from the crowd.

The panel popped open. Linaria peered inside. Running through the center of the column were several wires in a rainbow of colors.

"This is all you, mate. I don't know what any of this rubbish means. Good luck." Linaria stepped back.

Wendall took her place. He took a deep breath and let it out slowly. It was almost an exact duplicate of his science fair project.

"I know exactly what to do," Wendall said. "I know exactly what to do," he repeated, louder and with more confidence.

Wendall slung his backpack from his shoulders and tossed it to the ground. He removed a laptop, a paperclip, a screwdriver, and... panic set in.

Where's my glue?

He must've left it back in the forest at the bottom of the hill. Then his hand brushed something that crinkled. The silvery package reflected in the flowing electricity. Gum. It would suffice. Wendall felt his breath return to normal. He unwrapped a stick of Juicy Fruit, popped it in his mouth and started chewing, pushing the wrapper into his front pants pocket.

Wendall got to his feet. It was then that he noticed it. Stuck to the panel was a weathered note. The note contained one word, "Friends."

Wendall glanced over at Linaria, who gave him a big grin and two thumbs up in return. Wendall wanted to get back home, but he knew that if he did, he might never see Linaria again. Though their time together had been brief, he felt a connection with her that he hadn't found with any of the kids at school. His shoulders slumped.

"He's just wasting time," Blister shouted.

"Go on, mate, you've got this. I believe in you."

Wendall gave Linaria an appreciative grin.

Wendall plugged his laptop in a port that dangled from the opening, relieved to find it fit. He pulled up an operating system he had designed himself and rapidly punched in some code. With the code running in the background, he set down the computer and picked up the screwdriver. He loosened some things, tightened some things, and loosened and tightened again, until the things were exactly where he needed them. He took the paperclip and wrapped it between some of the wires, securing them together. Then, Wendall removed the gum from his mouth and wrapped the gray, juicy matter around a few other wires, combined them with the paperclipped ones, and then stuck them on the opposite side of the column.

He picked up his keyboard and hit "Enter."

There was a slow, drawn out *whomp*.

Then the electricity running between the orbs stopped completely.

Everything was silent.

Wendall felt his heart stop beating. The pace of his breath quickened. He was going to be stuck here forever. If he even made it that long.

The silence was replaced by grumbling in the crowd. A few fairies started to step toward him, anger and frustration in their eyes.

And then it happened. One by one, electricity passed through one orb to the next until The Beams were online again.

The crowd broke into a cheer. The surge toward Wendall was quicker, and he soon found himself lifted into the air and tossed around as the fairies chanted his name. Not one for jostling, Wendall begged them to put him down.

"You did it, mate!" Linaria beamed at him. "I never doubted it."

"I did, I doubted it greatly," Blister said. Then he turned toward Franzen and smiled, "And am I glad I was proven wrong. I guess sometimes it pays to take advice from others."

"How'd you do it?" Franzen asked.

"Science!"

Linaria stared at him. Her face said she understood, but Wendell could tell she didn't.

"Luck, Linaria. It was luck."

"Nah. We're the lucky ones, Wendall. Thanks, mate."

"But, you still made it so humans can't find us, right?" Blister chimed in, worry in his voice.

"I did. Until you're ready. Hopefully someday our races can join forces again."

"In time."

"Yes," Wendall looked glumly at Linaria. "In time."

"Go on then," Linaria said. "Get to it."

Wendall paused, unsure what to do. He felt like he should say something, but at the same time, he wasn't sure how long the portal he set up would allow him to travel back to the human world.

"Right," Wendall said and turned toward The Beams. He took a few steps forward, then Linaria rushed up behind him and gave him a hug.

"I'm going to miss you, mate."

"I'm going to miss you too, Linaria. But we'll stay in touch somehow."

Linaria let Wendall go. His shoulders slumped, but he knew what had to be done. He strode toward the electricity, somewhat confident, hoping he would return home in one piece. Linaria stared at the ground until she heard a gasp. She raised her eyes, swiped at the tears, and sighed.

Wendall was gone.

Linaria took a deep breath. This wouldn't be the last time she saw Wendell. She could feel it in her wings.

Wendall was back. He patted himself down to make sure he was all there, and as far as he could tell, he was. He had calculated it so he would end up at the top of the hill instead of the bottom and was pleased to find he was successful. Even if it meant he'd have to buy some more glue.

He walked out of the woods and headed for home. He knew the time in Faelleria had changed him. Wendall was excited for what the future would bring. And carried hope he would see Linaria again some day.

ABOUT THE AUTHOR

Ryan J. Schroeder lives in St. Paul, Minnesota, with his wife and two daughters. Ryan creates books for all ages based on the experiences of his children. As far as he knows, his kids have not been sucked into any portals, although they do disappear when asked to do chores. You can find Ryan on various social media platforms @vegetahbooks.

vegetahbooks.com

King Impulu & The Sky Pearl

BY ZIA KNIGHT

If I told you that I sprouted wings one stormy summer night when the air was sticky like syrup and glowing bright white with lightning bugs, would you believe me? No, right? Well, I wouldn't either. Until it happened to me.

My name is Ruby Freeman, and if you're reading this, *you* answered the call.

Are you ready to fly?

Grandma always told me that, way back when, our people could fly. But they were captured, forgot the old magic, and lost their wings. So, nobody flies anymore except the birds and the bees. Well, a few more animals can, but the point is that people can't make miracles anymore. Though I really wished they could.

I stood rooted to the ground, staring down at my muddy yellow boots as Grandma patted my back from behind. I didn't need to look up to know she was teary-eyed as she gazed over Sankofa Farm, our family's inheritance. My mama was beside me, holding my shoulder, probably flashing one of her fake smiles.

Grownups kept too many secrets. They never told the whole

truth, especially when it was bad news. But I didn't need to be older than twelve to know we were losing the farm and everything with it.

"Diamond, make sure you take good care of my baby," Grandma said.

The tips of her long, steel-gray locs brushed against my forehead as she bent over to give me a kiss.

"Of course, Ma, she's my baby, too," Mama responded, her voice so low it sounded like she was whispering.

The baby wasn't me or a little sister or brother. No, her baby was a leopard print kitten called Jinx nestled in my hoodie pocket. Every summer since I could remember, Mama made the long drive down from Baltimore to St. Moses, Georgia, and dropped me off at our second home. But this summer would be the last, and all the animals would need to find a new home.

I begged and begged until Mama finally caved and let me take Jinx. If we didn't live in an apartment, I would have begged some more to bring home a horse or chicken, but according to her, I was already pressing my luck.

"All right. Well, guess there's not much else to do other than load up the horses tonight. Let me take Ruby with me for one more night, okay? I have a present for her." Grandma insisted as she stepped from behind me, kneeling down to pinch my cheek with her calloused fingers.

It hurt and made me feel like a little baby. Something I really didn't like. But even I could tell she was trying hard to hold back tears, so I just smiled and took it, trying my best not to burst into tears.

"Sure. Does Jabari need a ride home?" Mama asked, sniffling softly as she flicked back her wavy black hair.

I wasn't sure if her allergies were acting up or if she was crying softly. You could never tell. Mama rarely showed how she was really feeling inside. A "corporate bot," Grandma always said, though I didn't know what that meant. She did look like she'd just come from work, which was typical. Even when she worked from home, she always "dressed the part." But no matter how hard I looked, I couldn't find any on/off button to confirm she was a robot.

"No. That baby is coming with me." Grandma finally stood up straight, and I wondered how she became so small. "He's basically a Freeman now after all these years I've raised him."

When I was younger, it felt like she towered above me, and now my head was almost to her shoulders. Grandma's colorful red and black headwrap was faded, her pale green sundress bleached from the warm summer rays, toes curled in her brown sandals. Mama liked to remind me that Grandma was a "happy hippie," but Grandma was always just herself to me. Not today, though. Today she looked far from happy.

"You go on and play," Grandma said, patting my shoulder lightly. "I'll call you in for dinna. If it starts rainin', come in sooner. And *don't* go near that gate, little girl."

Without another word, I slinked away with the kitten still in my pocket, glancing over my shoulder as they started chatting. The mood was heavy, and I knew it was already too late to save the farm. But I was praying for a miracle to come. Like the miracle that saved the Freemans, allowing our ancestors to inherit this farm.

The sun was about to set when I made it to the other side of the farm, close to the large wooden gates separating our property from the forbidden swamp. The morning had been filled with packing up boxes—with Mama ordering us to place them on a big moving truck. So I was more than happy to spend one last night relaxing under a blanket of stars.

I considered running up towards the gates for a split second but stopped short at the bottom of a grassy hill. My Grandma was the kindest woman around. But do something she told you not to, and you better run. Going there would be a big mistake. Besides, something else caught my attention.

I smiled, spotting a trio of familiar horses munching on grass: Amistad, a Tennessee walker with a gorgeous black coat, a black and white Pinto I named Moo when I was five, and a proud American Saddle named Chestnut, whose matching coat shined in the setting sun.

Grandma said this trio of horses was once feral and came to guard Sankofa Farm when I was a baby. It made sense they would be some of the last animals left. Knowing Grandma, she was trying every trick in the book to bring them with her to her new home. But horses don't belong in cities anymore. Just like people who can fly and rabbits that can talk, and all the other stories I grew up with on the farm.

Adults thought all of Grandma's stories were ridiculous, made up to entertain us kids. But, for some reason, I always felt like people in St. Moses brushed off Grandma's stories for a reason they wouldn't tell. When I was younger, she'd weave the most fanciful "tall tales," and everyone would ignore her or laugh it off. But as I got older, I started to realize their laughter was nervous, and their eyes filled with something like fear.

"Amistad! Moo! Chestnut!" I cried out, racing toward them, careful to avoid the pockets of mud left behind from last night's storm. "Where's Tilda?"

Tilda, a pure white Camarillo, was a very rare horse that was "way too expensive," according to Mama. Grandma had brought her last summer, and we bonded right away. But Tilda had been missing since last night, and I was beginning to worry that she had already been sold.

Moo and Chestnut raced away from me, neighing loudly. They never liked me much, even though I loved them. But Amistad stood still as I wrapped my much smaller body around one of his massive legs. When I heard a high-pitched hiss, it was only then I remembered the little kitten in my pocket and pulled away.

"Sorry, Jinx!" I reached inside to pat her head, and she nuzzled the tips of my fingers in a truce.

She saved me from making another big mistake. Free riding was dangerous, and Amistad didn't have a saddle on, so I didn't dare climb on his back. He had his bridle on, allowing me to maneuver him. However, Amistad was the fussiest of the horses, and I'd rather not end up with a cracked head during our last day together.

"You still afraid of falling, huh?" I jumped as Jabari's cheerful voice came out of nowhere.

I whipped around and grinned as he barreled towards me, stopping right in front of my face. His white t-shirt was stained with mud, and so were his blue jeans. Even though Jabari was only a year older than me, it felt like he'd aged three since last summer. He shaved the sides of his head, leaving thick, kinky black locs in the middle. Jabari's voice was deeper, brown skin a few shades darker, and shoulders broader too. That was also the first summer I had to look up when we were talking.

Those Lee's grow fast.

Another one of Grandma's favorite sayings. I didn't know how Jabari ended up on the Freeman farm, but I never really cared. I was just happy that my best friend was here with me and sad thinking it would be the last summer we'd spend together. People always thought of us as brother and sister, but it didn't feel that way when we only got to see each other for three months out of the year.

"You try falling off a horse and let me know if you'd be excited to jump on Amistad without a saddle." I rolled my eyes, pointing to an indent in the middle of my head, in between my braids.

Mama tried to convince me it was just a soft spot all babies had. But I wasn't a baby anymore, and I clearly remembered diving headfirst off Amistad's bucking back and nearly getting crushed when I was little.

Jabari crossed his arms over his chest, nodding slowly. "I get it. Anyway, come over here. I got something to show you."

We perched near an apple tree as Amistad continued grazing. From his back pocket, Jabari pulled out a cloth square. The background was jet black, and tiny spots that looked like stars were woven in it. In the center was a tree with the thickest trunk I'd ever seen, with thinner branches and huge green leaves reaching for the sky.

"The Tree of Life," Jabari murmured as if he could read my mind. "I looked it up online. It's called a Baobab Tree. It doesn't come from here. They're from Africa and Australia."

I nodded, not understanding what was so special about the piece of quilt or the picture it wove. Weaving was Grandma's favorite pastime, and we weaved a lot of them during the summer.

Skyweavin'. Remember, each stitch is a pattern to heaven. So let your fingers be nimble and swift.

That's what Grandma had called it during the rare times she took out the massive family quilt, each square completely different from the next. It told a story, our story, the people who could fly. We came from Africa, and while some used their wings and flew back home, the rest planted roots here in Georgia that grew until the Freemans were born.

That quilt was special. It told our history. Even Jabari, who lived at Sankofa year-round, wasn't allowed to weave anything on it. Had to have "Freeman blood" or something silly like that. When I turned sixteen, it would be given to me, and I'd keep it safe. Mama was supposed to receive it first, then give it to me. But for some reason, she insisted it be passed directly to me.

Which brought me back to the black square Jabari was all but shoving into my face.

"It's a piece of quilt. What's the big deal?" I asked as I took it from his hand, a strange feeling coming over me.

"What's the big deal? Ruby, this is it. This is what we need to save the farm."

My eyes shot wide open, and I was all ears. We were just kids, but Jabari always seemed to be able to outsmart anyone. If he had a plan, it was worth listening to. Maybe he found out that it was really valuable on some online auction, and we could get enough money to pay off the mysterious debt Grandma grumbled about all morning.

"It's a map! A map to a secret treasure the adults are too afraid to go after. But we can do it. I found more pieces... Pieces Mrs. Pearl was hiding from us. And when I put them together, it led from the farm to a place... A tree in the middle of the marsh."

"You mean the swamp? We can't go in there!" I hissed, feeling Jinx's fur stand on edge as I stroked her to keep myself calm.

"For the thousandth time, it's a *marsh*, not a swamp, Ruby! And yes, we're not supposed to. But if we don't, Sankofa is going to be sold. We gotta do something."

"...And what exactly are we looking for that would save the farm?" I murmured, flicking my eyes up to the sky. Storm clouds were rolling in from the East.

"A magical pearl. Remember, these quilts tell stories. And this map says there are worlds beyond our imagination. That the Freemans promised to guard something in exchange for their lives. In return, a King... or a bird? It's kind of hard to tell. Anyway, he took the Freemans' wings but gave them this land in exchange for something. I think if we find this 'Sky Pearl' and return it to him, we can save the farm."

For once, I finally understood how the people in town felt when they heard Grandma spinning tall tales. I stared at Jabari like he'd grown a second head. What did a magical pearl have to do with a real bank taking the farm? None of it made sense. And yet... my curiosity got the best of me, including Jinx, whose ears flicked wildly inside of my hoodie.

"How are you so sure? When did you learn about this?"

Jabari fidgeted against the tree, a few droplets of water falling on his knee. I reached out, palm up, to confirm a rain shower had come. We needed to get back inside soon before Grandma called us inside.

"... What if I told you Mrs. Pearl is hiding things from us?"

"Like what?" I asked, leaning in close.

"Like..." He glanced down at my hoodie pocket, Jinx's green eyes fixed on his. He seemed nervous, even a little suspicious of the kitten. Which was really, really weird.

"Do you trust me, Ruby?" Jabari asked, reaching out to grab my hand. "If you do, please try this with me. I think if we can make it, we can save Mrs. Pearl's home. *Our* home."

He squeezed it, forcing me to squeeze the cloth. My breath caught in my throat as something like electricity sparked in between our palms. We stared at each other for a long time, saying nothing, motionless as the winds started picking up.

Finally, I gulped and forced myself to speak.

"You really think we can do it, Jabari?" I tried to square my shoulders and be brave.

"I *know* we can do it, Ruby. Do you trust me?" he whispered, determination radiating from his dark eyes.

"I trust you. But if we get in trouble, I'm blaming you, Jabari Lee."

Never go beyond the gates. That phrase had been drilled into my head ever since I was a child. Besides critters and gators, there were other, more mystic dangers, dangers the adults were afraid to tell us about. All I knew was that kids were not supposed to go there. Not during the day, and especially not at night.

But despite every warning, I slipped out my bedroom window. My rain boots splashed against a puddle as I headed towards the gates.

We were supposed to be asleep after racing back home to avoid the storm and filling our bellies with Grandma's best chili. Instead, Jabari was probably already by the gates, and I was sneaking out as silent as a church mouse. I was never the type to break the rules, but if breaking this one rule could fix everything, I felt like it was worth it.

I tugged my clear rain jacket closer to my face, tip-toeing

around the house and toward the back door. Suddenly, a light flickered on, and I paused, trying to melt against the wall. I waited and waited, but the light didn't go out. Biting my bottom lip, I debated running back to my room to avoid a whooping or race ahead and pray Grandma didn't see me.

"Oh, quiet down! Nobody's coming or going this late at night," I heard Grandma shout at who, I didn't know. Only Jabari and I stayed there over the summer, and Grandpa passed away a long time ago.

Against my better judgment, I crept towards my window and went on my tippy toes. To my surprise, I found Grandma whirling and twirling around to her favorite record while singing so off-key it hurt my ears. I covered my mouth to stop myself from laughing.

That's when I noticed Jinx hunching her back and hissing. I rubbed my eyes, convinced water had gotten into them when I looked at her shadow. Because, instead of the arched back of a cat, it looked like a little girl with cat ears instead.

I don't know if the light was playing tricks with my mind, but it appeared as though Jinx's girl-shaped shadow also had a feline smirk that grew wider, like the Cheshire Cat from *Alice in Wonderland.*

"Oh, quiet down! Nothin's gonna happen. It's over. They won! Bloodsuckers have drained me dry. I couldn't pay back the debt, so now they're taking our land. And to top it all off, I can't find that contract anywhere!" Grandma grumbled as she swatted Jinx's paw away, stumbling around the office looking for something.

Jinx whined, jumping from a bookcase to the desk Grandma was rummaging through, her shadow returning to normal. She reached out to rub Jinx's head.

"There, there. I can't find that map anywhere either. I told that boy to *clean* the library, not rearrange it. But I guess there ain't no reason to fuss over things that can't be changed. This is *their* home now, Jinx. Now it's your duty to protect Ruby, not all this. That's what guardians do. My time is up."

Grandma sighed, plopping down in a big, green chair, defeated.

"They'll be here for me soon. I thought I could send it back, and that would be enough. Even sold my prized horse. You don't come across a unicorn like Tilda that often these days. But I'm too old to fly, to go and plead before the King. Had to sell off everything to the King's enemies so I wouldn't lose my head."

She tapped a wrinkled finger against her chin.

"Jabari's making no progress. Though I knew it was a long shot when I took 'im. Suppose I should've made Diamond try when I had a chance, or at least gotten her to see why Ruby needed training. But it's all over now... If only... Haaa... If only."

I cocked my head to the side, confused. Mama said the bank was taking the farm. So who was "they," and why were they coming for my Grandma? Who was this King? Was it the bird king Jabari saw on the map? And more importantly, what was Grandma trying to train Mama and me to do?

I tried to raise myself up to get a better view, only to choke on my tongue when Jinx appeared out of thin air, staring at me with her bright green eyes through the soaked window pane. I fell backward, hitting the ground hard.

"What was that?" Ice shot through my veins. Grandma heard me fall! I got up, my left side aching, and started running as if my life depended on it.

I ran so hard my legs shook from the force, the sky splitting apart as the storm picked up, thunder booming and lightning flashing all around. By the time I reached the gates, I couldn't stop myself.

Jabari, who was wearing a matching clear raincoat with black boots, shouted, "Stop!" as I kept on running.

My boots snapped twigs and were nearly ripped off in the mud. It was only when Jabari tackled me that I finally stopped.

"Ow!" I yelled as he rolled off of me. It felt like I got hit by a truck.

"Then stop next time! You can't just go runnin' around in the marsh!" With that, he dragged me to my feet.

Then Jabari pulled me underneath a large tree, arranging pieces of quilt on the ground. I kneeled down to see. He brought the same black one from earlier and four more he must have stolen from the library. Each looked like a completely different scene, one in the water, one in the sky, one on earth, and one that looked like the center of a volcano.

"We have to be careful. Remember, if Mrs. Pearl catches us, just blame it all on me."

I looked around at where we were. It was hard to see much in the dark, which didn't help, and I was feeling cold, covered in damp mud. This night was already off to a bad start.

"Maybe we shouldn't do this..." I started, wringing my hands nervously. "This doesn't seem like the best—"

"Please, Ruby, don't chicken out."

I frowned. Jabari wasn't the type to beg. Scratch that, Jabari *never* begged. So this had to be something really important to him if he'd risked being grounded for the rest of his life. This really had to be the key to fixing everything.

"All right, but the moment things get weird—"

"You'll leave me behind; I know."

"What?" I exclaimed, surprised. "No, I meant we *both* run away. I'm not that mean."

Jabari rubbed the back of his neck. "Sure. Okay. Anyway..."

He dug in his pocket, the heavy rain making everything slippery. Jabari pulled out five stones that matched the colors of the pieces of quilt: black, white, blue, green, and red.

"The quilt is the map, and these are the keys. Now listen. We need to go to this spot and conjure up... a spell. Erm... Incantation? It's pretty simple. We arrange these stones on the map. Bam! Portal opened."

None of what he said made sense to me, and my heart was still hammering against my chest, thoughts scrambled like an egg. Then I groaned, realized he'd taken way too much from her library. Grandma was going to be so mad.

He just shrugged in return, murmuring, "I didn't steal them. We're just borrowing them from Mrs. Pearl."

He grabbed my arm, stopping me in place before I could turn and run. "Wait, Ruby. I swear, it'll be fine!"

I didn't want to get caught stealing on top of going past the gate. Jabari reminded me that he would take all the blame, but it didn't make me feel any better. And yet, I stayed. Realizing I wasn't going to run away, Jabari took my hand gently and began guiding us through the marsh.

"Are you... Are you sure this Tree of Life is real?" I asked, shouting over the whipping wind. "That a portal will open?"

Jabari didn't answer right away, so I asked the one question I needed an answer to after hearing Grandma's strange conversation with Jinx. "Was Grandma training you to... make miracles happen?"

"Trust me, Ruby," Jabari grunted, struggling through the clumps of reeds and mud. "We'll make a miracle, or we can at least say we tried. Either way, we'll find out real soon if Mrs. Pearl's stories are true."

I nodded, struggling to keep the hood of my raincoat on, and kept my head low. We pushed through the wetlands an inch at a time, the water rising until our feet and legs were soaked, and Jabari and I were ankle-deep in muddy water.

We were walking around aimlessly, though Jabari pretended to know where we were going. I could barely see a few feet in front of me from the rain. If not for the mud clinging to our rain boots, I felt like we'd be swept up in the storm and blown away. It felt like it was all a lost cause until the lightning bugs came.

One lightning bug, barely struggling against the wind, landed in front of us, then a second, and a third. More and more came until they illuminated a pathway.

"See!" Jabari shouted over the heavy winds. "Just like the map! They'll guide us to the Tree of Life."

We waded through the water, our excitement growing as the bugs kept multiplying, lighting the way. He squeezed my hand as we turned a corner, and I grinned, realizing the stars I saw on the piece of quilt were actually bugs.

Soon we stumbled upon a tree trunk that was out of this world. It spiraled high into the sky, so high we couldn't even see the branches above. The lightning bugs that lit our path encircled the Tree of Life in a halo of bright, white light. They bobbed up and down, climbing skyward. There had to be thousands, like lights strung up on a Christmas tree.

We turned to each other, shouted, and hugged, overwhelmed that we had found it. We were closer to finding the answer to saving Sankofa.

"Okay, now we just have to do the spell," he said, digging into his pockets.

I tried to help him, but suddenly the water surged as if the storm knew our intentions. Then, the bugs scattered. We tried to get closer to the trunk, but the ankle-deep water quickly reached our knees.

"Jabari!" I screamed as we clung to each other. "What now?"

"I-I," he sputtered in shock. "I don't know! We can't do the spell... There's too much water. Oh no, the sto—"

He was cut off as water shot over our heads, pulling back until we were chest-deep. There was no time for magic, we had to swim!

But my legs felt heavy like stone, and the fear of Jabari's soaking wet face mirrored my own. We were sinking, then drowning as the water surged higher and higher until Jabari and I went spiraling underwater.

I was surrounded by a sea of darkness. I felt something like seaweed brush against my skin. I *thought* it could be seaweed, but when it wrapped around my ankle, I knew it couldn't be. I struggled to get away, but it gripped onto me tighter, long nails grazing against my skin. Terrified, I made the mistake of looking down and found bright yellow eyes staring up at me.

A gator? A swamp witch? Whatever it was, I didn't want to find out. I forced myself to swim upward and collided with Jabari. When we emerged, Jabari was hanging on for dear life on a smaller tree, my legs wrapped around it in front of him.

I tried to reach for him, but the more I moved, the more he slipped. My heart was pounding so hard my ears rang. I craned my neck to the side, only to see a wave splitting the trees and coming right at us.

This was no ordinary storm. Not even the wetlands flooded like a tsunami. I looked at Jabari, whose mouth hung open in shock, fingers barely gripping the tree trunk. Unsure of what I should do, I grabbed his hand, closed my eyes, and started chanting.

Fly! Fly! Fly!

I used to take a bedsheet and tie it around my shoulders like a cape. I would leap from my bed, horseback, and tree branches, knowing deep down my wings would sprout if I just believed enough. And then Grandma told me the people could fly, past tense, and nobody flew anymore. Miracles were a thing of the past. But tonight, I needed one more than I needed anything in my life.

The next thing I knew, the world went pitch black, and I felt as if I was free-falling. Afraid I fainted, or worse, drowned, I tried to paddle upwards. But to my surprise, my fingers weren't slashing through water. No, they were slashing air!

Slowly, I opened my eyes, and to my utter surprise, Jabari and I were no longer submerged in the wetlands. Sankofa and all of St. Moses were just tiny specks on the ground.

"It's true," I heard Jabari say, his voice filled with wonder. "Freeman's can fly!"

Sure enough, I was gripping him from behind as we soared high in the sky. My shoulder blades ached, and black feathers slapped my face.

My feathers! I had wings!

But the awe the miracle inspired was short-lived. The thousands of lightning bugs that guided us to the tree were flying directly toward us.

I wondered where they were all going until I turned around and saw it. The tree we had found below was still going, piercing the sky above where a black void had opened up.

"Is that the portal?" I asked as I was forced to fly upward, the lightning bugs pushing us towards the menacing black hole.

"We're going to find out!" Jabari screamed back as we were surrounded by the bugs blinding white light, piercing the spiraling void.

For a brief moment, I felt entirely weightless, soaring on what felt like a cloud and feeling the cool breeze against my skin. And then, I came crashing down, screaming as my arms pinwheeled around. Then, seconds later, my palms connected with a branch, and soon I found myself dangling mid-air.

"It's real..." Jabari's voice was faint, coming from below me, which didn't make any sense.

Jabari had been in my arms when the bugs forced us into the black portal. So why was I hanging from a tree?

"It's real!" This time the voice was clearer, almost right beside me.

My branch swayed as he climbed towards me, green leaves shaking. And they were humongous, the size of me once I really got a look at them. After a while, Jabari's head poked out from behind one of the leaves, using all his strength to move it aside as he scooted against the branch towards me. He reached down, and with some effort, he pulled me up. The branch was thick enough for both of us to sit down.

"Ruby, look!" he said, pointing outwards, and I turned my head.

What I saw nearly made me go tumbling back down to Earth. The ground, or more like the sky, was a sea of green. Giant trees pierced fluffy white clouds, each branch weaving into each other, creating what looked like miniature towns.

Between the leaves, super-sized animals appeared. The lightning bugs that had guided us to this world were now the size of cars, their bright white butts leaving a trail of white dust as they buzzed about. Honeybees the size of houses landed on equally enormous flowers that sprouted in mid-air, peeking through the clouds.

But what surprised me the most were the people. They weren't ordinary people, not like me and Jabari. They may have looked like people, but they were far bigger. Almost giant in size, with beaks for mouths. But what caught my attention more was that these people had wings like me.

They came in all shades, with hair that resembled human hair and wings in every color of the rainbow. Their long white robes had intricate stitches, not unlike the family quilt Grandma safeguarded. And on each of their heads was a beaded crown made of precious stones: gold, silver, rubies, emeralds, pearls, and everything in between.

"Woah!" I breathed, twisting slightly to see if I still had my own wings.

They were still there, fluttering softly. I looked to Jabari and grinned, who had dug out the stones and map to hold in his hands and smiled a toothy grin.

"We did it!" I whispered, afraid one of the giants would hear us. "But what now?"

"We find the Sky Pearl and give it to the King," he said, rolling until his back was against a cloud, laughing. "Mrs. Pearl was right, Ruby. The people could fly. Maybe the people that didn't return home to Africa built a new one in the clouds?"

I nodded, mind racing with endless, unanswerable questions. If Grandma was right, did that really mean all Freemans had wings? And what about the Lees? The possibilities were endless. But the more I thought about it, the more it didn't make sense.

"Look!" I gasped as something barreled through a cloud, followed by a loud rumbling that didn't sound good, darkness creeping through the sky.

My mouth flew open. I knew that white coat. It was Tilda! Or at least, it looked like Tilda. She didn't have wings before or a horn in the center of her head. I watched as she soared high into the sky and then nosedived, coming to a stop near Jabari and me.

My eyes flicked to her saddle and, to my surprise, curled up in a ball there was, "Jinx?"

The kitten mewed in response. Jabari and I shared a look, laughing.

"I knew there was something weird about that cat, Ruby."

I rolled my eyes. Of course, he'd focus on the cat and not the unicorn.

We continued to take in the new world around us, but it was becoming too hard to ignore the big, black shadow that had been slowly descending since Tilda and Jinx arrived. Thankfully, an impatient meow gave me the perfect opportunity to pretend it wasn't there.

"Hey, Jinx," I said, my voice going higher in pitch as I reached out to stroke her head, "How did you—"

King Impulu does not tolerate humans in his realm.

My hand stopped in place, and I blinked. Who had said that? I looked over to Jabari, who was in his own world, and then back to Tilda, her massive wings keeping her afloat.

I told Pearl that her descendant was planning to pierce the veil. If only she believed me. Now it's time to go home. As your guardian, I cannot allow you to do this.

Oh no. There was no mistaking this little voice was coming from Jinx, though her mouth never moved.

"What's... this?" Jabari asked, his voice confused and worried.

"What?" I turned to him only to find the stones beginning to glow in his hands.

Scooting closer, we both looked as the glow grew brighter before the stones fused into one jet-black ball, larger than before. Jabari rolled the orb across his hands, intrigued before it accidentally rolled from his fingertips.

We both screamed in horror, diving off the tree for it without thinking. Thankfully, Tilda swooped down to catch Jabari, and I was able to grab the orb, flapping my wings to stay afloat.

Uh oh. Jinx said in my mind once again. *We need to go. Now!*

I looked up to see Jabari on Tilda's back, cradling Jinx, her fur standing on edge. I was going to fly up toward them when I felt a prickle on the back of my neck. I turned to see hundreds of eyes on us, faces filled with shock and anger.

Looking down at the black orb, I noticed it hardening and turning white. Then I put two and two together.

What if...

What if we had the Sky Pearl the whole time?

My answer came in the form of a bird-woman opening her mouth and releasing a sonic boom. It forced us to scatter. I hurtled through a cloud while Tilda reared up to avoid the attack. Then it seemed everything and everyone was after us.

Insects slashed at me, bird-folk dove and tried to snatch the pearl from my hands, and even the trees seemed to shift and come alive, branches closing in, trying to block my path. I emerged on the other end of a cloud, almost colliding with Tilda. I threw myself on her back in front of Jabari.

"Hold on!" I shouted, not knowing if I could free-fly a unicorn when I could barely free-ride a horse.

"To what?" he shouted back, smashing Jinx into my back.

I didn't have time to answer as a pair of bird-women slashed at us from behind.

"Sister," one cawed, her hardened beak of a mouth clicking, "return King Impulu's core."

Leave them alone! I heard Jinx grit out as she leaped from Jabari's hand.

She twirled, shifting into a fairy tale creature part human and part animal. Part of Jinx looked like a dark-skinned little girl with a big, yellow puffball hairstyle, maybe four or five, with bright green eyes. But her legs were shaped like a cat and spotted, with long, sharp nails, a creepy grin, and ears on top of her head.

She landed on the back of one of the bird-women, swatting at her head until she was forced to flee. Then, Jinx somersaulted midair and landed back in Jabari's arms, transforming to her original size.

It was then that the skies began to rock with thunder and lightning, and we were forced to dodge the bolts. We screamed in terror as a large shadow flew above us, and I didn't need to look up to know it had to be: "King Impulu!"

"Ruby! Give him the pearl!" Jabari shouted, King Impulu's shadow stretching out as far as I could see, blanketing the realm.

"You dare disobey my order to never soar again in exchange for your life!" King Impulu screeched, his giant wings flickering downward, sending what looked like a tornado barreling downwards.

His people scattered, along with the animals and insects tending to the trees. It didn't look good for us. Not one bit as we whorled through the air. I whipped the reins to drive Tilda faster, knowing we didn't have much time before the King's claws snagged us and took us back to his nest or wherever bird king's lived.

Knowing we were running out of options, I screamed, "King Impulu! We're here to pay back our debt!"

With that, I flung the pearl upward and forced Tilda to dive downward, back to Earth, hoping another portal would open up. It was all I could think of in the heat of the moment. I clenched my teeth as enormous claws encased us, stopping our descent. But, just as fast, King Impulu let us go, and we were falling back to Earth again.

Jabari and I sighed in relief, thinking this was the end of it, but nothing came easy, it seemed. Especially making deals with celestial lightning birds.

"This is but a portion of your debt, Freeman. You will bring me the rest of my stolen treasure or face my wrath," he bellowed, and with that, the world began to swirl.

A rainbow pierced a cloud leading to another portal, another world inside this otherworldly kingdom. Our choice was simple: lose the farm and King Impulu's protection and maybe never make it back to Earth, or find his missing treasures Grandma was forced to sell. We had two guardians by our side and endless adventures ahead of us. And that sounded like a better deal than being crushed by a big bird with an equally bad temper.

Jabari squeezed my shoulders, Jinx squished in between us as Tilda neighed. I nodded, knowing our answer without even exchanging a word. I cracked her reins, and she galloped at the speed of light, piercing the new portal.

Grandma always told me that, way back when, people could fly. But then they were captured, forgot the old magic, and lost their wings. And now it was our duty to reclaim the lost magic and make miracles happen again. Starting with saving Sankofa Farm once we gathered King Impulu's lost treasures.

ABOUT THE AUTHOR

Zia Knight is an author of sweet romances, cozy mysteries, and whimsical adventures. She writes for adult, young adult, and middle grade readers. Keep in touch on social media @AuthorZKnight. You can also email zia@ziaknight.com.

www.ziaknight.com

BY BRITTANY HESTER

Keke stared out the bus window at the falling rain, trailing her purple, pink, and black painted fingernails over the smeared glass. Most of the other kids were huddled together, smushed between shared earbuds, or clustered over cell phone screens showing videos that made them titter with laughter. If she closed her eyes, Keke could imagine she was somewhere else. Her nose crinkled in concentration, and Keke knew she was probably making her freckles collect in odd ways over her dark brown skin.

She was almost there, safely tucked into a corner of her imagination where multiple moons glittered into existence as the sky became a painted symphony of colors like the aurora borealis. This was her favorite escape and, by now, felt as real to her as memory. A few more breaths and she would see the collections of granite carved buildings caked in shimmering starlight, she would then hear the sound of joyful laughing, but a scream cut through her mind instead, high pitched in a way only animals could achieve. Fire flashed in her mind, the heat so real it made her palms sweat.

Keke snapped her eyes open, breath caught in her throat as

she whirled around. She was on a bus. There was no fire. No sky with two moons.

"There's no way a cat could survive a fall like that. Right?" Dylan, a boy nearest to the window across from her, said, cutting through her thoughts. He widened his bulging eyes and peered down his thin, slightly crooked nose at his phone screen. Without meaning to, Keke glanced over in time to see Dylan showing her a video of a cat plummeting from a top floor apartment window.

"That's vile!"

"They're just animals," he said. Dylan sneered at her and moved his phone closer.

Keke thrust out her hand and knocked the phone to the floor. Her stomach lurched as the tell-tale crunch of a shattering screen brought everyone to a tense silence.

She darted to her feet to a few scattered "oohs" from her classmates. Not friends. They had never been her friends, even when they were younger. Always the odd one out, too much of a dreamer and too blunt to fit in, but too other to be completely ignored. "Hey!" The authoritative snap of the bus driver carried over the excited murmur of students. She knew how she must have not only looked odd to the driver with her wild, tight red curls on the top of her head and her smattering of freckles, but, with the broken phone as evidence at her feet, it also looked like she was the one bullying Dylan instead of the other way around. The bus driver frowned at her and pointed.

"If you don't sit down, I'll pull this bus over."

"But--"

"--Don't make me say it again."

Keke struggled for the right words to explain away her disobedience as tears pricked her eyes. She hated them for betraying her. It wasn't like she was sad. She was angry. Angry at the boy, angry at the person who took the video instead of doing something, and angry at herself for not being able to get her point across.

"Sit down, Kreepy Keke, " Dylan said low enough that Keke

could hear but not the driver. Keke turned toward Dylan and glared.

From behind her, the bus driver slammed his hand against the wheel.

"Didn't I say," the driver growled, "sit down. Now!"

"Just sit down, Keke," one of her classmates groaned from two seats over. "Some of us have places to be."

One look around told her that yet again, Keke had guaranteed no one who rode this bus would ever consider hanging out with her. *Maybe if I was braver, someone would want me.* She thought as she moved to sit back in her seat. *Maybe that was why people like them never seemed to be alone.*

"How was school?" Her mother's voice called to her from behind a large bush.

"I think I made a friend," Keke lied. At this point, it was easier than admitting she still didn't fit in.

"Really?" Her mother's face, just beginning to show signs of wrinkling, was instantly peering at her from behind the bush, her shoulder-length straight black hair with short bangs was pushed back by a broad headband Keke had made for her when she was six.

Keke knew they made an odd pair, but she liked it that way. Liked that people would see a very short, older Asian woman with a weed of a black girl with dark red hair and light brown freckles and have to stop and ask questions. What she liked most of all was that her mother never gave the same answer twice. Her mother was creative and mischievous in that way, and Keke thought she admired that about her most of all. Now her mother wiggled her eyebrows at her.

"What's their name? Tell me everything." Her mother punctuated the end of her sentence with a series of barking coughs that made Keke frown.

"How was your treatment? Did the doctor find...you know." She couldn't say the rest. She didn't want to think about how, one day, there could be a time when her mother wouldn't wake up. So, she pretended everything was fine. She was fine. Her mother would be fine. It was all fine.

"It went," her mother shrugged the question off. Keke flinched. They were always dancing this dance. Keke would ask how her mother's treatments were going, and her mom would do her best to pretend like she was fine. Just fine. But Keke wasn't blind. She saw the way the light seemed to be dimming in her mother's eyes. Everything was far from fine, and Keke didn't know if it ever would be.

She was afraid of being alone. She had too many things she wanted to do with her mother, too many questions she didn't have answers to that only a mother could help her with. She didn't even know who she was yet!

Was she supposed to just figure that out alone? How could she when other people--teachers, classmates, sometimes even perfect strangers-- were too busy telling her everything she did was wrong? *FREAK. LOSER. SCREW LOOSE. WEIRDO.* The words felt like they were materializing on her skin until she itched to be anywhere--anyone--else.

"I'm going to go on a walk," Keke said abruptly. "Maybe check on the hawk."

Keke quickly followed the worn dirt path around the side of the house through a broad stretch of meadow with waist-high grass. On one side, the meadow was fenced in by thick woods that Keke liked to explore as often as she could. On the other, a pond with waters so deep, she often wondered if its center was black as night kissed the meadow's shores.

Like a soldier on a mission, she marched towards the old rundown red barn that sat in the middle of the meadow. There was a hole at the bottom where the door had blown off during a particularly bad rainstorm, the roof was missing a few shin-gles, and the window to the hayloft creaked in protest whenever she opened it, but it was her favorite place in the entire world.

Ever since her mother had banned her from bringing her animal patients into the house, Keke had started nursing her creatures there. Rabbits, foxes, owls, and once--even though her mother had nearly fainted--two troublesome grizzly bear cubs. It only seemed right that Keke would go there to nurse her own hurting spirit.

As she drew closer, Keke discovered the hayloft door was wide open and clanged merrily in a slight breeze as if answering her disbelief with a cheerful hello.

Panic fluttered in her stomach as she realized her hawk might have found a way to escape. As she was being pulled by a string, Keke ran to the barn, clambered up the loft ladder, and slipped as soon as her foot hit the second rung of the ladder.

"Ouch," she hissed as she rubbed the spot where her chin had smacked into the ladder. Keke gritted her teeth and climbed slowly and more carefully up the ladder again. In the shadows, she thought she saw the outline of a wing tip.

"Hey there, buddy," she crooned as she pulled the rest of her body into the hayloft, "I'm glad you didn't fly away." As she drew closer, ice chilled her heart as she realized it wasn't her hawk in the corner. It was an angel with large wings folded against his back.

"Did I die?" She had every intention of keeping that question to herself, but when the angel turned his head to stare at her in what looked like disappointment, she knew she had uttered it aloud. In books she had read, angels were blindingly beautiful and terrifying with bright white wings or, sometimes, multiple wings to hide their immortal holiness for undeserving humans. But this angel looked a lot like a boy. A very tired boy who, Keke realized with a blush, was not wearing a shirt. Though, she supposed, clothing couldn't be easy when you have wings. He was crouched, balanced on bare feet with his hands clasped behind his head like he was trying to solve the world's most frustrating problem.

"You," he squinted pitch-black eyes at her, "are not what I

expected."

His voice was as soft as the wind whispering between the trees with a primal texture that made goosebumps crawl up Keke's arms. "Not what I expected at all."

"Sorry, I don't look nicer," she scoffed, forgetting that it probably wasn't wise to talk to a possibly holy entity that way.

He cocked his head at her in a very birdlike manner and wings, white like freshly fallen snow on the underside, speckled patterns of brown on the upper wing, twitched behind him. If Keke didn't know better, she would say his wings reminded her of a barn owl. Her fingers itched at her side as she suppressed an urge to stroke them. One of his covert feathers was slightly bent. Keke inched her way closer to him and stared at it. It was so tempting. She could just reach out her hands and pluck it.

"Do angels molt?" Keke couldn't help herself. It would be so nice to add an angel's feather to her collection--if she were still alive, that is. As if reading her mind, he snapped his wings in tight.

"I'm not an angel."

"Then I'm dreaming? That's a relief," she said, moving to sit across from the angel-that-was-not-an-angel-but-just-a-boy-with-wings. "I'm glad I'm not dead." The boy's eyes widened, and he rustled his wings.

"You," his voice trailed off as he studied her. "Are you," he tried again. He tilted his head to the other side. "I don't even know where to start."

"At the beginning would be best." Keke folded her legs over each other until she was sitting more comfortably. The boy groaned and then covered his face with his hands. "If you can't start at the beginning," Keke offered, "start with your name. I'll go first. I'm Keke."

"No, you're not."

Keke rolled her eyes. "If I'm not, then you showed up at the wrong house, secret not-an-angel boy." She narrowed her eyes at him. "Are you Dylan's older brother? Did he send you here to mess with me because I broke his phone? Because that was an accident." She looked away guiltily. "But he did deserve it."

"You don't know who I am?"

"Why would I?"

In one fluid motion, he fluttered his wings, lifting himself as high as the barn loft ceiling would allow, and sprayed Keke with dust and scattered bits of hay. Lightly he pumped his wings until he paced in the air above her.

"How are you so," he paused and glanced at her before throwing his arms up in confusion, "so human?"

"Because that's what I am."

"No," he landed softly on his feet and looked at Keke. For a moment, her head buzzed, and she swore she saw something like understanding dawn in his eyes. "But that is what you believe."

Keke frowned and reached down to pick up a few fallen feathers from the loft floor. There was nothing fake about them.

"What are you?" She whispered.

"I'm not from this world."

"Earth? You're not from Earth?"

"That's right."

Keke stumbled back. Every book, every movie, everything she had ever heard told her that she should be running as far and fast as she could right now.

"You are not from this world either," the angel-boy continued.

Keke couldn't help it. She laughed.

The boy squinted in confusion. "You and I are from another dimension, a world called Aril," he said seriously.

"Aril?" Keke repeated, wondering if it would feel like a familiar word. It didn't.

He frowned as if he had been waiting for her to react to the word, too. "Somehow, your parents opened the portal and sent you here to live as a human. Surely you remember something of who you were? Who you are supposed to be?"

"I'm not human?" The world was spinning faster and faster,

and no matter how deeply she tried to breathe, it wouldn't stop.

"You don't remember home, Keke?" He whispered softly. "Warm skies splashed with vibrant colors?"

"Brilliant stars and carved granite buildings?" She asked in shock. The boy nodded gently.

"Two beautiful moons--"

"--that you can see no matter the time," she finished in disbelief. "I'm not human." She looked down at herself in wonder. She wasn't a freak. She just wasn't like everyone else on Earth. She looked at the boy again and frowned. "Am I still me? I mean, the me that I am here on Earth? Or do I have wings or horns or giant hairy feet or something like that on Aril?"

"You are still you, but you're also not. There are certain parts of yourself that you can't access here since there are dampers throughout Earth's mantle that hold back all but the most powerful magic of Aril. "

"Right," she whispered, "That makes sense, I guess." She sighed. "So what was I supposed to be? If my parents hadn't sent me to Earth?

"You are a Nevolean."

"Nevolean? Is that what you are and why I should have recognized you?"

The boy shook his head. "I am an Aviaon," he said proudly. "We are the ones with wings who patrol the skies." He spread his wings to their full length, and Keke gasped as the light from the sun highlighted the distinct marbling in them.

"Do Nevolean have wings? Is that a normal thing for Aril?" She tried hard not to let hope creep into her question. Keke wondered what it would feel like to fly, and warmth filled her chest at the idea of her own wings sprouting if she ever went back to Aril.

"No," he said promptly. "Only the Aviaon have wings. Nevoleans are known for something else."

Dread crept into Keke's stomach. "Like what?" Maybe she would have hairy feet or something worse.

"Perhaps you should journey with me to Aril to find out?"

"You want me to leave Earth? What about my mom? My life?"

"You could come back. Time passes differently on Aril than it does on Earth. It would be like you had never left here."

"This is happening so fast," she mumbled. The offer was tempting. She could go back to where she came from, learn about herself, and maybe finally understand why she was the way she was. Keke picked at her nailbed. But would going to Aril mean letting go of the person she was on Earth?

"Please," the boy said as he reached into his pocket and pulled out a large, raw gemstone colored with veins of turquoise, rusty brown, and glittering black. As she gazed at it, something in her chest, behind her heart, thumped like a beast awakened from a thousand year slumber. THUMP. THUMP. Each pounding in her chest echoed in the stone as it pulsed in time with the vibrations stirring within her. The boy stepped closer to her and held the stone out in a silent invitation to touch it, hold it if she dared. Something inside her stirred, and she felt the gemstone answer. *Come home*, the stone seemed to whisper. *Aril needs you.*

"My given name," the boy continued with an air of gravity as the stone seemed to glow brighter, "is Averialidocix, first of my name, son of Devidas, Captain of the Free Skies, and I ask you to Keke, daughter of the Nevolean people, to return to Aril and aide me in my quest."

"How can I help you? I just learned that I'm from Aril."

"You're exactly who, or rather what, I need."

"I am not a what," she said firmly. "At least, I don't think so." She looked away. "Are Nevoleans a what in your world?"

Averialidocix took Keke's hand and brought it to the stone. Suddenly, the hayloft turned the inky black of night. Keke tried to pull her hand away as small, bright burning dots shot from the spaces between her fingers that were touching the stone, but Averialidocix held her hand in place.

"Nevoleans are the watchers of stars," Averialidocix said

gravely. Wonder made Keke laugh breathily as the tiny starlight dots began raining down around them. However, she stopped abruptly as she realized that where the stardust hit the hayloft floor, outlines of yellowed bones and full skeletons rose like illusions. "They are the master of death," Averialidocix finished.

"Make it stop," she said with a shudder as she tried once again to pull her hand away.

"It is your magic the stone reflects. There's nothing to be afraid of."

"No!" Keke protested as she finally freed her hand from Averialidocix and the stone. She had never liked death and never felt a dark surge of evil power.

"Like calls to like, Keke," he urged. "The magic in you called to the magic within the stone. It is as I had hoped it would be. You have the true power of a Nevolean. You are a necromancer."

Finally, Keke yanked her hand away and the hayloft returned to normal.

"I didn't even know this was who I was until you showed up, and now you want me to just accept the fact that I can raise the dead? I like to fix things that are broken, mend them and leave them better off for knowing me. Living things! Not dead ones."

"Come with me to Aril then. Helping me would be leaving me better off for knowing you." Averialidocix gritted his teeth in frustration like he was fighting the urge to tell Keke a long protected secret. "You know how I mentioned calling to like? Well, I'm looking for," he paused, clearly uncertain on what to say next.

"A thing? A person?" Keke offered.

"Something like that," he said with a brush of his hand. "You and your magic can help me. Your magic is connected in a way, so it shouldn't be an issue for you to guide me where I need to go."

"But I don't know anything about Aril. How can I help you if I don't even know what we'd be looking for? Or even where it would be? I've never been to Aril. I've never even been more than a three hour car ride from my house!"

"Your magic will guide you and you'll guide me." Averialidocix lifted the stone towards her. Keke wanted to touch it again and see the stars dance across the illusion of the night sky, but she was also scared.

"What if you're wrong? What if I can't do what you need me to do? What if I can't help you? What if my powers," she sputtered to a stop as she realized what she said. *My powers.* They were hers, and even though just the idea of it felt foreign and wrong, she wanted to understand how it fit with who she was. She wanted to see the two moons for herself instead of remembering it like a dream. Most of all, she wanted to go to a place that felt like she belonged. A place that felt like home.

"I need you," Averialidocix said, cutting through her thoughts. "And you," he jostled the stone towards her, "need answers. You deserve to know who you are. So, say you'll come with me."

She had never been wanted, let alone needed, before. Even in group projects, she was always overlooked and pushed to the outside. But here Averialidocix was, a perfect stranger who somehow felt more familiar to her than the classmates she had gone to school with from kindergarten to seventh grade, saying he needed her. A vivid image of the boy on the bus calling her creepy flashed through Keke's mind. They had never asked her for anything. Keke took a deep breath. "I'll go with you to Aril, Averialidocix."

"You can call me Avery," he said with a broad grin. "We won't need to be so formal since we'll be traveling companions." Briskly, he put the gemstone back in his pocket.

"So when do we leave?"

"Now." Quicker than a human could, Averialidocix closed the distance between them and wrapped an arm around Keke. "I haven't flown anyone else before, so hold on tight."

Instinct made Keke dig in her heels as Averialidocix started tugging her towards the open hayloft door.

"I think I'd rather walk."

"Don't be silly. I opened a portal in the middle of the pond over there." He gestured with his free to the pond Keke had purposely skirted on her way to the barn earlier. "I didn't see a vessel and unless you can walk on water, the only way to get there is to fly." In a neat trick, Averialidocix bumped his hip against Keke, throwing her weight off balance. Despite her best efforts, she stumbled forward and Averialidocix pumped his wings hard as he used her momentum to propel them out the loft.

In seconds, Keke felt like she was riding a rollercoaster ride as solid ground disappeared from under her. Tears stung her eyes as they gained speed but soon began losing altitude.

"Avery," she warned as she clung her arms around his neck. Below them, grass turned to rippling water. Averialidocix grunted under their weight as he strained to move higher and towards the center of the pond.

Keke squeaked as she realized they were now higher than the roof of the barn and directly over the center of the pond. The air around them seemed to still as Averialidocix pulled the large turquoise stone from his pocket again. For a moment, Keke thought he would try and give it to her again, but instead, he held it out in front of him. Sweat dripped down his forehead as the stone began to pulse.

Without needing to be told, Keke looked down and watched as ripples spiraled out from the center of the pond as if something had disturbed the surface. While she could see herself and Averialidocix in its rippling reflection, she could also see something in the depths begin to glow and rise. It was terrifying and mesmerizing all at once.

"I'm going to close my wings so we can dive through the portal, alright?" Averialidocix said loudly so she could hear him over the pounding of his wings. "If you close your eyes, it will help with the crossing. Ready?" Keke tightened her grip but she didn't close her eyes. Not as she looked down and saw a glowing gate in the shape of a ring beneath the dark waters. Not when Averialidocix dived, fast and sure, towards that gate's blossoming center that shimmered with the colors of the stone he held out in front of them. Not when she felt her skin tingle like something within her had been unleashed. And not when they appeared on the other side of the portal in Aril.

As soon as Keke's head broke the water's surface, she gasped, but not for the need for air. No, she gasped for the splendor that surrounded her. Above the sky seemed to be permanently fixed with a rainbow array of blues, purples, yellows, and soft amber pinks with two luminous moons, one large and one small, hanging almost ornamentally in the eastern and southern sky. Directly overhead, the sun warmed Keke enough that the chill ocean water felt refreshing rather than shocking.

She wasn't sure when she had let go of him, but Keke treaded in the turquoise water that was the same color as the gemstone water and tried to take in more of the world around her. The scents seemed sharper than the things she smelled on Earth, the colors more vibrant, and for a moment Keke wondered if this was part of what lay dormant within her while she had been masquerading as a human on Earth. *If my senses are sharper, what else will I discover about myself here in Aril?* At her thought, something behind her heart seemed to twitch as if just beginning the process of waking up.

Ahead of her, Keke noticed Averialidocix swimming slowly towards a massive bridge-like object in the distance. However, it wasn't until she had swam there and clambered up the bumpy exterior that Keke realized it wasn't a bridge but a massive tree root. Covered in a silvery brown moss-like substance, the sun bleached root shot from the ocean's depth and curved its massive bulk like a boa constructor towards the horizon with other massive roots sprouting nearby or branching off of it, creating a network of paths all leading in the same direction.

Far in the distance was the largest tree imaginable. Every root from the ocean led to the sun-bleached tree that reached for the sky. Keke looked up for the top but could only see the trunk going up past the clouds, maybe even past the stars, and into the heavens. The further away from the ocean the roots got, the closer together they came until land formed between them. First beaches and plains, then immense mountains that rose like waves around the central tree but only reached a third of its height.

"Aril is centered around a tree that is an island?" She called out to Averialidocix as she brushed the water out of her eyes.

"Aril is the Mother Tree, and the Mother Tree is Aril. Aril rose from these waters, and we rose from Aril." He said, but his voice sounded far off.

Looking around, Keke noticed Averialidocix digging through a rucksack a few paces away on a secluded sandbar nestled between two gnarled roots that made a small private beach. As she jogged over to him, she looked curiously at the treeline where smaller, dense trees along with thick-stemmed flowers with massive onion-shaped baubles the size of her house in the middle of the stems sprang up from the roots embedded deep within the sand.

She was surprised to discover that even after swimming to shore and climbing on top of the giant tree root, she barely felt tired. Was this part of her magic, too? Or was her body just different in Aril?

"Avery?" She asked. "Is there a way to know what exactly about me has changed now that I'm back?"

"Hmm?" He didn't turn towards her as he pulled out a black scaled shirt with two slits in the shoulder blades that glinted like fish scales and slipped it over his head. "Better," he mumbled to himself. "Now weapons." Next, he pulled an intricate harness filled with knives, swords, and other weapons she couldn't name and began strapping them to himself. He looked fierce and terrifying and so much more unapproachable than he had in the barn.

"Averialidocix," she said with more reproach than she had meant. He snapped his head up at her and furrowed his brows. Keke repeated her question. "How do I know what's different about me on Aril? Other than my magic, I mean."

"Well, for starters, you look more like a Nevolean. On Earth your hair was frizzy, but it's not anymore. And your hair and eyes were dark brown there. They're red here, and they match your freckles." Keke blinked in surprise. "Take a look for yourself."

Keke didn't hesitate as Averialidocix gestured to a large flower cupping a mirror size puddle of water in its center. As he returned to the contents of his pack, Keke studied herself. She touched her hair that was now tamed into neat spiraling curls and smiled as she realized its normally mahogany color was a beautifully vibrant garnet that matched her eyes and freckles.

"Do all Nevoleans look like this?" she asked Averialidocix.

"The ones with magic tend to have red hair or red eyes like you, but they don't usually have both."

Keke touched her hair again and twirled one of the perfect spirals around her finger.

"Will I stand out because of it?" she asked.

Averialidocix huffed as he pulled out a purple flowing skirt, a gold sash with bells fashioned along the seams, and a black shirt with scales like his.

"You'll stand out less if you put these on." He held up each item as he explained, "a skirt so you can blend in with other women your age, a sash to tie your hair, and--"

"--a shirt to match your own?"

Averialidocix rolled his eyes. "Light armor to protect you during our travels."

"Why didn't you wear that on Earth?"

"Earth doesn't have dangers like Aril." He tossed the clothes at Keke one at a time.

"What? Do you have, like, werewolves, dragons, or evil witches?"

"Among other things."

"Among other things?"

"Shhh," he hissed at her and glanced towards the water. "Something will hear you and we don't know if you can use your magic yet."

"And how would I use my magic to help you? Blind an enemy with stardust?"

"How do you think necromancers fight, Keke?"

She gulped. "I already told you, I don't like death or dead things. I don't even think I could raise the dead even if I wanted to. And I don't."

"You haven't even tried it."

Keke rolled her eyes and turned towards the ocean.

"Then can you really say you don't like the things you have a magical connection to?"

Keke didn't bother responding. She had had to say goodbye to plenty of animals on Earth. Animals she couldn't nurse back to health or creatures she had taken in just to give them a few pleasant memories before they passed. No matter how long she had cared for them, it always hurt when they were gone. Just like it would hurt if her mom was gone.

What if my magic could keep me from having to say goodbye? She glanced over her shoulder to see if Averialidocix was paying attention. Keke turned her attention back to the sea. Maybe he was right. She didn't really know how she felt about her powers until she tried them. Besides her senses, stamina, and appearance were different on Aril, perhaps her feelings about death would be too.

She closed her eyes and imagined a fish or whale skeleton rising from the ocean. The way she supposed it, if it worked and she didn't like it, then at least the creature would be trapped by the water. And if she didn't mind what she brought to life, then at least she would know for sure that her powers weren't something to be afraid of. When Keke opened her eyes a moment later, she saw that the ocean water in front of her boiled as green, purple, and silver scaled fish floated to the top.

"Um, Avery," Keke said as she took a step forward. She'd meant to bring something back to life, not turn a spot in the ocean into fish stew. "I think I messed up."

"What do you mean you--" Averialidocix froze mid sentence

as a maw the size of an elephant rose from the water, followed by two russet eyes and four whip-like whiskers on each side of its snout. "Seadragon," Averialidocix breathed as he grabbed two long knives.

The seadragon roared as it slashed its head from side to side. Suddenly, one of its large eyes focused on Keke and it screeched so loud Keke covered her ears and yelled along with it.

"Go away!" She yelled at it as it moved swiftly through the water towards her. "I didn't mean to call you!"

"How did you summon a seadragon?" Averialidocix asked as he shot into the sky above her and twirled his blades so the light from the sun bounced off their gleaming surface and momentarily blinded the monster. It hissed in pain and blasted scalding water in the place it had last seen Averialidocix. Luckily, Averialidocix was already speeding out of the way.

As the seadragon's vision cleared, it roared in fury and slashed its fish-like tail out of the water. Keke gasped as the seadragon's tail smacked into Averialidocix and sent him crashing to the sandy beach.

"Avery!" Keke called out to him only to realize he was lying unconscious where he had fallen. She glanced around her for a weapon, any weapon at all, but all she could see were tall, double decker sized flowers with basketball sized barded seeds that reminded her of poison dart frogs with their mirage of yellow, blacks, and bright blues.

The seadragon gave an earsplitting whistle as it slithered its mammoth form onto the shore. The sand seemed to shift as its short, stubbed centipede-like legs hammered their way towards Averialidocix's fallen body.

She wasn't sure what had gone wrong when she tried to use her magic, but Keke knew she was somehow responsible for this. Perhaps there was something dark within herself that called to the destructive nature of the beast. Averialidocix had said that like called to like in Aril. Keke gulped and ushered a silent plea that she was wrong. Sure, it had been silly for her to think she could just close her eyes and use her magic, but she didn't want to make Averialidocix pay the price for her recklessness. She had only wanted to test her magic and raise a dead creature to see if she could really do it like Averialidocix said. Accident or not, she wouldn't let someone else suffer for her mistake.

She looked back at the flowers and quickly considered what she had learned in science class. Poison dart frogs, like other highly venomous things in nature, were vibrantly colored so predators would know not to eat them. Taking a shot in the dark, Keke grabbed a large leaf from a plainly colored plant and used it to pluck one of the barbed seeds. As soon as the leaf touched the seed, Keke heard a faint hissing sound and saw angry yellow, blood red, and midnight black smoke rise from the disintegrating leaf. Faster than she thought she could run, Keke raced with her improvised projectile back towards Averialidocix and the seadragon.

"Leave him alone!" She bellowed at the seadragon as it paused one step away from crushing Averialidocix's wing.

The seadragon bared its teeth at her and then stomped down on one of Averialidocix's wings. Averialidocix's wing bent in an unnatural angle towards the Sky before blood as bright and vibrant as a summer sky gushed from the impaled wing and began dyeing the sand around them.

Keke was too far away to hear the sickening crunch of bone, but she could hear Averialidocix's scream. She didn't think she would ever be able to forget it for the rest of her life.

"Avery, no!" Keke screamed. The thing inside her seemed to be screaming in defiance and rage with her. Beneath its bulk, Averialidocix thrashed as he fought to free himself.

The seadragon lifted its leg from Averialidocix's wing and hissed at Keke. Seeing his opening, Averialidocix tucked both his wings in close to his body and rolled away. This was her moment. It was now or never.

Keke charged forward and hurled the seed towards the eye Averialidocix had injured early on. The world seemed to move in slow motion as the seed exploded against the seadragon's face in a cloud of angry yellow, blood red, and midnight black. Through the haze, Keke could see the serpent's scales bubbling like it had been sprayed with acid. The serpent shook his head in pain and opened its jaws to release a burst of scalding water with no clear target.

A cold sensation spread through her, freezing her heart in her chest as she watched the giant serpent's legs buckle underneath it.

"Run, Keke!" Averialidocix called loudly over the sound of the falling seadragon. "It's dying. This is your chance to get away!"

But she couldn't move. Tears stung her eyes as the monster tried to reach its claws towards its boiling face. She had done this. She had taken a life. The cold sensation within her began to burn like frostbite. Instinct made her take a step and then another towards the creature until she was right next to its shuddering body on the beach.

She reached tingling fingers towards it. After healing so many animals on Earth and being present for the last moments of the creatures she couldn't help, it was all Keke could do not to reach a comforting hand out to the creature in its final moments. Instead, she stood next to it with her hand out in indecision.

It had just tried to kill us, a voice inside her side. *It does not deserve your pity.*

She was so wrapped up in her thoughts that she didn't even notice Averialidocix limp over to her side with a handful of silvery moss pressed against his wing as it dragged heavily behind him.

"Don't touch it." Averialidocix warned. "The mist from the seed will eat away anything it touches."

Keke turned away but didn't put her hand down.

"It shouldn't feel alone."

Her outstretched hand began to shake as she held it there, but she didn't care. Even if she couldn't touch the seadragon in its last moments, she wanted it to feel her presence. She wanted it to know it didn't leave Aril without a single creature noticing its departure.

"Keke," Averialidocix gasped quietly.

When Keke turned back to the seadragon, she noticed a trail of starlight black magical essence flowing like a river between her outstretched hand and the seadragon.

"What's happening?" Keke tried to yank her hand down but the magic held her in place. The thing within her seemed to grow until it was wrapped around her heart like a comforting blanket as her whole body turned ice cold.

The black magic grew brighter until shimmering crystals materialized in the ebony river. Suddenly, the magic seemed to swell until it formed a bubble around Keke, Averialidocix, and the seadragon.

The seadragon's now deceased body shimmered and Keke thought she saw the outline of a tall man leaning over the muzzle of the seadragon and pet it affectionately. Although she couldn't make out any distinguishing features on the form, Keke could tell it turned towards her and bowed in gratitude before it gave the seadragon's form one last hug. The figure glowed brighter until it seemed to disappear in a flash of light.

However, when Keke finished blinking away the stars from her eyes, she realized she could still see the form, now accompanied by the seadragon's spirit, walking down the beach towards the Mother Tree.

"I had heard," Averialidocix whispered, "that the Nevolean had familiars, but I never dreamed to see something like this."

"And what was whatever just happened exactly?"

"It was a necromancer welcoming its familiar in death."

As warmth slowly returned to Keke's body, she blew on her fingers, impatient to feel like a living person again. "Is that why the seadragon attacked us? I have the same magic as its master?"

"I-I don't know."

"What do you mean you don't know?"

"The intricacies of necromancy were a well guarded secret among your people." Averialidocix hung his head.

"What do you mean 'were'? Was telling their secrets the reason that seadragon was waiting for a necromancer to find it?" Avery wouldn't look at her anymore. "Are my people so careless that they let their dangerous little pets run loose to hunt people?"

Avery flinched. "No," he said slowly. "You're people were never careless. If anything, they were too trusting." Avery sighed. "You are the last necromancer." Hands trembling, he said, "my people hunted yours to near extinction. Any Nevolean left are powerless or hiding because they would be killed if they were found out."

Keke's mouth dropped open in shock, and the thing that had been guarding her heart recoiled like it had been struck.

"So you took me from my own safe dimension and brought me back here to finish what your people started?" She stuttered. The thing behind her heart uncurled and then seemed to prowl under her skin, comforting her with warmth.

"Of course not," Avery lifted his hands in defense. "I won't let anything happen to you, I promise." He looked at her and pleaded for understanding and forgiveness. "What my people did was horrible. It should never have happened. What they did threw our world out of balance, and I need your help to fix it. With your help, I could find the heir to the Dead Throne and restore the governing powers of Aril to what it was meant to be. My people thought the darkness of your people's powers were corrupting Aril, but mine have been no better. Things are wrong here without the Nevolean, and I think," he sighed like he was used to someone cutting him off there. "I think you are the key to setting things right," he finished.

Keke took a breath to steady herself. His people had been wrong to hunt hers. They had been wicked and cruel, but Averialidocix wasn't like that. He was trying to fix what had been broken by their parents' generation. The force within her stretched like a cat as Keke realized she wanted to help him, not the Aviaon race, but Averialidocix, who seemed to carry the burden of his people's actions on his shoulders and who wanted nothing from her but for her to embrace who she was born to be.

"If we're going to find the heir and restore the natural ruling order of Aril," Keke said with a small smile, "we'll need to get your wing healed. And," Keke looked down at her hands before clinching them into fists, "and find some place where I can get a good grip of my magic without endangering us."

Averialidocix returned Keke's hesitant small with a broad grin of his own.

"I know just the place. I think your old home may be just the place for us."

"And where's that?"

"The Caverns of Starlight and Silence." He flicked a finger across her spattering of freckles. "When I saw your constellation birthmark, I knew you had to be from their clan. They were academics, scholars, and healers before they..." he fell silently briefly, "before they were attacked. Maybe if we take you there, you'll be able to tap into your abilities with more control. It's a long hike from here by foot, but it should be abandoned now. You can practice and I can heal."

Keke gazed at the sky above. *Home.* Where she could learn more about her people, her powers, and herself.

While she wasn't sure what she would find there, a part of her hoped it would be more than answers. Hoped against dumb, persistent hope that it would be belonging, family, and understanding of who she was and where she fit in this world. For that hope and her new friend, she would continue this crazy adventure. No matter the cost. Keke didn't take her eyes from the sky as they moved towards the blackwood forest. Deep within her, the force that felt as ancient as the Mother Tree wrapped itself around her heart and peaked one glittering red-eye up at the stars, too.

"Okay," she said as she wondered which of the barely appearing stars above would mirror the patterning on her face. "Let's go to the Caverns of Starlight and Silence."

ABOUT THE AUTHOR

Brittany Hester is a young adult fantasy and science fiction author who loves creating elaborate worlds filled with diverse characters and fantastical creatures. When not writing, you can find her tucked away in nature, spending time with her kids, obsessing over her new favorite anime, or playing video games with her husband. Keep in touch on Instagram @_brittanyhester_ or Facebook @ AuthorBrittanyHester or Tik Tok @brittanyhesterauthor.

www.brittanyhester.com

Fae-Took

BY MARIE MCHENRY

I'm the last person who should have been fae-took. Maybe everyone is right, and Auntie and I speak of the fae too often. Maybe they heard us talk about them. Or the magic of that realm lingered on her and rubbed off on me. Perhaps I brought this on myself.

The fae weren't the only monsters outside the Wall that snatched children. While some wanted to eat us, fae took children they considered beautiful, unique, or special. In some people's stories, the taken became playthings to the fae. Servants or entertainers, exotic pets or a toy to be broken, forced to serve until death. Some were treated very well, like courtesans of the king's court. Others were abused horribly, sold like cattle.

If they were taken, they would never be freed or ever seen again so who knew, really? It wouldn't surprise me if they ate them when they were done with them.

It isn't fair they took me, but maybe it's just as well. I've heard the stories from the only woman to ever escape.

Passing into the fae realm is like a fever dream where you start in one place and then all at once you're somewhere else. The details of are fuzzy until you look right at it.

I remember birds' songs and the river's laughter mingled with my family's presence. I remember a dark, strange mist. I saw a fox with clever eyes. The world then goes out of focus, and it's a swirl of colors and sound. It's like spinning in a field of colorful flowers, and is dizzied.

I realize that the world is wrong, that the sky shouldn't be made of water, that I shouldn't hear the birds speak human language, and I'm passing through something. But once I noticed that it's wrong, I woke up.

That's what it was like.

One moment at the river's edge, the next I'm in the forest feeling weary as though I've walked for miles. There's a boy who doesn't look older than my thirteen years walking beside me. A jolt of panic shoots through me. I stop, and my new companion does as well.

I've met hundreds of people traveling with my family. Sitting with my father as he bargains, I've learned how to read people very well, whether they're trying to cheat us, or are desperate, or clever and kind. But even for a stranger, this boy is confusing.

His skin is brown, his eyes are red, and he has a fox tail. He is a monster, a kitsune, and in Auntie's stories, they're viciously clever. But he's young and only has one tail. There's a pinch in his brow that makes him look guilty and scared.

Those feelings aren't monstrous at all.

"I'm not going to hurt you, but you need to do what I say so it stays that way," he says. He has the same tone as the boys when they're trying to soothe startled animals.

"Absolutely not, don't be ridiculous." I cross my arms.

"What?" He tries to growl the word, but his voice cracks like my cousins who think they are so manly now that whiskers are sprouting from their chins.

He's a fox, but he's also a boy. Auntie had handled his kind before when she'd been here. What would she do? Auntie, were she in my sandals, would be brave and clever. She had made it home. So would I.

"I don't even know you," I say, "So I can't possibly be expected to blindly do what you say. Perhaps if we were friends I could be persuaded. I'm much more agreeable to my friends."

He seemed like he was going to refuse, tail bristling behind him and ears flattening, until I said "friends." Surprise softens his features.

"Oh, uh...I guess we can be friends?"

"Excellent! Friends it is then," I say, smiling and sliding my hand out of my sleeve to offer to him. "Tell me, what is your name?"

He stares at my hand a long moment before grasping my forearm instead. "Jovi."

"Lovely to meet you. This has been such a nice time, but I do think it's time I get back home. If you would be so kind as to tell me how?"

His grip tightens painfully around my arm. "Wait, what? No, you can't *go* home. You're here so *I* can go home!"

Instead of cowering or snapping back, I force myself to calm down. This is a negotiation, and I can't afford to let my emotions get away from me. His fingers are claw-tipped, still gripping my arm.

"Help me understand that, Jovi. Because if you're my friend, then I can help you. And maybe we can both go home."

He's breathing hard, on the verge of panicking. Maybe he didn't expect his kidnapping to go this way. I didn't expect to be kidnapped but here we are.

"Jovi," I said, trying to stay calm. "You don't want to hurt me and I don't want to be hurt. We both want to go home so tell me who is stopping that from happening. Please?"

"I don't...Did you mean it when you said we're friends?"

"Yes, I did. We're friends, Jovi."

He releases a shuddering breath and starts to cry. His story comes in pieces, halting between his cracking voice. I try to balance between pulling him back from a full breakdown and pushing him to tell the story.

It's very long and very sad.

But human children are not the only ones who are taken.

Jovi should have taken me to his master's home. He tells me that his master is a powerful fae of great wealth. He'd instructed Jovi to bring him a new girl, a new assignment for the fox boy. His success would have removed decades off his service.

Instead, he leads me to his burrow in the base of a huge tree. We take a slow stop-start, backtracking path there. His master has many eyes here. The birds talk, he says, and I remember the white bird that had watched us.

These unfamiliar woods are quickly growing dark. Time here and back home are different, and I worry that days may pass there while only moments pass here. Decades could go by, and my family could be gone. I could be forgotten and become one of those they tell stories about.

Jovi holds my hand as we go, squeezing when we need to stop. We hold still, and I watch his ears flick and his nose twitch as he leads us.

As the sun sets, I feel both fear and excitement. It surprises me that the fear belongs to my new friend rather than me. I should be terrified. I was in an entirely different world to what I knew. A world many didn't return from. I certainly shouldn't trust Jovi with my safety. But he doesn't want to be here anymore than I do.

We squeeze our way through a tangle of roots and vines to reach the entrance, a hole in the ground. I stumble on a root as we enter the burrow, but Jovi steadies me. Inside, the burrow is dark as night. Jovi releases my hand and a moment later, fire sparks to life. The flame hovers above his fingers before flying into a rough hewn fireplace with a simple flick of his wrist. The walls around us are dirt, and tree roots peek out at us. The fire shows a small round room and a dark path beyond it, across from where we came in. Many smaller dark passages dot the walls, some so tiny only bugs could enter from, others large enough to crawl through. Yellow and red eyes glitter from the darkness, and I can't suppress a shudder.

I despise bugs.

From how easily Jovi moves around this place it is clear this is his own home. Scrapwork woven rugs and a bundle of blankets lay near the fire. He leads me to sit at a low table with a stuffed cushion for me to sit on. Nearby lay a dented pot, kettle, and dishes. He puts the kettle onto a hook and positions it over the fire. The burrow is cozy and soon it's warm as he moves about the place, talking nervously the whole time. Jovi seems to be someone who likes to talk but has been punished many times for doing so. He looks at me and flinches a few times, uncertainty and fear apparent. The water is boiling soon enough, and he pinches dried herbs from chipped porcelain dishes with his claws and sprinkles them into a cup.

"So your parents owed the fae a debt," I say slowly, wrapping my mind around his tale. As well as his tail. It has a life of its own, reflecting the emotions of its owner and flicking around like a candle flame. "And you're the payment?"

"Only partly. I'm to serve for the price of a life debt. Kitsune can live hundreds of years, you know, so it's a pretty rough deal. I can work it off. Or I could have…"

He places a cup of tea and a little plate of dry biscuits on the table before sitting across from me. I accept the tea he offers with no intention of drinking it. He isn't a fae himself, and maybe eating their food doesn't apply to his kind. I don't sense a trace of deceit in him so maybe he's merely polite. All the same, it is better to be careful than to be tricked.

"Not having second thoughts, are you, friend?" I ask and force a little laugh.

Jovi gives me a flat look and shakes his head. "Too late for that. I've taken too long to bring you back anyway. I'm sure his spies have reported me to him. Being a servant might not be so bad if I worked for his brother."

"His brother?" I lift the cup and sniff the contents. It smells delicious, and my mouth waters. I'm a little sad that I can't drink it.

"Lord Lobo. He's different from his brother. Bassel values power. He hurts people weaker than him and competes with his brother all the time. But his brother is actually all right. I'd even say he's honorable."

"I think I know that name," I reply, laying my cup down on the table. "My auntie told me stories about the fae realm, and she made it out. She made friends here too, and I think one of them was this Lord Lobo."

The name Lobo is familiar, but I don't remember Auntie saying anything about him being a lord. From her stories, he sounded like a companion, almost a servant.

"Really?" Jovi asked, surprised. He follows his question up with a frown. "If he helped your auntie, maybe he'll help us?"

"Well, all we really need is to get me home first, right? I don't think I'd do well in a fox den. And I don't suppose you could just...?"

"No, only noble types know where the ins and outs are. They have their spells that can guide you like Bassel used for me, but I'd never be able to find it again. But if we get you home, then what about me?"

"You would come with me of course. I think my aunt might be able to help you find your way home. It's just that I'm not sure how I'd do in a whole den of foxes. No offense."

"None taken. To be honest, I'm not sure I really want to see my family again."

"Oh," I say, somewhat stunned by his bluntness. "Well, that's...um."

His situation is different from mine. I was taken. He was given away. I turn the tea cup around. It's not chipped like Jovi's, but it's not a set. is a mismatch, as if all of it had been thrown out and then found by my new friend.

"How do they cast the spells? How do they know the way?" I ask him.

"All their words sound like gibberish to me. It's a language, sure, it is just like nothing I've ever heard before."

The spells, he explains, are the truth. The words are the truest words that can be spoken and must be spoken in the truest way.

"It's all got to do with their goddess or other and what they say about creation," Jovi says, unimpressed with the whole thing.

My mind whirls at that. For some reason, fae having a deity is not something I ever considered before. Did the other creatures all worship some form of god? Auntie had never mentioned anything like that before. As interesting as that is, I need to focus on the task at hand.

Besides, if Jovi really does come with me, I can ask him all about that later.

"Do fox people have spells?"

"Yeah, but not like that. It's different. We learn some on our own, and other stuff we're taught. And I wasn't taught a whole lot of techniques. I was a lot younger when...when I left."

His sadness is almost suffocating. I almost want to cry just looking at him.

"What do fae value?" I ask.

He brushes his short, fire-red locs aside and scratches his ear. "What do you mean?"

"Well, humans value things like family and money and power. Gold, land, people's opinions. Fighting over ridiculous things like that."

His ear, soft-looking and exactly like a fox, twitches, and I struggle to not stare at it.

"Fae are like that too. Lord Lobo and Bassel are always competing with each other, trying to outdo the other. It can be entertaining. When you're not the one being used as a pawn."

Oh.

His brother...and competition and honor. My aunt's stories.

"Tell me about his brother," I demand.

He tells me, and as he does, a plan begins to form in my mind.

I start talking, a plan developing as I do. Jovi stares at me, his disbelief obvious. Then he makes an odd, choked sound which I realize is a rough, unused laugh.

"You really are crazy," he says. "You think that things work like that?"

"It works," I tell him, and I let my conviction wash over him. "However I say it works."

Because that's part of the way the fae realm works. It is even more susceptible to bending to the will of people, to making impossible the possible. But you can't doubt it.

The plan will work. It has to. It's the only plan I have.

When I wake up the next morning, the light has just begun to touch the edge of the burrow. Jovi is already awake, drinking tea at the table. I roll out of the nest of cushions and blankets and pick up my bag as I go to the table.

Dried meat and a few dates from my bag are my breakfast. It's not enough to fill me, but I'll have plenty to eat later. Jovi looks pointedly at the food on the table, and says, "I'm not fae, and this isn't fae food."

"It's fox food," I say with a wink. "But it's in the fae realm. I don't want to risk it."

He shrugs and eats more of the food. "Suit yourself."

After finishing his meal, Jovi yawns and scratches at his ear. His tail catches my attention, twitching behind him. After a moment, I realize he's staring at me staring at him.

"What now?" Jovi asks. After I explained my plan, I spent some time asking Jovi every question that came to mind, and he willingly answered all of them. This went on until a centipede had crept onto the table, and I made a fool of myself shrieking at it.

But at this point, he could easily see when I had a question brewing.

"Are you a boy who turns into a fox or a fox that turns into a boy?"

He narrows his golden eyes. "Yes," he says.

I stick my tongue out at Jovi while he smirks.

He's nervous so I try not to be. Fear is always present with him. It had followed me into my sleep and gave me nightmares. Of course it could be my own. I'd been very tempted to drink the tea he offered, hoping it'd soothe me.

It's been so long since I've seen Auntie, and I wish she were here. In her stories, she ate nothing or only what she was lucky to have with her. To eat food from the fae was to tie yourself to their realm forever. My food might last two more days. But we might be home by then. My older cousins have said I should fast more so now is as good a time as any.

"Pass the honey, Girl."

"What did you call me?"

Jovi grins, like he'd been waiting to tell a joke. "You never told me your name so what else am I supposed to call you?"

Names are powerful things. Giving a name to a fae would be a foolish thing to do. Even though he's kitsune and we've agreed to be friends, even though he claims to have no spells, I can't simply give him my name. And he knows that.

"You are the worst," I say and nudge the honey pot closer to him. "Fox-Boy."

"Human Girl." He spoons a disgusting amount of honey into his tea and laughs.

After our short breakfast, Jovi cleans up. He puts the dishes and tea away, stores the biscuits back in their tins. He pauses as he's about to tidy the sleeping area, stepping back.

"What am I doing?" he asks with a chuckle. "I'm not coming back here anyway, right?"

I hum in thought at his comments. "Well, think of it this way.

Someone else might find this place one day. They'll be glad to find the place so nice."

I try to look at the den through his eyes. This place must have been home and a haven away from what had to be a terrifying life. I'd even found it comfortable enough to fall asleep.

"Maybe," he says. "But I—"

He goes completely still except for his ears, like he had in the forest. The birds, which had been chattering and singing up until now, were dead silent.

A twig snaps.

Someone is outside.

He holds up his hand with his fingers spread wide. Then he makes a fist, and the fire goes out. It's pitch black inside, and I nearly shriek when something touches me. I realize it's Jovi's hand as he pulls me almost off my feet as we rush to one of the larger passages. We have to stoop to enter.

It grows darker and cooler, and the ground slopes downward. Our feet crunch in the dirt, and the smell of damp, rich earth fills my senses. I can feel the presence of the ground surrounding us, pressing in. I grip Jovi's hand tighter, aware that if he leaves me here, I might never find my way out.

But he wouldn't do that. He can't. We're friends.

I keep reminding myself of that and breathe through the panic that threatens to overtake me. The den had felt like a home. This tunnel feels like a tomb.

After what feels like eternity, we come out of the ground and into a clearing. The way out is the base of a tree stump. The sky is open above me, and the grass is high here, brushing my waist. Eyes watering from the bright light after the dark underground, I raise my hands to the sky and turn in a circle, breathing deeply. The forest is far, far behind us, and the rest of the clearing is flat land for as far as I can see.

"Sorry," Jovi says, "I didn't think about you getting scared in there. I didn't think about it."

"It's ok. I'm fine."

"Don't lie to a trickster. You don't have to be fine. It's ok if you're scared."

"Fine." I snapped, finally letting go of I'd been holding in. "I'm scared. I'm terrified, and I'm angry and I want to go home and cry, and I think I want to hit you!"

Jovi nods, like that's all completely understandable. "Well, you can't hit me, and I can't do much else about you being scared or mad. Might help us. So let's see about home." He points behind me, and I turn to look.

There's a massive door, suddenly there from nothing. It looks like it was made for giants ages ago, ancient wood and runes carved into it. It creaks open inward and reveals an entirely new space.

I walk around the doorway, but it is still just as impossible. The door to nowhere hangs there in space but shows the way into a maze. I try to look inside without entering it and can see that even the sky is different on the other side, a hazy gray rather than noon blue.

It sparks a memory.

"Auntie's stories...she told me about the maze. This is how she got home. Jovi, our plan will work!"

"Yeah, sure it will, Girl," Jovi says. "Lord Lobo's dwelling is the center of the maze. You have to leave that," he says and points at my bag.

I grip the strap tighter where it rests across my chest, shaking my head.

"Why? It's only food and things."

"There's a safety ward. You can't bring stuff like that. I think it's to make sure no one can bring weapons. A pretty good trick against that brother of his."

I want less and less to meet Jovi's master. But I don't want to leave my bag. It feels like leaving behind a piece of home, not to mention my food.

"Weapons?"

I step forward, refusing to believe that someone could be that paranoid. And besides Jovi and his fire, I really haven't seen much magic. I can see the walls of the maze move through the portal. I reach my hand out, and the thorns, branches, and vines weave themselves together and threaten to crush me. I step back, and the wall recedes.

Then the wall goes watery as tears fill my eyes.

"Yeah, see?" Jovi says, oblivious to my distress. "You might be able to get away with some in your pockets, but not a lot. Eat what you can and leave the rest. It could take a while to reach him."

It's hard to eat past the lump in my throat and the knot in my belly. I eat, and I openly cry, and Jovi pretends not to notice, walking away from me. I'm making him uncomfortable, but I don't care. I eat as much as I can and stuff the rest in the pockets of my linen trousers. They're dirty and ripped in places after trekking through the forest and crawling through the dirt. They were so fine and bright only a day ago.

That only makes me cry more. It's silly to be upset over a bag, but it's everything.

What if the plan doesn't work? What if we don't make it through? What if this is a trap?

But no, Jovi wouldn't need to trick me into doing anything. I need him more than he needs me. What if none of it works though, and I never see home again?

I cry harder, standing in front of the thorny maze while birds chirp in the morning light. Suddenly, Jovi takes my hand. He's only done that to drag me around from place to place. I'm so startled that I stop crying for a moment.

"Hey, it's ok, you know. It's just a bag, and you can get another one from your family, right? And we're friends now, so that means I'm right here with you. So you're not by yourself. We'll be ok, Girl."

His calm is greater than his ever-present fear, and I latch onto it like the lifeline it is. After a moment, I'm fully calm. I dig through my bag and take a scarf out to wipe my face. Then I tie it around my hair, securing it over my locs. I leave the bag and take Jovi's hand again.

We walk through the door together.

The maze is as tedious as the underground was dark. Complete and ongoing. We walk for hours. I have no idea if we're going the right way or not. I hate not knowing. Jovi seems to know the way or, at least, he acts like it.

When I ask, he says he's following his nose. All I can smell are the roses that grow from the maze, the walls higher than either of us. I couldn't see over the top even if I stood on Jovi's shoulders. The sky is gray, and I can't tell where the sun is. It must be hours, and we don't stop often. I offer Jovi one of the biscuits from my pocket, and after insisting a few times, he eventually accepts. I drink a little water, but it's not nearly enough to satisfy my thirst. My stomach grumbles even louder at me than before.

There are no birds or animals to fill the silence, so Jovi talks. I let him, not needing to participate in the one-sided conversation to keep it going. He speaks of his past and everything and nothing. Recipes he's tried at his home, places he found the best herbs, or interesting things he'd seen. He's certain that he once saw a dragon dive into a river, but those creatures are rare even in this realm.

We turn a corner that looks the same but enter a new space. Here, we enter a garden, with rows of manicured shrubs. On one side, there are rows of trees bearing delicious looking fruit. A pure white bird sits in one of the trees. A river runs nearby it and disappears into the maze.

Just before us, a figure sits at the edge of a long stone fountain with crystal clear water. It's as still as glass and reflects the world in a topsy-turvy way, as if it were a circus mirror.

The fae in front of them is the most beautiful being I have ever seen. With skin the blue black of night, and his locs a stark white, it's almost like looking at a star. His robes are a deep, rich blue with silver thread running through it. I lose my wits for only a moment, but a sharp pinch to my arm brings it back. I glance at Jovi, and he winks at me.

One must have a clear head when it comes to bargaining.

"Well met, good Lord Lobo," Jovi says with a small bow. I mirror him.

"What fine manners you have," he says, and his voice is deep and cool. "You're my brother's boy, aren't you? Is the girl a new one of his as well?"

"No, I am not," I say, surprised at the strength in my voice. "Your brother Bassal stole me from my family. I've eaten and drank nothing from the realm, so by right, I'm not bound here. I request passage home."

He stares at me, and I can barely look him in the eyes. My hands start to shake so I reach for Jovi's and squeeze tight. Lobo watches.

"What of the pup? I doubt my brother will be happy with his failure."

"He's to be my companion to ensure my safety, and as, uh, reparations for my suffering."

"Your suffering..." he says, a laugh in his voice. "You mean to keep him? How splendid. However, that's no reason for *me* to meddle with Bassal."

"If I can be so rude, my lord," Jovi says, wearing a sly grin. "But I'd think the meddling should be reason enough."

"You owe a debt, don't you, pup? What will become of that? These things have to be balanced, after all."

"My parents owe that debt. So I suppose they'll have to pay for it themselves," Jovi says.

"You're bold for such little creatures, I'll grant you that," Lord Lobo replies, a smile to his voice.

"Thank you," I say, "My aunt shared many stories and lessons from when she visited this realm. She is called Thandie. I think you might know her?"

"Thandie," he says, and his sharp gaze looks at something past us. Something in his past. "You're her little niece? She spoke of you as a baby. She must have grown."

"Yes, my lord. She told stories of a friend, my lord, who she always trusted and was quite good and fair. Though quite aggravating at times."

"That's only because she insisted on being disagreeable," he says and his eyes meet mine again. "Tell me, has she a man?"

"Has she what?" I squawk. Next to me, Jovi snickers. Lord Lobo waits patiently as I splutter. It seemed my aunt might not have told me *all* of the stories. "No, my lord, not to my knowledge."

"Indeed... Very well. I accept on your word that you haven't partaken of the fruit and water of this realm and find no doubt. I accept, on behalf of my brother and by my name, your claim to the fox as due reparation for your inconvenience. On one condition." He reaches out a hand and picks a rose from a bush at his feet. It's so deep and rich a scarlet that it's almost black. "You'll deliver this to Thandie. Are we agreed?"

My mind races. Fae bargains always have a catch, and I knew we risked one. But I don't see one. He didn't weave a spell by words or any motion. It was merely a rose.

What's the trick?

I look at Jovi, but he doesn't seem to notice anything wrong. He would tell me, wouldn't he? Could Lord Lobo truly want something so simple?

"Deliver the flower. Nothing more?"

He smiles and it's a little sad. "Nothing more, child."

I look at Jovi, and he shrugs. It's too simple. But if that is the bargain, then that is the bargain. I accept the rose, careful of its thorns. "Agreed, my lord."

He nods then speaks words over us, and my hair stands on end. The syllables all flow together, nothing like gibberish but a melodic song. I don't understand a single word, but something in me does. The mist that appeared before when I was taken swells through the garden and spreads over the water of the fountain. The fae lord stretches his hand out, and the dark mist parts the water, piling it high on either side of us like walls.

Jovi tugs my hand, and I follow, clutching the rose in my other hand.

There is shouting, but I'm not afraid. I know those voices. I let them guide me through the mist. My steps grow more confident as the dark mist that gathered at my taking now heralds my bringing. I'm going home. Soon, I'm the one tugging Jovi.

The mist clears, and the world twists dizzily again in a swirl of colors and sound.

The others hesitate, but Papa sees me first and runs to me. He grabs me up and pulls me to his side, embracing me and backing away from Jovi. He smells like sweat and cedar oils, his clothes rough beneath my palm.

"Child, where have you been? What happened?"

"All is well. I've journeyed to the realm of the fae, just like auntie! I bargained, and I won."

Just like the fae, Papa's eyes widens and his jaw drops. His entourage is equally bewildered. Behind me, Jovi chuckles.

"How, my child?" Papa asks, awestruck as he takes in the fox-boy behind her for the first time.

"Papa, I have such a good story for you."

ABOUT THE AUTHOR

Marie McHenry is an author of fantasy, cozy mysteries, and adventures where the good guy wins... eventually. She writes for young adult audiences mostly as well as nonfiction as Christianna Johnson. You can follow Marie on Instagram @bymariemchenry or email her at bymariemchenry@gmail.com

Magiks and the Tale of Two Kings

BY LOUP GAJIGIANIS

One wizard, one warrior, and two kings.
The story that changed the magik world.

Nearly one and a half thousand years ago, in a wondrous place, where wizards and fairies were plenty, and sorcery wasn't just a tale told to children, there were many great kingdoms governed by magiks. In the region of the Islamic empire, during the reign of the Abbasids, two magical kingdoms, hidden from humans, were ruled by the most powerful brothers across the lands; Mighty kings that believed the power of shapeshifters and shadow walkers was untapped.

As princes, during the age when shapeshifters and shadow walkers were known only as changers, and their magic was feeble, the brothers were inseparable. They played together, grew together, laughed together, and side-by-side toyed with the limitations of their power. Prince Kazar believed in the way of shapeshifting. He turned himself into objects, and he embodied citizens of the empire. However, by taking the form of another, he was also bound by their weaknesses. His brother, Prince Zaeg, did not like accepting the weaknesses of other bodies. Thus, he discovered the magic of shadow shifting. He practiced daily and enjoyed pranking the castle guards with his unfathomable power. The two brothers loved each other dearly and were rarely seen apart. But, alas, as kings, a rift formed between them, for each believed they had discovered the best way to conquer the magical limitations of changers.

After the death of their father, they split his kingdom into two great empires; The Kingdom of Shadow Walkers took the lands south of the Euphrates River and east of the Nile. The Kingdom of Shapeshifters took the northern lands, from the Black Sea to the Indus River. For decades, each king devoted his life to breaking the magical limitations of changers. Their knowledge spread like wildfire, beyond the borders of their lands, and across the world.

THE RETURN OF THE PRINCE

King Kazar

The distant horizon pinkened. A soft spread of orange cascaded across the hills, reflecting a golden hue off the grassy tips. A subtle glow illuminated the high domed chamber where King Kazar sat impatiently. It was the same, vaulted solar that once belonged to his father, the King of Kings, and it has changed little through the years. Now it was his own personal chamber, though he rarely used it, except for special occasions like this. His tired face turned to the windows as the sun rose. *Finally,* he thought. A king was not made to wait for anyone, not even the sun. Dawn should have risen hours ago. For if the king had to wake, so should the sky, and the birds, and then the people to follow. Instead, he'd woken alone, save for the servants tasked with gowning him.

Even now, a servant fumbled oafishly over his embroidered

silk robes, black as wet ink. They matched his dark hair and ebony eyes as he narrowed them and were chosen by his tailor for that reason. With his life spent as a Royal, he had acquired a regal demeanor, but black added the daunting edge that suited him well.

The heavy tap of a heeled boot announced the arrival of one of his men-at-arms, but King Kazar didn't need to look up. Only Firoza, the fiercest fighter in his kingdom and captain of his guard, would dare enter without announcing herself first.

"Has my general arrived?" King Kazar let the servant finish. There was no reason to move yet. If only the man would hurry.

"Yes, My King." Firoza replied. "Moments ago. Along with five thousand soldiers. He is hiding them around the palace and in the city as you commanded."

"And the Elves?" His voice curled, with a daunting edge to his tone.

The servant stepped back, and King Kazar faced his warrior captain. Gold earrings dazzled her sharp features, and dark hair tumbled down her back. Two crystalline wings fluttered behind her. If he hadn't known how dangerous she was, he would have been captivated by her beauty. Knives decorated her hair, her earrings picked locks, and her wristlets were armor.

"They have refused the invitation . . . as you predicted."

"Good. We don't need their interference," King Kazar grunted. "Leave us," he ordered the servants, and they departed directly. When they were alone, he spoke softer and with an openness he shared with few. "My brother has always been an ambitious prince, and now, as ruler of half my father's kingdom, he has pushed magic beyond even what I thought possible." The king stared down at his marred hands. Years of breaking the boundaries of magic had left deep scars that even the innate power of changers couldn't heal. Nor the elven elixirs made of ash, from The Land of Fire. "His army has tripled the size of mine. And with it, he has taken other lands. Azhir warns me against an alliance." By habit, he pulled on the gloves he had accustomed himself with wearing. The soft leather creased familiarly over his marred hands. "They say my brother can soar weightlessly across the lands." His voice tightened.

"We have been experimenting too."

"Yes. But unlike shapeshifting, my spies say there are no limits to the possibilities of shadow shifting," he gritted.

"There are limits to all things, My King."

"Yet I hear of none."

"Just because you do not hear it, or see it, doesn't mean it is not true." Firoza hesitated before delicately suggesting, "Ask your brother to confide in you and share the challenges of the shadow ways."

"How, when my brother and I do not even speak? He is my blood, and I barely know him. Once, when we were children, nothing could have torn us apart. But now, our kingdoms are split with walls, our castles are filled with spies, and I must hide that I am in trouble."

"Perhaps this secrecy is not necessary. Tell your brother of the troll raids. Tell him of the impending invasion. Tell him tonight, at the celebration."

King Kazar faltered. He stared back at Firoza, wanting it to be so easy. But years of bearing the weight of a king had hardened him. "I cannot. Not until I am sure he can be trusted. The safety of my kingdom rests on my shoulders." He crossed the chamber and unfolded a map across a weathered table. His gloved finger traced the marked points along the boundaries of his empire and the lands beyond. "Everyone is a danger to our kingdom. We are surrounded on all sides. The mountain trolls have come down from the Alps and crossed the Danube River. Sea trolls attacked our southern ports by the Arabian Sea. And Desert trolls have gathered to our eastern borders along the Khyber Pass. The elves wait for our army to deplete. The fairies do nothing. And then finally, to the South is my brother, who wishes that every changer had learned the way of shadow shifting. I'm surrounded on all sides. We must only let my brother see a strong, unbreakable empire of shapeshifters. One whose alliance he will wish to join."

"But if you were—"

"I must be certain you understand this." His eyes turned to a withering glare that sharpened. "Or perhaps you aren't fit to be head of my guard."

Firoza bowed deeply. "I seek only to be the blade that protects you, and the voice that guides you."

King Kazar's hardness faded, and he sighed. Bearing the weight of a king was wearisome, and he wished he could be a boy again, playing in the fields with his brother.

"Rise," he commanded, ashamed of his quick anger. Firoza was his most trusted soldier. She had followed him into every battle and fought beside him, guarding him with her life. Over the years, she had become family. And though she wasn't an advisor, her words held weight. His voice softened. "My apologies, Old Friend."

"None is needed from a great king." Firoza reminded him.

King Kazar rubbed the bridge of his nose tiredly. "My father would have wanted peace. He would have wanted our kingdoms to remain one empire. We were wrong to divide it." He moved to the window and stared out as far he could see. "Even now, troll armies assemble beyond our borders. They envy our lands. Our prosperity. Our wealth. They want our trade routes and our fertile land. They may even have the strength to take it. If they attack, they'll kill everyone. And those that live will have fled."

"You have built a great army, My King. You could defend us."

"That may be true. But many lives would be lost. "I need my brother's help. I must convince him to join me." He turned his back to the window. Convincing his brother to unite would not be easy. "I want this to be the grandest celebration in magic history! But my brother must be kept safe. If the trolls see him approaching, they may attack. Our enemies will not want us to make an alliance."

"He will be in danger. Should we warn him?"

"Not until I'm ready. I want to tell him of the coming days myself. Send soldiers to escort him to the city, and while he is here, you will guard him personally."

Firoza bowed deeply, her armored hair swung forward, revealing more daggers on her back. She had never failed him, and for that, risen higher than an exiled soldier should have been allowed, even if she was a fairy. She would not fail the king now. Not when peace for the entire realm was at stake.

By mid-morning, the castle was buzzed with life. Servants bustled from chamber to chamber carrying flour for cakes, sweeping mud from the stone hearth, and preparing for the elaborate celebration. By noon, the cavalcade arrived. Nearly a hundred of the shadow kingdom's finest soldiers, richest merchants, cleverest advisers, and noblest magiks. King Kazar easily spotted his brother amongst them. He rode the back of a manticore surrounded by beautiful dancers that turned to shadows and back again, in rhythm with the music.

The procession drove King Kazar's subjects wild. They cheered and threw favors, celebrating the return of their lost prince, now King of the Shadow Lands. His brother laughed handsomely with the natural charm he had as a child. But he was a man now. His face had hardened and matured, and his beard had filled in, angling out from his chin. He was unrecognizable except for the mischievous play in his smile, and the way he dazzled the crowd.

"They adore him," King Kazar admitted reluctantly.

"He is your father's heir," Firoza said shrewdly. "As are you."

"And yet they love him more." He remembered the many times his brother won the affections of those around them. "They have forgotten he was the cause of the divided kingdom and that he abandoned all who did not follow in his ways."

"You are a forbidding king," Firoza admitted truthfully. "He is playful. His charisma is easy to love."

"He is a better king."

"Enchanting others does not equal moral character." Firoza's voice hardened. "Do not undermine what you have accomplished. You rebuilt treaties with your neighbors, expanded the lands of your kingdom, spread the knowledge of shapeshifting, and brought wealth and peace to all. Look again. They have prospered because of you."

King Kazar turned back to the parade. A ruckus broke out below, and he watched his brother show off amidst the swooning crowd. His brother had always stolen the hearts of those around him, and lost in the enchantment, King Kazar leaned further over the balustrade. He longed to be beside his brother, dazzling the crowd.

King Zaeg's glance flickered up, catching sight of King Kazar. His impish smile vanished. Hurt, hardened over time, flickered across his features, and he looked away. At the base of the castle, he dismounted and strode up the grand staircase.

King Kazar returned inside the high vaulted solar and braced himself. Cool bumps tingled down his arms and he shivered. Strange, he could not remember the last time he had been nervous. He watched the closed chamber door. The safety of his kingdom depended on making peace with this King of the Shadow Lands, now a stranger to him. If he did not make an alliance, his kingdom would be torn apart before the next summer's end. Of that, he was certain.

King Zaeg strode through the doors, pausing only when he caught sight of King Kazar waiting. His back stiffened. To conceal his hesitation, he smiled handsomely and swaggered forward to greet the king of the shapeshifters.

King Kazar clasped his brother in a tight embrace. "Welcome, Brother," he grunted uncomfortably. Forgiveness was hard for men, harder for brothers, but hardest for kings. "It's been too long." A feeling of longing squeezed his chest, and he hugged his brother tighter.

King Zaeg blushed at the embrace. When they broke apart, the warm flush lingered, and he circled the vaulted chamber that had once been their father's, his cheerful spirit returning. "Thirty years," he counted.

"Thirty-three." King Kazar corrected. He inspected his brother closely. Dark shadows swelled beneath his eyes, and there was a thinness about his handsome features. Tolls from his own pursuit of magic. Memories flooded back from untroubled times. "The last time I saw you in this room, you chased the tutor from the solar." King Kazar's eyes glinted humorously. "You demanded he not to tell you what was impossible. That nothing was impossible. He only lacked imagination."

King Zaeg smiled crookedly. "You remember that?"

King Kazar smiled bigger. It felt foreign and stiff but good. "I'll never forget it."

King Zaeg's brow tightened, and his smile dimmed. He walked to the window where their mother used to sit, clearly lost in memories. "Why have you called me here?"

King Kazar's chest squeezed. There was a time his brother would have come to him gladly, without suspicions or doubts. Now they were older and wiser from ruling their kingdoms, and his brother was too keen to be fooled for long. But when words of the troll raids came, he could not speak them. "We must reconcile. We must align our kingdoms, join our armies, reinforce our borders, and encourage our subjects to live together as allies."

"Align? That is not possible. Too many years have passed."

"It is my wish."

King Zaeg swallowed hard. "I'll admit I'm surprised." He lifted his eyes and met his brother's gaze. "We have spent many years at odds. Shapeshifters and shadow walkers have come to distrust each other. Fear each other even."

"Which was never our intent." King Kazar's eyes cut into his, meaning the words fully.

"In that I agree." King Zaeg's taut muscles loosened, and he slouched against the window. "When we began our dreams of developing our magic, it never occurred to me that I would lose my brother.... Perhaps it was best you sent for me."

King Kazar let out a breath he was holding onto. "I worried you would refuse my invitation."

"I thought of it," admitted King Zaeg.

"But you didn't?"

"We're brothers." King Zaeg straightened from the window. His carefree smile returned and the handsome sparkle played in his eyes. "Why should I not come, when my brother asks for me?"

A wistful smile wavered over King Kazar's features. "Because I pursued a different path than you. One that you did not favor."

"It was not your choice of path that drove me away. It was your disapproval of mine," King Zaeg reminded him. "I wished to rule our father's realm together. I never wanted a kingdom separate from yours."

"Forgive me then," King Kazar said hurriedly. "I feared your abandonment of the ancient rules of magic. I see I was wrong. Let us start anew. We will learn from each other. Grow from our newfound knowledge. And turn our kingdoms into brothers like they once were."

"Do you mean it, Brother?" King Zaeg's voice wavered slightly.

"I do." King Kazar pulled his brother into a tight embrace, meaning it truly in the depths of his heart.

Mist dappled King Zaeg's eyes.

Feeling whole again, King Kazar released him. "I have a gift for you—crafted by Azhir Izzat Ibn Al-Ghaazi himself."

King Zaeg's surprise curled into a grin. "The rumors are true then? Azhir is here? The Great Warlock of the East?"

"In the caverns beneath this very castle, tinkering away."

"I must stop by and see what mischief I can find."

"Ha! You haven't changed a bit," laughed King Kazar. "But you must be tired from your journey. Use this solar as your own. Your guard may rest in the adjoining chambers while Firoza watches over you. Tonight will be a glorious celebration."

King Kazar left, feeling lighter than he had in years.

Outside he spoke to Firoza. "He wishes to align our kingdoms as much as I!" His voice burst from his chest, and he rocked forward on the toes of his slippers.

Firoza showed no change in manner and replied with a straight face, "Is he not a threat to your borders, as you said?"

"I was mistaken."

"Yet, you did not tell him of the troll raids."

"When the time is right. I will do it then."

Firoza's distrust was apparent across her features, so King Kazar continued. "I believe him to be earnest. This may work as planned. No, better than planned. He misses me. I can tell."

"It would appear so." Firoza toyed with the hilt of her dagger, as she did when considering matters of state.

"I see your hesitation. Speak openly," the king urged. "Dare I hope that my kingdom is saved? Dare I dream to have my brother by my side?"

"You must always hope and dream. But you cannot take a few, carefully chosen words and form judgment of one's character," she said wisely.

"He is my brother."

"And a stranger. With no allegiance to you."

King Kazar shook his head stubbornly. "We are brothers, and I was wrong. He is not as different as I thought. Nor has he changed much, from when we were children."

"But this is your kingdom at stake." Firoza pressed. "Their lives depend on you."

King Kazar considered her. "Watch him then, but keep him safe. My brother may have reached the castle safely, but that does not mean he is no longer in danger. Our enemies know if we align, our forces would be unstoppable. And when the trolls meet us in battle, the fairy king will no longer be able to sit idly by as they take the free lands. He will have to join us... or the trolls."

"He will not join the trolls," Firoza assured him.

"I'm counting on it, and I await the day he comes with gifts and apologies and beseeches to join my armies." He offered a fiendish smile. "I should make him beg."

"You are too great a king," Firoza reminded him.

"Then I shall enjoy the thought of it," he groused. With that, King Kazar shapeshifted. Feathers sprouted, his nose hardened, and he shrunk in size. He took flight, soaring through the castle, feeling at ease for the first time in a long time.

Perhaps, all would be well after all, he told himself.

The Warrior's Wisdom

King Zaeg

King Zaeg strolled about the elegantly furnished room. He stopped at the balustrade. Below, dozens of carpenters, smiths, and merchants prepared for the feast. They laughed and sung with ease and gaiety. His brother's kingdom had prospered far beyond anything he'd imagined. His own kingdom was poorer compared to this spectacle below. But his army was the greatest in the world. No company, command, or artillery could face the dark shadow walkers without annihilation. But perhaps he had warred too long. The disparity of wealth disheartened him, and he wondered what choices, as king, his brother had made that were better than his.

For some time, his thoughts wondered. Did his brother really miss him? Could their kingdoms truly be allies? And if they were, would the Shadow Lands prosper like the Kingdom of Shapeshifters? He stood like this for some time, leaning over the balustrade deep in thought, as he watched the villagers below.

A lone soldier quickened across the yard, and King Zaeg let his keen eyes trail after him. The sun gleamed off freshly polished armor. A curved sword glinted in the light, and a short dagger hung from the warrior's belt. The soldier glanced around and scurried beneath the low-hanging rooftops. Using them for cover, he hurried out a sight.

King Zaeg's soft smile disappeared. His suspicious nature flooded with new thoughts, and he turned to the door, where Firoza stood watch.

"Firoza?" He called out, not certain she would answer. But then the door opened, and the beautiful warrior stepped inside. "My personal guard will protect my chamber—if there is need. You're free to go. I'm sure my brother has need of you."

"My orders are to take watch here, outside your chamber."

King Zaeg forced back a frown and kept his expression light. "Well, if you wish to attend other matters, he will not hear of it from me." He offered the crooked smile that usually gave way to the effect he wished for: a trick he learned young and mastered years ago.

"My King wishes to strengthen our kingdoms. He wishes to reunite with his brother. I have no other matters than to guard the King of the Shadow Lands. It is my honor to keep you safe." Firoza bowed.

King Zaeg's gaze never left hers. He was excellent at reading others. He searched for a sign she may break if pressed. There was none. He made a show of sighing. "As you wish then. I will take a nap. Please do not disturb me."

"Yes?" His brow quirked, naturally curious, though beneath it, his pulse was racing, and his heart pounded against his chest.

"My king wishes only for peace. You should trust him."

King Zaeg's lips curled into his most handsome smile, and he inclined his head. "You are as loyal as word has told."

Firoza bowed and left as quietly as she entered. The moment the door snapped behind her, King Zaeg's politeness dissolved. He knew a soldier readied for battle as well as anyone. He glared at the door. He also knew when his chamber was being watched rather than guarded.

He furrowed his brow, thinking fast. Decided, he crossed the room, making the heel of his shoes clap heavily against the stone. He would discern the truth for himself. Instead of climbing in bed, he shadowshifted. His majestic turban and robes whirled up into soft wisps of black night. His skin flaked from his body, and he became a shadowy remnant of what he once was. Soundlessly, he floated across the room, dove from the window, and soared across the yard.

Though it was harder to stay hidden in the daylight, shapeshifters weren't accustomed to the magic of a shadow shifter. The villagers excused his apparition as a this or that and went on about their business with hardly another thought. And for that, stalking from above, the king of shadow walkers was able to move freely. He quickly spotted the lone guard and followed him to a vast garrison. Armed soldiers lined the streets in battle formation, alert and ready. His brother was preparing for war, but with whom? He had heard of no troubles with the Kingdom of Shapeshifters. The only kingdom at odds with the lands of shapeshifters was his. Perhaps it was him, that his brother wished to make war? Which could only mean this celebration was a trap.

A dark, furious haze crossed King Zaeg's shadowy face. Anger and hurt swelled, and his shadow whipped daringly. *If I get a better look*, he thought, *I can see if my brother does intend to betray me. And if he does, I can prepare my kingdom for this snare he has set.*

A commanding soldier snarled and shoved the lone guard into formation. "We're supposed to stay hidden." His spit sprayed across the dirt, and his hand shot out at hundreds of soldiers. "The king does not want his brother to know we're here." He jabbed his thumb into the soldier's chest.

"Won't happen again, sir."

"No, it won't!" he snarled.

From the rooftop, King Zaeg stared down in stupefied horror. There it was. Proof. His brother had assembled this grand army and was hiding it from him. Hurt bloated in his gut, and he did little to hide his shadow, blatant in the afternoon light. Voices rose below. Soldiers pointed at his ghastly shade. Still, he didn't care. His brother had assembled a great army. And there could only be one purpose—to take the Shadow Lands.

King Zaeg plunged from the rooftop. His shadow billowed out as he returned to the castle and swept back through the crannies of the stone walls, leaving not a trace he had ever left.

Shocked and furious, he paced about the balcony. His brother had never approved of the way he'd forsaken the ancient rules of magic. He had called it unprincipled, dark, and corrupt. But just because something was unfamiliar did not mean it was evil. King Zaeg trembled. He should never have come back. He wiped a tear before it fell. What he needed was a plan. And the answer came, as his treacherous brother slipped across the courtyard below.

THE WARLOCK'S GUILE

King Kazar

King Kazar hurried across the castle grounds. The eccentric warlock kept a workshop deep beneath the castle in an underground cavern. Why? King Kazar couldn't fathom. It was dark and damp. Torches never stayed lit, and boewood died in their lanterns. Only fairy fire survived the thin, stale air, and it cast a golden hue that was frightening against the cavernous walls. Light was not much easier in the warlock's laboratory. Piles of books and vials collected dust from the stone ceiling. But the warlock had insisted. Here, his potions and brews stayed cool. And when King Kazar, desperate to avoid the deep labyrinth, tried to gift the wizard with the beautiful dome spire in place of the chilly cell, the wizard replied by taking both. Now both the highest tower and deepest dungeon belonged to an obstinate magic maker who hardly ever did as he was bade.

King Kazar took a last breath of fresh air and entered the stone cave. The cheerful festivities and lively music playing above quickly became a dream as he trudged down the steps. The walls creaked and groaned at the intruder, as if by magic, and the warlock's rats spoke. Their chitters echoed off the stones so it was impossible to tell if there were three or a hundred. Inside the storeroom, potions bubbled and brewed. Usually, at least one book read itself aloud to the perked ears of Azhir. Sometimes two books babbled together, competing for the attention of the bizarre wizard. But today, they were silent and still, lying listlessly in their disorganized fashion. And inside, the rats didn't speak. The only sound came from the soft cackle of the fireplace, for Azhir needed silence to complete his complicated piece of magic.

King Kazar hesitated at the entrance to the workshop, inside of which, Azhir leaned over his grimoire with a candle of golden fire. His long brown hair was knotted and braided out of his face, and his piercing black eyes devoured the words on the page. Flowing robes with sleeves trimmed at the elbows were belted at his waist by a round stone that changed colors with the skies. And his pointed slippers stuck out from beneath his robes, adorned with metal knickknacks like pliers, rods, picks, and spoons. He wasn't an old wizard, merely a century or so, but he was an unusual one. Even at half his age, he was the most powerful warlock in the world, save for Merlin himself, and some questioned even that. It was a miracle really that he had consented to come to the lands of the shapeshifters to practice his arts, and King Kazar knew it.

Careful not to disturb the warlock, King Kazar treaded lightly as he entered, in the gentlest of manners, but magic couldn't be fooled. A soft gibber carried through the room and warned the magic maker. Azhir lifted his head from his grimoire, grudgingly. "I know why you're here." He waved his wooden staff, and the blue crystal, nested within it, glowed. A gold crown encrusted with rubies, emeralds, and sapphires soared between them. "I call it the Crown of Guilledon."

King Kazar gazed up at the glittering crown and said tightly, "It's of the western world."

"It is," agreed Azhir. "The borlaugs that forged it are of Cologne, from the Kingdom of the Franks. So naturally, it is of their world." He turned back to his grimoire, trailed his finger over the page, and continued scouring the page, hungrily. "But I've made some adjustments."

"Adjustments?"

"Yes." Azhir smiled coyly. Had it been an ordinary crown, the spells might have been simpler. But it was forged by borlaugs. Terribly powerful beasts that hammer magic from the elements into the very cores of the chattels they create. And unable to wipe the crown of the borlaug's spells, Azhir had overlapped one enchantment with the next and then went back, carefully sewing them together.

"I am aware of your troubles. That is why I'm compensating you so generously." King Kazar's gaze slid from the brilliant warlock to the marvelous crown flickering between them. Borlaugs turned junk into masterpieces. Even King Kazar knew that. A borlaug's magic was nameless. It couldn't be learned nor stolen. Only Azhir, The Great Warlock of The East, would have found a way around their enchantments.

Azhir finished reading. Satisfied, he shut the grimoire. "Would you like to see its power?" He waved his staff. The crown floated to him and rested gently on his palm. The moment it touched the warlock's skin, it transformed. The metal twisted and melted into a shimmering gold ribbon that flickered of a thousand colors in the soft light. It twirled and danced and spun into a beautiful, gold turban. Centered in the middle was the largest blood stone King Kazar had ever seen.

"It's magnificent."

The warlock nudged it into the air, and the crown floated between them, shifting back into the jewel encrusted crown. "It's a dangerous gift."

"It's dangerous for any magik to have the power of all magiks. But I trust my brother."

"Are you certain?"

"If he were to understand the simplicities of shapeshifting—if he could know its power as I do—perhaps he will accept our alliance." He laughed half-heartedly. "He may even give up his pursuit of shadow walking."

"Or he will use the power you give him to take over your empire as he took the wizard lands."

"I will trust my brother," King Kazar declared obstinately.

"I've thought as much." Stubbornness sharpened the bones in Azhir's cheeks, making them appear hollow and unforgiving. "I've added another spell."

"What spell?"

"Too much is at stake. Not only your lands, but the ones you promised to return—the ones stolen from the wizards."

"What spell?" King Kazar growled fiercely, in a tone no one dared use when speaking to Azhir.

"If the King of the Shadowlands betrays you—if he were to overpower you or attempt to steal your kingdom—the crown will seize his will, chain his mind, and cloud his memories. He will forget his desire for power. For as long as he wears the crown, his memories will fade, never lasting long enough to realize his mind is imprisoned. He will become magicless; unable to oppose you. You will take his kingdom, lands, titles, and with his army all that you desire will become yours."

"No—"

"The trolls will not be able to raid your lands," Azhir interrupted him, "and with your kingdoms aligned, your enemies would be outnumbered. Your reverence would be returned. It is all you've wished for."

"Remove the spell!"

Azhir's eyes twinkled with bewilderment. "It cannot be removed." He flicked his staff, and the crown spun. Dazzling light reflected off the stones. "It's sewn into the fabrics of the metal."

"You will remove it, or our agreement for the wizard lands is forfeit."

A glower shrouded Azhir. The crystal rainbows disappeared, and the cavern dampened with his anger. "You gave me your word."

"I promised the return of your lands peacefully—with the consent of my brother."

Azhir tugged a metal bead, knotted in beard. "I can, perhaps, quiet the spell."

"Do it... and I will keep my word."

"As you wish." The warlock threw back his head, and terror filled his face. His pupils blackened. A deep unnatural voice spoke, though his lips didn't move. The incantation chanted, echoing through the room. The lights did not return, but the floor shook. Stacked books tumbled over, and vials of liquid burst, one pop after another—

King Kazar covered his face from the shards. Then the sound was gone, and the cave was quiet. "Did it work?" His voice shook.

Azhir wiped sweat from his forehead and pointed his staff at the broken flasks and beakers. The staff glowed of its deep crystal hue, and the glass flew up. The sharp edges glittered dangerously and reassembled themselves, but the ruined potions didn't return. "The curse is contained—for now. If your brother wishes you harm, you need only say these words to unlock it...." The warlock whispered in low tones, so soft the king couldn't hear him. But then, the words fluttered across the room like butterflies and spoke in his ear.

Amazed, King Kazar nodded slowly.

"Speak them with care. Once spoken, they cannot be taken back."

A cool dread dampened his brow. "I understand."

Above them, a dark shadow crept through the crevices of the stone. It slithered down the shadowy walls, past the spilled potions, and slinked behind the warlock, tucking itself in a tight corner.

Unaware of the intruder, Azhir turned his attention to the potions, now bubbling and smoking precariously. He swept his staff, crystal blue light erupted from the tip, and the hazardous potions lifted off the floor. "Venit," he commanded. Herbs and dried ingredients mobilized from scattered places and convened around the warlock. They danced around him, speaking to him, urging to be chosen. But ignoring their pleas, Azhir kept his gaze transfixed on the frothing elixir and choosing his preferred ingredients, calmed the volatile glop. Once it was done, he bottled the remnant and sealed it.

The king cleared his throat. "May I test it?" He hesitated with his fingers stretched out to the crown.

The warlock blinked up. "As you wish."

King Kazar plucked the sparkling crown from the air. The moment his fingers touched it the heavy metal transformed. It molded, swirled, and dazzled, and a new turban formed, woven of blue silk, encrusted with hundreds of pearls, and lined with the blue stones of lapis, turquoise, and sapphires.

King Kazar sucked in a breath, and reverently placed it on his head. The turban retied itself magically.

Nothing happened.

"What now?"

"Use its magic," Azhir said cryptically.

"How?"

"You've seen your brother shadowshift? You must have some idea of what he does."

At this, the shadow tensed, condensing darkly, and two eyes, masked within the gloom, stared down astonishedly.

King Kazar thought of his brother, the tales of his transformations, and the strange experiments from when they were younger. His hands wisped away. His robes faded. And his flesh turned to shadows. The air around him felt heavy and warm. And then, as if he'd done it a thousand times, he lept into the air and soared around the cave. He glided past a foggy orb, behind a casket of scrolls, between a dangling candelabra of fairy fire, and then landed in front of the eccentric wizard.

"Spectacular." King Kazar stared down at his billowing robes and gem-encrusted slippers, and then removed the turban. "I want to keep this for myself," he said, breathless. His eyes sparkled at the stones. "It's too powerful."

Azhir's mouth quirked knowingly. "Which is why I added spells." He waved his staff and the turban lifted into the air. "Without this gift, you may not be able to deliver on your promise. I want the far lands of your brother's kingdom. I want them returned to the wizards." His lip curled firmly.

"And you will have it," the king swore.

The shadow twitched and jerked forward with a vengeance—but Azhir's firm voice halted it. "Or your kingdom will face more grievous enemies than you can imagine," warned Azhir. "You do not want me for an enemy."

King Kazar sucked in air, aghast. He stepped back. "You dare threaten your king?"

"You are not my king." Azhir held up a skull-ringed finger. "My allegiance is to my own. That is the way of magiks. Your expansions and invasions—constantly trying to transcend your brother—have taken what belongs to my brothers. I want it returned," he finished firmly.

"I gave you my word, and I will see it done," assured the king. Offended, King Kazar stomped for the arduous stairs. He was not stupid enough to challenge Azhir, but his patience was wearing on him, and the dark cave was dampening his mood. As he reached the door, the warlock's voice called him back.

"Don't forget the words," warned Azhir. "Exactly as I said them."

Remembering the whispered chant, the king shivered, and his blood turned cold. "I could not even if I wanted."

THE KING'S FALLACY

King Kazar

King Kazar hurried through the final hour, dressing in his finest robes; a soft linen ghilala, an exquisite silk qamis, a stately qaba crafted of rich brocade, and a high court mantle made of silk and gold thread. Music and laughter drifted through the castle. Impatient to join the festivities, King Kazar ushered his servants from his chamber and shapeshifted into his usual guise. He shrank, grew scruffy fur, and turned into a cat. On four padded paws, he swaggered from the room and through the castle.

At the towering doors of the golden hall, King Kazar darted between the shuffling feet of his subjects, and proudly strutted down the carpet to the dais where his brother awaited, regally dressed, on a raised platform, and surrounded by his own shadow guards.

At the foot of the throne, when guests were beginning to notice the bold cat, King Kazar shapeshifted back and standing tall, adjusted his jewel encrusted turban. He held his arms wide as he addressed the crowd.

"Welcome travelers and neighboring kingdoms! For many years, the discordance between the Kingdom of Shapeshifters and the Kingdom of Shadow Walkers has grown. Yesterday, we were two empires divided by distrust. But today, my brother has returned. He will sit on the throne our mother once sat upon and eat at the table our grandfather built. We will align our kingdoms and our empires will be brothers once again."

He beamed at the merchants, viceroys, chamberlains, and courtiers of each kingdom, standing together. This was what his father would have wanted. United, his enemies would be defeated. Overcome with joy, he leapt up the stairs and embraced his brother, but having not seen him in many years, he didn't notice the forced smile.

A servant came forward, interrupting them. In her arms, she carried a sparkling crown on a cushion of delicate silk. King Kazar pulled his brother forward. "May I present... the Crown of Guilledon."

King Zaeg's eyes raked over the magical crown, but King Kazar didn't notice the thirst sparkling in his gaze, and he mistook his brother's desire for delight in the amusement of the celebration. As King Kazar was not aware that his brother had spied and already knew the power of the crown, he explained its magic. "This crown is enchanted. It will show you the power of shapeshifters. With it, you can see the world as I do, and as any creature you desire. You—"

King Zaeg swirled down the stairs, in a daze, before King Kazar finished. The moment his fingers grazed the buffed gold, the crown changed. The metal melted and molded, intertwining around itself, and a black turban, pitch as the darkest shadow with sparkling peridots and blue sapphires took shape. The crowd gasped... and then broke into applause.

King Zaeg placed the turban on his head. The silk rewrapped itself magically.

"You don't seem surprised?" wondered King Kazar. "How did you know..." his voice trailed off, stunned by the anger on his brother's face.

King Zaeg signaled to his guards, secretly placed around the golden hall. They marched forward, swords clanging, and seized Firoza, the palace guards, the nobles, and then his brother, the king. King Kazar's soldiers drew their weapons, but as they were caught off guard, they were outnumbered.

"Yield." King Zaeg demanded.

King Kazar's eyes widened, and his face filled with hurt. "Brother?"

"Yield!" King Zaeg shook with anger

King Kazar nodded. His soldiers dropped their swords, and they were swiftly disarmed.

King Zaeg turned to the startled room. "I am king now. My brother cedes the throne. You are all subject to my rule. From this day, shapeshifting is forbidden."

The crowd looked on fearfully.

King Kazar stepped forward, arms raised, but a soldier stopped him with a blade to his chest. "I thought we agreed on peace."

"Don't speak to me of peace!" King Zaeg spat. "I know of

your peace. You think I'm not clever enough to uncover your schemes!"

"What schemes do you speak of?"

"You assembled an army!"

"I am a king," he said simply.

"They are readied for war!"

King Kazar fumbled as he tried to understand what had led to his brother's betrayal. Why would assembling his own army cause his brother distress? "The trolls have pushed into shapeshifter lands and attacked my cities."

King Zaeg shook off his brother's reasoning. "You promised my lands to the wizards!"

"I did," King Kazar admitted slowly. He was beginning to understand. "Through a treaty. You have pushed your boundaries too far. I hoped to reason with you. It is rightfully theirs."

"You've expanded your kingdom too," his brother accused in reply.

"I don't deny it. But not the lands of the magic makers. We need the wizards. I'll give you some of my lands to account for it."

"You say this now only because I have your kingdom."

"It was my intention all along. I wish to reunite with my brother and face the trolls together."

"Lies!"

"It is no lie, brother. You are seeing blindly and forming judgment with only partial truths. Calm down and look again. I've assembled this celebration for you. I've had a borlaug's treasure crafted to honor you and welcome you home."

"Welcome me home." King Zaeg snorted. "You wanted to keep the crown for yourself. I heard you—"

"You spied on me?" King Kazar's voice shook. His subjects looked away, ashamed and afraid.

"Your trickery and dishonesty left me no choice," King Zaeg flared. "Now your kingdom is mine."

"You cannot take over the Kingdom of Shapeshifters. Surely you know this."

"I believe I just did." King Zaeg shapeshifted. A beast ripped from his body. It took the form of a manticore with a hulking lion's body, poisonous scorpion's tail, and enormous dragon wings. It roared savagely. Screams pierced the room, and his subjects fled. They trampled over each other, pushing for the doors.

King Kazar faced the beast and squared his shoulders. Brown eyes were all that was left of his brother, but that was enough. "This is not the way. Change back, and we will speak openly." His jaw tightened, refusing to let fear show in his face. He would need to tread carefully with whatever came next. His brother didn't understand the laws of shapeshifters. He didn't know the power he held wavered precariously. If he wasn't careful, the creature would take control of his instincts, and he would become more beast than magik.

The manticore spoke in an inhuman growl. "Was I to be taken in chains?"

King Kazar took another step. "That would never have happened."

"More lies!" The manticore lashed its venomous tail and hit a statue, crumbling it to the floor. "Concede, or I will take your life as you would have taken mine." He lashed out again. His tail hooked around another statue and brought it down over his brother's head.

From a dark corner, Azhir mumbled, his lips moving quickly. He struck his staff against the stone floor. Tap. It came to life, and a deep wave of blue magic rippled from the staff and struck the falling statue. It cracked, split in two, and the chunks fell on each side of King Kazar, leaving him unharmed.

A swell of hope fluttered. Though King Kazar didn't delude himself into thinking the wise warlock cared for him, at least he did not face his brother alone. The warlock cared for the balance of power. And he would want the lands of the wizards returned. That was enough to tie their fates together. And it gave him a chance at beating his brother now.

"Stay out of this warlock!" King Zaeg growled.

Azhir uttered softly, barely above a whisper, but his voice echoed off the walls, magnified with magic, repeating itself a dozen times. "Speak the words!"

King Kazar stuttered—the words stuck inside his throat. He never wanted the curse. Not in his heart. He had wanted his brother.

Spiked with anger, and unused to the cravings of a wild beast, King Zaeg began to lose control. The beast's snarl turned to a rumbling growl. The last of King's Zaeg's brown eyes transfigured, and golden slits glared down at King Kazar. The manticore attacked.

King Kazar stumbled back, shielding his face with his arm.

Clang. Firoza caught the manticore's teeth around her armored band. Snarling, the beast bit harder, tearing into her flesh. "Get back," she cried.

"No," King Kazar sputtered, unable to believe what was unfolding before him.

Firoza swept the hind legs of the lion's body and tumbled the manticore on its back. Free of the beast, she drew her sword—

"NO!" King Kazar bellowed.

Firoza stopped, the blade inches from the soft fur of the glorious manticore. The beast whirled, its tail flashed, and its pointed stinger sunk deep into Firoza's chest. Her eyes rounded, and she fell back into the arms of her king.

Realizing what he'd done, the manticore slunk back. Brown eyes teared, the beast faded, and King Zaeg knelt beside her. "Why isn't she healing?"

"She's a fairy. Not a changer," King Kazar cried. "Bring the healer!"

The guards retrieved their weapons. Several hurried from the golden hall in search of the healer. Others stationed themselves around the room, arresting the shadow guards and restoring the order of the king.

King Kazar cradled Firoza in his arms as she struggled with each breath. His eyes misted, and he pleaded with the warlock.

"Azhir! Save her with your magic!"

"I cannot."

"If you're truly the greatest warlock," King Kazar challenged, "then I command you to save her!"

"Firoza is a fairy. That power is beyond me," claimed Azhir.

Firoza tried to speak, but the words choked in her chest.

"Shush. You will be fine." Tears spilt down King Kazar's cheeks. There were many times he had been too harsh to her or unfair to her. He had not shown he cared like he should have.

The strength left Firoza, and her hand drooped. He caught it and held it tightly. "Hang on. Help is coming."

"In the fairy kingdom, by her own kind, she can be saved," said Azhir.

"If she returns to the Kingdom of Fairies, I'd never see her again. I'm not ready to part from her."

"She cannot be saved here," Azhir spoke sensibly. "You must say goodbye. For if she doesn't go, she'll surely die."

King Kazar choked on a sob. He pulled her tighter. "Take her then." He gently laid Firoza against the stone and whispered in her ear. "Thank you, my friend."

The warlock knelt beside them and lightly touched her shoulder. "I will return shortly," he told the king.

A blue swirl of clouds burst through the windows, banging the stained glass against the walls. Shattered pieces sprayed across the golden hall as the blue cloud swirled around them. Then Azhir and Firoza were gone. The glass clattered to the floor, and the hall was silent.

King Kazar stood and faced his brother, taller than he had in years. "I brought you here for peace. Only peace!" He said fiercely. "A legion of trolls gather at my borders. They mean to kill us all! If they take my kingdom, they'll come for yours. I only wished for our kingdoms to align and face the darker days ahead. It was my fear you would not support us that delayed me telling you."

King Zaeg's eyes dawned. Sorrow swelled in his chest. "I've been a fool. I saw only treachery and deceit. I thought you meant to betray me."

"I did not!"

"I'm truly sorry for your friend," said King Zaeg.

"Your regret changes nothing. Some choices cannot be undone, no matter how much you wish them." King Kazar pointed to the turban, still resting on his brother's head. The stones glistened black against the candlelight. And he spoke the words.

> *Cast of magic, blood, and stone*
> *Born the Crown of Guilledon*
> *Cursed in love, hate, and fear*
> *Twisted the metal of fate near*
> *A veil of good deceives thy nature*
> *And on my blood, I release thee.*

The turban luminated. An incandescence flushed warmly against the black silk. It spread through King Zaeg, igniting him in a smoldering afterglow. When he was fully ablaze, the glimmer dissipated, leaving a dark coolness.

Dazed, King Zaeg's eyes fell on King Kazar. "Brother?" Bewildered, King Zaeg touched the jeweled turban uncertainly. He blinked and looked around the golden hall, now in crumbles. "What happened?" He locked eyes with his brother and reached out to him, concern and love etched across his face. "Why are you angry? Is everything alright?"

King Kazar softened, feeling the innocence of his younger brother many years past. The crown had imprisoned him, just as Azhir had said. A thick tear fell down his cheek. But then his eyes settled on the disturbed dust, where Firoza had once been. Even now, she may be dead. He had been helpless in saving her, though she had kept him safe for years. And if by some miracle she was alive, the fairy king would never let her return. She was lost to him forever. His heart chilled. "Take him," King Kazar commanded.

The remaining guards stumbled forward awkwardly, uncertain if the king meant it. Metal armor clambering, they seized King Zaeg and bound him with glowing shackles.

"What's going on?" King Zaeg tried to shadowshift, but nothing happened.

"Take him to the east tower." King Kazar's jaw hardened. "When our kingdoms are aligned and all changers live together in harmony—and when I've forgiven what happened here today, I will release him from the curse."

The soldiers dragged King Zaeg from the hall, and King Kazar looked away, sickened with hurt and grief. When the golden hall was quiet once more, he knelt where Firoza had once been, now empty, cold stone. He remembered the first day she'd arrived in the Kingdom of Shapeshifters with a treaty, to bring peace between the kingdoms. He could almost feel her presence, though it was only a memory.

For some time, the king knelt in despair. A majestic figure with sweeping robes glided in on a blue cloud and landed on the stone. "Firoza will heal," said Azhir. "In time."

"She lives?" King Kazar scoured the warlock's face, needing to hear it again.

"She will live."

He dropped his face, in sorrow. "And yet she is gone forever."

Blue robes billowed behind Azhir, dragging softly against the stone, as he approached. He laid a hand on the king's shoulder. "You can care deeply for someone and not have them with you. Did you know that?"

"I don't know how," he wept.

"You must wish her well, and then let her go," Azhir said kindly. "You have pressing concerns that need your immediate attention."

"It is too hard."

"It will be a tremendous weight to bear, as will uniting the kingdoms, but you must do it all the same."

The king rubbed the wetness from his eyes and staggered to his feet.

Azhir cleared his throat. "Will you be a good king?"

King Kazar's square jaw flexed, hardening himself for what lay ahead. "Until the day comes that the kingdoms rule themselves."

"It sounds like a good beginning."

"I owe it to the shapeshifters and shadow walkers of our kingdoms—of my kingdom. There must only be one."

"And what of the lands of the wizards?" Azhir quirked a brow.

"Are henceforth returned."

"Then I shall take my leave. Like you, I suddenly have many things to accomplish. My friends will want to know the good news. Farewell." The warlocks' eyes turned crystal blue. Speckles of light glittered. The robes spun with him. Then he vanished.

ABOUT THE AUTHOR

Since childhood, Loup wanted to be many things—a jockey, a sailor, a fencer, a treasure hunter, an artist, and even an amateur mixed martial artist. While she wrote short stories as a child, she never imagined she would be an author. Like all things she does, the Magik Series came from the heart.

You can follow her on social media @enchantedchronicle

enchantedchronicle.com

Enjoyed the Anthology?

We hope you've enjoyed *Tales from the Otherworlds.*

This was put together by a band of authors who find extraordinary joy in the youthful outlooks of imagination and wonder.

If you enjoyed *Tales from the Otherworlds,* it would mean a lot if you could leave a review for it on your favorite retailer or social media so that the stories can get discovered by new readers.

And don't forget to tags us!
We'd love to see and hear what you think!

Acknowledgements

To our Kickstart backers:

Alex Gates
Ally
Amy Lynn Conners
Ann Schroeder
Arias Williams
Arthur Bowling
Aure Nash
Brian Lambert
Brittany Hester
Cheryl
Christian Humes
Courtney Cannon
Darcy Colemon
Diane Helander
Elise
Emily Claypoole
Ev
J.A. Benson
Jace Chretin

Jamie
Joyce Sherri
Katara Johnson
Kristina Conners
Lisa Moment
M.L. Wang
Markita Staples
Matthew Chatman
Nikki VandenBerg
Princess Isis Asare
Ruth Valadez
Seth McNitt
Sherry Burch
Tim Conners
Tim Mojica
Toni McDonald
Tyler Kieler
Wendy Blaeser
Yolanda Leilani

Thank you for your time, dedication, and support of this project.
The story wouldn't be what it is without you wonderfully whimsical
wonderers.